W.W. MITCHELL

The Legend Of Sky City

To my wonderful children — my worlds are nothing without the ones who inspire me to create them. You fill my heart with wonder and my mind with endless dreams. In your eyes, I find the courage to imagine; in your laughter, I rediscover the joy of possibility. You are the heartbeat behind every story I tell.

"It is not the strongest of the species that survives, nor the most intelligent, but the one most responsive to change."

— CHARLES DARWIN

Contents

Acknowledgments

I am nothing without the love, lessons, and strength of my parents. You've shown me what true resilience looks like—how to stand tall in the storm and rise again with grace. Because of you, I've learned to chase dreams without hesitation and to face every challenge without fear. I carry your love in everything I do, and I love you both with all my heart.

To my incredible wife—your joy, your faith, and your boundless enthusiasm have lifted me higher than I ever thought I could go. You cheer for every story, every step, every impossible goal, and somehow make me believe that nothing is beyond reach. You are my constant reminder of why I create, and for that, I am endlessly grateful.

To my brothers and sisters—my lifelong support-ers and unshakable foundation. You remind me where I came from and encourage me to keep climbing, no matter how steep the road.

And to my family and friends who've walked beside me on this journey—thank you for every prayer, every word of encouragement, and every moment of belief. Your support has carried me through the long nights and quiet doubts. You are part of every dream I've dared to chase.

Prologue

"Head down, everyone!"

My voice thundered through the echoing halls, ricocheting off riveted steel and vibrating through the bulkheads. Each pounding step against the berthing doors reverberated with the tremor running through my hands—as if the ship itself mirrored my dread. Stifled squeals rose above the deep groans of *The Demeter's* strained hull—high-pitched, grating, like nails dragged across bone. Each jarring note pulled my heart into a frantic, erratic rhythm.

There was no room for compassion. No time for coddling. The world had emptied itself of such luxuries long ago, leaving only survival in its wake.

Something was coming. I had felt it for days—a pressure beneath my skin, a taut string waiting to snap. The air carried a weight, heavy and ancient, forbidden. I should have heeded the whispered prophecy of the blind woman who wandered into my world like a ghost from the depths. She had spoken of this danger, her voice thick with an anguish I hadn't understood until now.

"They're coming," she had said, her sightless eyes wide as the ocean, brimming with unseen terrors. Her child shifted restlessly in her arms, sensing the same unspoken menace. She had pleaded with me to prepare, to turn back, to do anything but press forward into the abyss. But I dismissed her—brushed aside her words as the ramblings of a desperate woman. My pride had been the greater force then, an immovable tide that drowned reason.

Now, as I made my way to the bridge to meet McGrady, her warning wrapped icy fingers around my spine. *The Demeter* groaned underfoot, her rhythm off-kilter, as if the sea itself resisted her passage. When I reached the bridge, McGrady stood frozen—broad shoulders hunched, eyes locked on the horizon.

"What's wrong?" I asked, placing a steadying hand on his shoulder. His silence answered before his lips moved. Slowly, he turned, his face ashen, his eyes unblinking as they pointed past me.

I followed his gaze.

In the distance, cutting through the grey haze of the horizon, a massive vessel emerged—its silhouette bloated and menacing. It moved with unnatural precision, its hull gleaming like a predator's tooth, slicing through the waves without sound.

"Do you think they're hostile?" McGrady's voice wavered, the tremor betraying the fear he tried to mask.

"I don't know," I admitted, my voice low, raw with doubt. My hand lingered on his arm a moment longer before I turned, leaving him to his thoughts. Deep down, I already knew the answer. Hostility hung in the air like the scent of gunpowder before the first shot. The ship was closing in, its purpose clear even without the raised flags of intent. Lawlessness ruled these seas now—governance had drowned alongside the old world, and this hulking specter was no envoy of peace.

I hurried back to my quarters, each step heavier than the last. Inside, Alana was already stirring, her thin frame rising from the bunk as if she'd felt the shift in the atmosphere. In her lap, the boy Ahmed lay curled, his small body wrapped in threadbare blankets, his face serene in sleep.

"What's going on out there?" Her voice was tight, searching the space around her with the urgency of someone who could only see in shapes and sounds.

"They're here," I replied, my voice barely above a whisper. The weight of those two words hung between us like the blade of a guillotine.

Alana's face paled. She clutched Ahmed tighter, her fingers trembling as she shook him awake.

"Ahmed, come on, baby," she murmured, her voice cracking under the strain. She rose unsteadily, the boy limp in her arms.

"It's us they want. Let them take us," she pleaded, desperation rising like floodwater.

"No!" I snapped, shaking my head violently. "We stick to the plan."

"Remember what I told you," she said, her words sharp, biting. "If something happens to me, take him. Promise me."

Her grip on the boy tightened, and his sleepy eyes fluttered open, gazing at her with a mixture of confusion and trust. I nodded once, solemnly, before leaving them behind and making my way to the top deck, where the tension among the crew was palpable.

The ship loomed closer now, cutting through the waves with chilling precision. Figures swarmed its decks, preparing for what could only be an invasion. And then they came.

They descended with the fury of a storm—agile and ruthless, their weapons gleaming like polished fangs under the pale light.

Amidst the chaos, a figure emerged from their ranks—a towering man with broad shoulders and a face chiseled into a permanent scowl. His hook-shaped sword gleamed menacingly as he stepped onto *The Demeter's* deck, his presence a shadow over the frenzied clash of blades and shouts.

"Your willing surrender is appreciated," he said, his voice carrying an unsettling calm. "But not necessary. What's yours is ours."

"Remove yourself from *The Demeter*," I shouted, my voice cutting through the din. "Or we'll remove you ourselves."

The pirate laughed—a low, guttural sound that resonated with unshakable confidence.

"You don't know who I am," he said, stepping closer, his boots slamming against the deck. "But you'll learn."

The fight that followed was chaos—a whirlwind of steel and blood. My crew fought valiantly, but we were outnumbered and outmatched. The pirate leader's hook-sword swung with brutal efficiency, its edge slicing through the air, narrowly missing me as I ducked and countered with my blade.

One by one, my crew fell. The deck ran red, and the cries of the wounded filled the air. A sharp blow to my chest sent me sprawling, and before I could recover, the pirate loomed over me, his blade poised for the killing stroke.

"A general rule," he sneered. "A Captain goes down with her ship."

His fist met my face, and darkness claimed me.

Darkness didn't release me gently. It spat me back into reality with the groan of failing metal and the cold kiss of seawater lapping at my legs. *The Demeter* was dying—her proud hull listing dangerously, her spirit broken. She trembled beneath me, her final death throes echoing in the cavernous silence of my failure.

The pirate's words still rang in my skull: *A Captain goes down with her ship.*

I had believed it. I had accepted it. But survival has a way of rewriting convictions.

I staggered to my feet, each movement a struggle against the shifting deck. The air reeked of salt and blood. My crew had done what they could— lifeboats dotted the churning waters, carrying what remained of us away from this ruin. Yet, as Captain, my duty was clear. A Captain must go down with her ship.

But then I heard it—a whimper, faint but unmistakable.

Turning, I saw her: a young girl, no older than six, curled in the shadow of the taffrail, her eyes wide with terror. Her presence was impossible, yet undeniable—a ghost of innocence in a place that had long since abandoned it.

"Where's your mom?" I asked, kneeling beside her.

"I don't know," she sobbed, clutching a ragged doll to her chest.

There was no time to think. Scooping her into my arms, I plunged into the freezing water. The sea roared around us, eager to claim what little remained. I kicked hard, the weight of the girl pressing against my chest as I fought the current. The nearest raft bobbed just ahead, its silhouette a fragile promise against the chaos.

"Captain?" one of the dwellers called out, his voice trembling with shock as I reached the lifeboat, hoisting the girl into the vessel.

"Take her!" I commanded.

"What about you?" someone asked, their voice thick with fear.

"I'll find the others," I said firmly, and dove back into the abyss.

* * *

I plunged into the icy water, the chill biting

into my skin like a thousand tiny daggers. The wreckage of *The Demeter* loomed above me—her once-proud frame reduced to a fractured silhouette against the churning sea, a monument to defiance and ruin.

Re-entering the sinking wreck felt like willingly stepping into a grave. Every instinct screamed at me to turn back, to save myself. But something stronger—something stubborn and unrelenting—drove me forward. Duty. Guilt. The promise I'd made.

The flooded corridors offered no respite. The water rose steadily, its chill numbing my limbs, sapping my strength with every stroke. *The Demeter* groaned and pitched violently, her bones cracking beneath the pressure, threatening to collapse in on herself and drag me down with her.

"Hello?!" I shouted, my voice echoing through the submerged halls, bouncing off fractured metal. The sound came back distorted, eerie—like the ship itself mocked my efforts. Another tremor shook the gangway. A surge of water slammed through the corridor, and I clung to a rusted pole, my grip slipping as the current tried to tear me away.

Navigating the tilted, waterlogged hall was a waking nightmare. Angles twisted unnaturally. Shadows flickered in the dying emergency lights.

My breath came in ragged gasps, lungs burning as I pushed forward. Then I saw it—a cavernous gap in the wreckage, jagged and wide.

Across the chasm, barely visible through the gloom, two figures clung to the edge of a broken walkway.

Alana and Ahmed.

Alana's voice was hoarse, urging him to hold on. The boy's small hands gripped the metal rail, his face pale with terror. The ship lurched again. A violent shudder. I watched in horror as Alana's fingers slipped.

"Alana!" I screamed, but the sea claimed her before the sound reached her ears. She vanished into the depths, swallowed by the cold, merciless dark.

I froze. The moment stretched, unbearable. But Ahmed's cries shattered the paralysis.

"Mommy!" he wailed, his voice raw, breaking with anguish.

"I've got you!" I shouted, forcing my body to move. The metal beneath me was slick with oil and seawater. I crawled, clawing my way across the twisted wreckage until I reached him.

"You're going to be okay!" I promised, though my voice trembled with uncertainty.

His wide, tear-filled eyes met mine. I wrapped my arms around him, pulling him close. "You have to hold onto me, Ahmed," I urged, my voice low but firm. "I'll get you out of here. You just have to trust me."

He nodded, his tiny hands clutching my soaked jacket. The ship groaned again—a final, thunderous cry. We were out of time.

I propelled us toward the nearest breach in the hull, water rushing in behind us. With Ahmed clinging to me, I leapt into the sea. The cold hit like a hammer, but I held him tight, kicking hard to keep us afloat.

Gasping, I spotted a raft bobbing not far away. Figures leaned over the edge, shouting, reaching. My limbs screamed in protest with every stroke, but I pushed forward, the boy's weight anchoring me to purpose.

Strong hands reached down, pulling Ahmed from my grasp. I clung to the edge, coughing, shivering, my breath ragged. For a moment, I allowed myself to look back.

The Demeter, proud and resilient, was gone. Her shattered remains slipped beneath the surface, swallowed by the unforgiving sea. The last bubbles rose, marking her grave.

A heavy silence fell. Not peace—just absence.

Ahmed's soft cries reached my ears, and I pulled myself fully into the raft, wrapping a protective arm around him.

"You're safe now," I whispered, though the words felt hollow. Safety was an illusion in this world. And the sea held no promises of mercy.

I

The Old World

2031, March 10th

My name is irrelevant. What matters is the data. Rapid polar melt, atmospheric destabilization, and anomalous tidal shifts—none of it aligns with known geophysical models. Sea levels are rising at catastrophic rates. If my projections hold, lunar gravitational influence will destabilize. A global hydrospheric event is imminent. If this is my final log, let it serve as a warning.

Something is Coming

A rjes clutches his satchel to his chest, lungs burning as he bolts down the tiled corridor of the college. His shoes slap against the waxed floor, echoing like gunshots. Students wave, call his name, try to catch his attention — he doesn't slow, doesn't answer. No time. Not now. Not when the numbers are still screaming inside his head.

He bursts through the glass doors into the pale daylight, cutting across the street toward the cracked stone stairwell of his apartment building. His heart hammers against his ribs, but the fear that drives him is larger than exhaustion. It is dread. Cold, suffocating dread.

The key rattles in the lock as he shoves the door open.

"What's all that for?" Tammy's voice greets him from the kitchen, half-laughing, half-concerned — until she sees his face. He is pale, sweating, eyes wild, breath coming in uneven gasps. Her own voice sharpens, drops low. "Arjes. Talk to me. What's wrong?"

Arjes doesn't answer. He stands frozen at the window, staring at the sun where it hangs fat and distorted above the horizon, its glare bleeding strangely against the clouds. His fingers twitch at his side. Finally, he turns to her, his voice raw.

"We need to leave."

Tammy sets the wooden spoon in her hand onto the counter, slowly, cautiously, as though he's a spooked animal ready to bolt. "Leave? What are you talking about?"

"I told them this would happen," he mutters, fumbling through drawers, pulling out keys, stuffing them into his bag with shaking hands. "And none of them listened. Not one."

From the hallway, a smaller voice cuts through the air. "Dad?" Tymond stands in the doorway, no more than twelve, his head tilted in confusion. He sees his father's frantic movements, the sheen of sweat across his brow. "Work go that bad?"

Arjes spins on him, his tone sharp, commanding. "Tymond — your room. Grab clothes. Enough for three days. Stuff them in a bag. Go!"

The boy flinches at the bark of his father's voice but obeys, vanishing down the hall.

Tammy grabs Arjes's arm, forcing him into the chair at the table. Her own fear trembles at the edges of her voice, but she forces it down. "Honey, sit. Look at me. Breathe. Explain what's going on. Please."

He leans forward, his eyes hollow, voice stunned. "They acted like they didn't believe me. Mocked my reports. Laughed at the simulations. But the whole time, they were preparing. Quietly. Quietly building their way out."

"Who?"

"There's a roundtable. Officials. Not just academics — people with power. People who decide who lives and who drowns."

Tammy swallows hard, but she doesn't interrupt. He digs into his coat pocket, producing a flash drive that trembles between his fingers. He jams it into his laptop on the counter, the machine whirring to life. Images bloom across the screen: massive hulls under construction in dry docks, blueprints of towering vessels — not ferries, not liners. Arks. Cities on the sea.

Tammy's breath catches. "They… they already built them."

"Started years ago," Arjes whispers, clicking furiously, pulling up lists. Names cascade across the screen, columns of them, highlighted, coded. "I traced the manifests. The passenger rosters."

Tammy steps closer, eyes narrowing as she scans the list. "These are politicians. Corporate heads.

Military." Her voice falters. "That's it?"

"That's it." Arjes slams the laptop shut, his hands shaking. "Twenty vessels. Twenty floating fortresses. And only their names fill the lists. No workers. No students. No families."

"They're going to leave us," Tammy breathes, horror rising in her throat. "Leave everyone else here to die."

Arjes looks at her, eyes wet but burning. "They're not going to leave us. They're going to erase us. My research showed them the timing, the inevitability — and they've decided who matters."

Her face hardens, anger blooming where fear had been. "But you're the one who warned them! Your work gave them this chance! And they'd just—"

"They will," Arjes cuts in, his tone low, certain. "They'll let the rest drown, starve, claw each other to pieces while the seas rise. Only the chosen make it aboard. The rest of us? We are ballast."

Silence hangs, broken only by the ticking of the wall clock. Then Arjes's voice drops further, urgent, desperate.

"We don't have time. I've secured a space in the Vizer Building, top floors. Reinforced. High above the floodline — for as long as there is one. It will buy us days, maybe weeks. Enough to survive while the city drowns."

Tammy stares at him, mouth half-open, mind reeling.

"Tammy." His voice cracks now, stripped of authority, of reason, down to something raw. "They know I know. I've been followed since the briefing. We have to move. Now."

Sky Rise

T he elevator doors groan open onto the twenty-eighth floor, a hollow mechanical sound swallowed by silence. The hall stretches long and dim, its carpet worn, its windows smudged with fingerprints of rain.

Tammy steps out first, her heels clicking softly as she drifts toward the glass. The city yawns beneath her, a maze of streets and glowing signs, the rush of cars threading endlessly below. She presses a hand against the cool pane, her breath fogging the surface.

"Is this high enough?" Her voice is barely more than a whisper.

Arjes lingers behind her, his satchel clutched tight to his chest. His eyes flick from the floor number stamped on the wall to the storm-colored horizon beyond the glass. His reply comes low, uncertain.

"I hope so."

He doesn't say more. He can't. Because he

doesn't know. He has seen the projections, the simulations — rising tides like jaws, swallowing coastlines whole. But simulations cannot measure panic, or the speed of collapse once it begins.

Tammy keeps staring downward, transfixed by the people below. A mother tugging her child across a crosswalk. A street vendor ladling soup into a paper cup. Strangers bustling, shouting, laughing, their lives unfolding as if nothing waits above them.

"It's like they don't even know."

"They don't," Arjes murmurs. He pulls the keys from his pocket with shaking hands and forces the apartment door open. "And the elites intend to keep it that way." He pauses in the threshold, his jaw tightening. "But I won't let them."

He pushes the door wide, and the three of them step inside.

The apartment is too lavish for its silence. A cavernous living room unfurls before them, glass walls offering a sweeping view of the glittering city. Plush furniture sits untouched, a rug thick enough to swallow footsteps. Everything is staged — polished, sterile, like a hotel suite waiting for ghosts.

Tymond lets out a low whistle, wandering toward the panoramic window. "How did you get this place?"

"It's been in reserve," Arjes says flatly, setting the satchel on the counter. His voice carries weight, the kind that presses against the air. "For when it was needed. That time is now."

Tammy's eyes dart across the room, taking in the untouched surfaces, the faint smell of stale dust. A corner of her mouth curves into a smirk. "Anyone else been up here before us?"

Arjes finally turns toward her, forcing a faint smile, though it never reaches his eyes. "No one but you, honey."

He twists open a bottle of water, the plastic crackling too loud in the hush of the room. He drinks deeply, but when the bottle lowers, his face is grim again. The shadows have returned.

"I won't abandon the world," he mutters. "Not for their false superiority."

Tammy drops into the sofa, her shoulders sagging. Her voice sharpens with disbelief. "I never thought people could be that corrupt."

"There are," Arjes answers, his tone clipped, final. He paces, restless, the window glow painting him in stark light. "People who discard life the second it becomes inconvenient. They will watch the seas swallow millions and still sip their wine on a deck chair. People like that have always existed. And they always will."

The silence that follows is heavy. Tymond shifts

uncomfortably, glancing from his father to the horizon. The city lights shimmer, but already the clouds beyond the skyline look wrong — bruised, swollen, like the sky itself is rotting.

"What are you going to do?" Tammy asks at last.

Arjes stops pacing. He stands with his back to the window, framed against the world he swears is ending.

"It may be months before the first signs show. A storm that will not end. Floodwaters gnawing the edges of every coast. That is time — time to force their hand. Time to make them build more arks."

Tammy leans forward, her elbows on her knees. "And how are you going to do that? What leverage do you possibly have?"

Arjes reaches into his pocket. Slowly. Reverently. The flash drive glints between his fingers, catching the city lights like a shard of glass.

"With this." His voice is hoarse, but burning. He holds it high, as though it weighs more than gold. "Their secrets. Their ships. Their plans. Everything they've hidden. It's all here. And I will use it."

For a moment, the room is silent but for the hum of the city far below. Then thunder rolls across the horizon — deep, distant, and hungry.

The Warning

"You lied to those people!" Arjes roars, his voice cracking against the gray sky. His hand slams against the wooden podium, rattling the microphones wired to it. The crowd, a restless sea of bodies pressed shoulder to shoulder, shifts uneasily. Some lean forward, curious. Others cross their arms, scowling.

News vans idle along the curb, their antennas stabbing into the low clouds. One camera swings to frame him in sharp focus, the red tally light burning like an unblinking eye.

"If you're just joining us," the anchor's voice cuts through from a speaker, tinny and detached, "breaking news from Essex County — a former meteorologist, recently dismissed from the Vizer R&D Corporation, has called an impromptu press conference. He claims that an elite coalition has prepared an escape plan to evade a catastrophic lunar event. His words… have ignited a storm of confusion and outrage."

Arjes grips the podium with white-knuckled hands. The sweat on his brow gleams beneath the harsh floodlights. His voice drops low, urgent, almost pleading.

"I am here because the truth has been buried. They told me my work didn't matter. They told me your lives didn't matter." His gaze sweeps the crowd — the mothers holding children on their hips, the students with half-torn backpacks, the workers in dirty uniforms still clutching lunch pails. "But it does. It matters because when the water comes, when the tides rise and keep rising, it won't care about your politics. It won't care about your paychecks. It will swallow us all."

A voice cuts through the murmurs: "Prove it!"

The words strike like a thrown stone. Arjes' head snaps toward the sound. A woman in the front row pushes forward, her eyes narrowed with fury.

"Prove what, exactly?" he fires back, his voice echoing off the stone facade of the town hall.

"Prove the conditions!" she shouts, her fists balled at her sides. "You're fearmongering! You're spouting doomsday trash without showing evidence! You're just a political extremist looking to divide us."

The crowd ripples with murmurs — doubt, suspicion, anger. The air thickens. Someone laughs bitterly. Another man jeers.

Arjes slams his palm flat on the podium, his chest heaving. His voice erupts like a crack of thunder.

"There is nothing political about survival!"

The microphones squeal with feedback, a shrill cry that makes the crowd flinch. He leans forward, pointing a trembling finger skyward.

"Pull your eyes from your screens. Look at the tides. Look at the skies. The moon itself is dragging the world out of balance, and you sit here demanding paperwork like this is some committee hearing! The ice is melting! The seas are rising! The weather you think you understand is breaking apart, piece by piece!"

A young man shouts back, his face twisted in disdain: "Everything's always changing! Storms. Politics. Governments. Always have, always will. What's your point, Dr. Toran?"

The crowd chuckles nervously, but Arjes does not smile. His voice drops, steady now, sharp as a blade.

"My point is this: if you stay silent, if you do nothing, the elites will survive. They've built ships you will never see. They've written lists your names will never be on. And when the waters come, when the horizon itself breaks, it is their children who will live… not yours."

A hush spreads across the assembly, broken only by the click of cameras and the low hum of news drones circling overhead. Thunder growls in the distance, a rolling tremor that makes windows rattle.

Arjes leans closer to the microphones, his eyes bloodshot, his voice hoarse but unyielding.

"I am not here to scare you. I am here to tell you that survival is not theirs to hoard. It is ours to take back. But if you do not fight for it — if you do not demand it — then when the flood comes, you will drown with the truth still locked in their vaults."

The last words hang in the air like smoke. The crowd stirs, torn between disbelief and terror. Some shout for proof again, others cry for justice. The first drops of rain patter against the podium, darkening the wood.

Arjes raises his arms to the sky, and the storm answers.

The Wave

T he television hisses to life as Tammy flicks it on, her weary eyes expecting the usual monotony of late-night chatter. Instead, a news bulletin overrides the broadcast with urgent tones.

"Several coastal cities remain under catastrophic impact from the unprecedented floods. Death tolls have already tripled last week's totals, with entire districts submerged. Multiple states and sovereign territories have declared states of emergency and have called upon the Worldwide Ark Vessel Corps to coordinate mass evacuations across the oceans. Citizens are urged to seek higher ground immediately."

Tammy clutches the edges of the couch, her throat tightening. The screen cuts to aerial footage: helicopters skimming above drowned metropolises where only rooftops pierce the rolling surface. Highways curve beneath black water, cars bobbing like toys. Faces press against broken glass as flood currents tear buildings apart in real time. Bridges collapse like paper, vanishing into the tide.

Her pulse hammers. This is it. This is what Arjes had shouted from the rooftops, what he lost his job over, what the world dismissed as paranoia. It was all here, on the screen, undeniable now.

Then — a sound. A warped *howl* of air pressure, like reality bending inward. It rattles the glass of the sliding window behind her, vibrating deep in her chest like the groan of a collapsing hull. Tammy rises on shaking legs.

"Arjes?" she calls, her voice breaking.

She draws toward the sound, toward the window, her bare feet sticking against the cold polished floor. She pulls the curtains aside—

And the horizon is gone.

The city is already half-drowned, but now the waters churn with a violence that no storm could explain. Whole blocks buckle beneath the currents. The sky darkens, the daylight fading as something enormous eclipses the sun.

Her eyes widen. The ocean itself is rising.

A wall of water towers in the distance, higher than skyscrapers, as if the sea has decided to stand upright. A tidal wave — no, something greater, something alive in its enormity — rises on the skyline, its sheer face blotting out the world.

Shadows stretch across the metropolis, turning day into an apocalyptic dusk.

Tammy's throat clenches. Her knees lock.

"Oh… my God…"

"Get away from the windows!"

Arjes bursts into the room, chest heaving, hair slicked with sweat. Tymond is clutched in one arm, his small face pale with terror. Arjes lunges, seizing Tammy by the arm.

The roar of the oncoming wave is deafening, like a thousand freight trains colliding at once. The apartment trembles as if sensing its doom.

Then the world breaks.

The wave collides with the city. Glass detonates, concrete fractures. The luxury tower groans before its façade explodes inward. Water doesn't just crash — it *invades*, a hyper-pressurized wall ripping through steel and stone.

The window shatters, and Tammy screams as the flood hurls into the room with impossible force.

The family is lifted, spun, swept into the current. Their bodies smash against furniture, the hallway warping into a drowning tunnel. Tammy claws for air as the torrent slams them down the corridor.

"Hold on!" Arjes bellows, his words shredded by the roar of the flood.

He locks his arm around a railing, muscles

screaming. With his other hand, he clamps onto Tymond, his knuckles whitening. Tammy flails, desperate, then seizes her son's leg. For a breathless instant, the three of them hang in a fragile chain against the fury of the water.

The current is relentless, a monstrous physics that seems to tilt the world sideways. Their bodies are pulled at angles that defy gravity. The stairwell groans, metal twisting, beams ripping free.

Tammy's nails dig into her child's leg, but the water is merciless. Her grip is slipping. Her eyes meet Arjes's — wide, terrified, shimmering with tears — and he knows. He knows in that single look what is about to happen.

"Baby?!" she screams, her voice ragged, her face distorted by the rushing torrent.

"Just hold on!" Arjes yells back, straining with every shred of strength in his body. But his words feel hollow even as they leave his lips.

Tammy's fingers slide free.

"No—!" Arjes's scream fractures as she tumbles, limbs flailing, vanishing into the liquid abyss.

"Mom!" Tymond's shriek pierces the roar, and in his panic he thrashes. His small hand slips from Arjes's grasp.

"Tymond! No!"

The boy is ripped away, his figure flung into the maelstrom, swallowed alongside his mother.

One instant they are there, the next they are erased, carried into the watery void as if they never existed.

Arjes's chest constricts with agony. His grip falters. He pulls himself upward, hand over hand against the torrent, forcing his broken body into the stairwell where the waters crash but do not fully consume. He drags himself onto the landing, coughing violently, his lungs burning with salt and blood.

He looks back down the corridor, eyes wide, desperate for any sign — a hand, a shadow, anything — but there is nothing. Only the churning flood, receding into silence.

His wife. His son. Gone.

The city beyond screams with sirens and collapsing steel. The wave still pounds, splitting towers like matchsticks. Arjes grips the railing until his hand bleeds, his teeth grinding. His mind collapses inward, wracked with a grief so deep it almost unmakes him.

But beneath it — buried like embers under ash — something else ignites.

Not surrender.

Not despair.

Something sharper.

Resolve.

II

Never-Land

55 Years Later

**Captain's Log — Kara Logan, Calvina
Ark**

*The seas have been calm, but a shadow
rises on the horizon. Massive. Intentional.
I feel fear, sharp and biting, yet I am ready.
My crew must be ready too. Orders are set:
double watch, battle stations at the ready.
Whatever comes, the Calvina Ark will
meet it with resolve—and I will not falter.*

Hooked

S alt burned in every cut.

Kara's face—slick with blood, sweat, and sea—twitched with every lash of murky water that slapped against her skin. Her lips were cracked, eyes swollen half-shut. Lacerations carved across her brow and jaw like the memory of a storm, reopened with each movement, each breath.

The catwalks groaned beneath her body, warped metal moaning as the rising water surged through the lower levels of the ship. She lay twisted in a shallow pool just above the ballast tanks, where the bulkheads had given way during the last skirmish. Every breath she took felt like it came with a blade between her ribs.

She reached upward—blindly—fingers grasping at cold steel. The railing was slick with oil and blood, but she latched on, pulling herself up with the trembling desperation of someone who knew the ship wouldn't stay afloat much longer.

Her boots scraped across the grated deck, dragging sea-slick puddles as she rose. Her knees shook, her shoulders sagged—but she stood.

Barely.

The dim light from a broken ceiling lamp above flickered intermittently, casting fractured shadows down the corridor. The interior of the vessel smelled of seawater and diesel. Beneath it, the coppery scent of blood lingered in the air like a ghost refusing to leave.

She wasn't alone.

Not anymore.

But whoever remained wasn't on her side.

"Dracor..." she rasped, voice thin and broken. She swallowed hard. Her throat ached, raw from crying out in the fight and breathing smoke. "Dracor!"

Her words carried poorly through the flooded steel corridors. The name hung like a dying breath.

She dropped to one knee and clutched the short sword lying in the shallows beside her. Its hilt was wrapped in soaked bandages, the blade nicked and painted with old blood—some hers, some not. She clutched it close, her fingers wrapping around it with fading strength.

"Dracor!" she called again, louder this time, the name now laced with something more dangerous than pain: doubt.

Silence answered.

Not a soul stirred above or below. Only the rising slosh of ocean water licking up through the seams in the decking, like the ship itself was bleeding out from its lower chambers.

Had the entire crew been taken? Executed?

Her thoughts churned as wildly as the sea beneath the vessel.

The invaders were children. That was the most humiliating detail. Preteens—some no older than ten—dressed in patchwork armor, wielding chipped blades and electric prongs like pirates born of myth. There was a fury in them, but worse, there was *discipline*.

They weren't feral. They were trained.

Someone had taken these children and forged them into precision weapons. A cult of silence and cruelty. A nightmare set afloat on rusted hulls and desperate ambition.

And worse—every rumor had been true.

First, they stalked their targets from the mist. They didn't strike until they'd isolated a ship— usually smaller, slower, under-defended. Then came the deception: a distress call, a lifeboat adrift, a child in need. And every damn time, a soft-hearted captain welcomed them aboard.

Then came the seizure. Quick. Coordinated. They moved like predators on instinct—sabotaging power conduits, severing communication lines, locking hatches from the outside.

By the time anyone realized the truth, it was too late. Supplies gone. Power gutted. Hull compromised. A sinking coffin left behind, barely afloat.

Kara stumbled forward, limping deeper down the catwalk, her sword held loose in one hand. Her shoulder slammed into a wall to steady herself.

She could feel the weight of the water now. It surged around her calves. Her ship was sinking. The *Calvina*—a third-gen Ark, old but proud— was going under.

And the bastards who did this had vanished like shadows.

Her breath hitched. She reached a torn control panel sparking dimly on the wall and tried to access the command override. Nothing. The interface was fried—clever sabotage. They hadn't just attacked.

They'd *studied* them first.

Her heart thudded.

She glanced back into the corridor.

Still no sign of Dracor. No sign of anyone. Only the faintest echo of dripping water. And then… something else. A whisper. Soft. Impossible. Like a child's giggle muffled behind a bulkhead.

She froze.

No movement. Just the dim flicker of dying light.

And yet… the giggle lingered, twisting beneath her skin.

She wasn't just beaten.

She was being *toyed* with.

She backed into a wall and tightened her grip on the sword. Her hand bled where the hilt bit into her palm.

Then a noise from the shadows ahead. Bare feet slapping metal. Small. Light. Faint as a memory.

Kara breathed slowly, a thin whimper escaping her cracked lips.

She didn't know who these children were.

But she knew who had sent them.

A whisper passed through her mind like a sickness:

He trains them like dogs.

The sea hissed louder now. She could feel the ship sinking by degrees.

And in her mind's eye, beyond the rising water, beyond the salt and blood and terror, she saw a figure. Not a child.

A man.

Watching.

Always watching.

Wrecked

O verhead, the great ark's masthead light swung wildly with the listing hull, casting slow, pendulum arcs across the carnage.

Kara's eyes locked on a boy sprawled before her—a scrap of life in a war-torn corridor. His uniform was not the tattered civilian garb of the refugee children huddled behind her, but the crude patchwork rig of the Renegades, sewn from scavenged sailcloth and rusted insignia plates. His tunic was soaked black where he pressed a trembling hand against his gut, trying to hold himself together.

One of *them*.

Now, one of her prisoners.

Her voice was low but shaking with fury.

"Why should I waste breath—or bandages—on you?"

The deck beneath them groaned again as the ark's keel screamed in protest. Somewhere deep below, water flooded the engine room with a

40

deaf, crushing roar. The vessel was dying—its thousand-ton frame slowly surrendering to the abyss. Kara's gaze swept over the boy, her mind as turbulent as the sea battering the hull.

"The price for treachery," she said, stepping closer, "should be the endless spilling of blood from your black heart."

The boy's reply was steady, almost defiant. "Then so be it."

He could not have been more than nine, but his eyes were old—flat, calculating, carrying the weary cynicism of someone who had seen too many suns rise over too many corpses. "Orders kept me alive," he went on. "Orders are what's killing me. Either way, the orders don't matter anymore. So do what you must."

The surrounding silence was only broken by the whimper of the other children and the hollow clang of a loose davit arm swinging in the wind. Kara studied him. Something in the set of his jaw stirred an unwilling respect in her. This was no ordinary deck rat.

"What's your name?"

"Dover."

"Dover," she repeated, tasting the name like a challenge. "You're coming with us on the escape craft. The last thing I'll do is leave your soul to be swallowed before it's truly held to account."

She extended her hand. Dover accepted it without hesitation, and she pulled him upright, his knees buckling as she caught him against her chest. His lips were already paling to a ghostly blue, sweat sheening his brow. He hung there, suspended between life and the long pull of the deep, but his gaze never left hers.

That was the last survivor she found. No more shouts in the passageways. No more scraping of boots on steel. Just the hollow wail of the wind through the breached superstructure.

She turned, leading her ragged clutch of survivors toward the internal mayday chamber—a cramped, steel-walled refuge where the escape craft were stowed. They boarded the cutter, a stubby, triple-hulled craft with the paint scorched from its flanks, and the locking clamps released with a metallic shudder. Gravity took hold, and the vessel dropped down its chute into the heaving black water below.

As the cutter's twin screws bit into the waves and pulled them clear, Kara looked back.

The ark was listing hard to port now, her great prow rising like the head of a dying beast before the stern vanished into the churning dark. Masts snapped one by one, the sound sharp as gunshots, and the vessel that had once combed the forever seas slipped beneath the horizon of foam.

She turned her gaze downward. Dover's forehead was damp and hot under her palm, though the color in his cheeks was fading fast. She pressed harder on the knife wound, feeling his pulse flutter like a trapped fish beneath her fingers.

"Come on, kid. Stay with me. We put out a distress call. Someone will answer."

His eyes were half-lidded, his voice barely more than a breath. "Don't make promises."

A pause, then a faint, strange smile. "I'm perfectly fine with destiny. That's all that truly guides the boats."

His chest rose once more—then stilled. A final sigh escaped him, warm against her collarbone, and was gone.

The cutter's prow cut onward through the black swells, carrying the living into the uncertain dark.

* * *

The horn tore Kara out of the shallow, broken sleep she had collapsed into, her cheek pressed against the blistered rim of the evacuation boat. She blinked hard, her throat dry as salt. For a moment she thought it was another dream, the same kind that taunted her with phantom ships and false landfalls. But this sound carried across the water like iron—low, resonant, alive.

Her pulse quickened. She forced herself upright, her neck stiff from days of half-sleep against the metal. The small raft groaned under her shifting weight, its battered pontoons sighing against the swells.

It may have been days—maybe longer—since they'd drifted from the wreck, and the survival kit had been picked down to crumbs and drops. The rations had been meant for seven days, maybe eight if stretched carefully. They'd lasted half that time. The children beside her had stopped asking for food; their silence was worse than the begging.

Kara twisted around toward the stern, squinting against the sting of salt spray. And there, hazy through the mist and distance, was a hull cutting the horizon. A leviathan compared to their dinghy. Letters stenciled in white across its battered plating: *VESTA.*

Her breath caught. Her heart rose like a flare fired skyward.

"I knew it," she whispered, the words cracking but real, spilling out before she could stop them. Relief surged through her chest like a tide, fragile but enough to hold her upright.

The sea shifted beneath them, the swells growing as the ark's displacement churned the water. Kara's hands closed on the nylon safety lines that rimmed the raft, bracing herself as the little craft rocked against the pull of something vast approaching.

She glanced downward at Dover. The boy's body was curled awkwardly against the inner bulkhead of the raft, wrapped in a foil blanket no longer meant for warmth. His face was pale, lips parted slightly, eyes closed forever. She'd done what she could—kept him apart from the others, away from the children's line of sight—but still she felt the sharp twist of guilt every time her eyes found him.

She tightened her grip, knuckles blanching.

"Everyone hold steady," she called, forcing her voice into something commanding. "That ship's coming for us. Just sit tight, don't panic."

Some of the younger dwellers lifted their heads, hollow eyes staring past her, straining to catch sight of what she promised. Others clung to one another, silent, skin sunburned and lips cracked. A few adults stirred at her words, but none of them looked convinced.

The waters heaved again, harder. Wind cut across the raft, carrying the scent of ozone and churned brine. Kara tilted her head back and froze.

Above them, a formation of clouds was rolling in from the west—dark, roiling, monstrous. A squall line. The kind that could swallow a dinghy whole without even leaving wreckage. Lightning flickered within its belly, a grim warning stitched into the sky.

The swells began to stack, steep and breaking, sending the raft lurching sideways. One of the children whimpered; another vomited into the bilge water at their feet. Kara wrapped her legs under the bench plank and gripped harder, eyes locked on the *Vesta.*

It loomed larger with every swell, its blackened hull scarred by old fires, streaked with salt and rust. The ship looked less like salvation and more like a fortress dragged unwillingly into the deep— but still, it was a ship. Steel. Decks. Provisions. Protection.

And for Kara, it was all that stood between her and the storm's teeth.

Her gaze flicked once more to Dover's body, tucked into shadow. The storm might have him yet, might scatter them all into the abyss. But not if she could help it.

Not yet.

She fixed her eyes on the ark, refusing to look away as the wind clawed at her hair and the sea threatened to roll them. Hope and terror braided together in her chest until she could barely breathe.

The *Vesta* was coming closer.

But so was the storm.

III

The Vesta

Commandment of the Vesta
Order, balance, and resilience. The Vesta shall navigate with dignity, offering humanitarian presence where safe and practical. Strength lies in restraint. We do not chase storms—we endure them.

—Senior Councilman Balthazar Dach

Nice to Meet You Ahmed

"Truth or dare!"

Billy snapped, his voice sharp as a cracked bell in the steel belly of the ship. He jabbed a finger at Ahmed like he was issuing orders on a war deck.

Ahmed sat cross-legged, the rusted bulkhead behind him sweating with condensation. He rubbed his hands together for warmth, then sighed. "Truth," he muttered, already regretting it.

Billy groaned like the ship's old hull. "You always pick truth."

"That's 'cause you always dare me to do something dumb."

Billy's grin cut across his dirty face like a scar. "Just say dare, coward."

Ahmed narrowed his eyes, jaw tightening. He wasn't about to get punked in front of the others. He was ten now—older, sharper, and tired of being underestimated. "Fine," he said, low and bitter. "Dare."

Billy's eyes lit up. "I dare you to sneak into the

brig."

Ahmed threw up his hands. "I knew it!"

Billy shrugged, victorious. "You said dare. Rules are rules. What, you scared?"

"No," Ahmed snapped, already stuffing his things into the under-compartment of the bulkhead. "If I get caught, you're the one scrubbing bilge for a month."

The group of kids—half-feral, smudged with oil, and starved of entertainment—followed him like a pirate crew tailing their unlucky captain. They padded through the narrow passageways of the *Vesta's* lower decks, their laughter fading under the hum of the ship's power core and the creaking of pressure-stressed steel.

The *Vesta* was a behemoth—one of the last of the Arc Fleet, retrofitted to sail the salt-choked waters of the planetary flood they called Neverland. Earth had drowned beneath rising oceans and atmospheric collapse, and the survivors clung to whatever floated. Onboard, discipline kept people alive, and the brig was a line no kid was meant to cross.

Ahmed crouched beside a coolant conduit that pulsed with blue light, the others huddled close behind. "I can't just waltz in there. Someone's gotta come out first."

Minutes passed. Then more. The stale air

thickened. Somewhere down the passage, boots echoed. A guard emerged—naval armored, re-breather mask hanging loose at his hip, oblivious.

Billy was about to whisper something smart—then sneezed.

The guard's head twitched.

Ahmed didn't wait. He launched himself down the passage and dove into the shadowed stairwell. He tore down the grated steps two at a time, each clang a death knell. At the bottom, he nearly slipped on condensation pooling along the grooved floor panels.

The brig.

It stank of rust, salt, mildew, and despair. Dim yellow emergency lights cast sickly shadows over the walls. The metal bars that separated the cells from the walkway looked ancient, warped by salt corrosion. Leaks ran down the bulkheads like tears. This was the end of the line—the place where the worst of the *Vesta's* remnants were chained and forgotten.

Ahmed took one step forward.

Snoring. A mutter. The faint sound of someone scratching something onto the wall.

He froze.

"I can hear you from here, boy," came a voice—gravelly, ragged like netting torn in a storm.

Ahmed's eyes darted around. "Who's there?"

"Follow the voice."

He crept forward, passing shadows curled in hammocks or sprawled on mats. Eyes watched him—some curious, some hollow, none friendly.

"That's it," the voice croaked. "You ever hear what happened to the curious cat?"

Ahmed blinked. "No."

"Then I ain't telling you," the voice wheezed out a laugh.

"Why not?"

"'Cause you're still curious. I ain't here to kill the fire in ya."

Eventually, he saw him—a wiry old man hunched inside a corner cell, skin like wrinkled parchment, eyes sunken but alive with mischief. He pulled something from beneath his moldy pillow. It was a sliver of ham—so thin it looked like a breath. He peeled a strand from it and placed it on his tongue like it was gold.

"That all they feed you?" Ahmed asked.

The man looked at him as if that was the dumbest question he'd heard all week. "If I had more, you think I'd be rationing crumbs like a squirrel in winter?"

"Maybe you're a light eater," Ahmed replied, straight-faced.

The old man laughed hard, belly shaking like a warped cargo drum. "Name's Arjes."

"Ahmed," the boy replied.

"You think you should be down here, Ahmed?" Arjes asked, tone suddenly parental.

"I think you need more food. They've got tons upstairs."

"That they do," Arjes nodded, licking his lips. "But down here? This place don't have half what we were promised. *Sky City* was supposed to fix all that."

Ahmed furrowed his brow. "Sky City?"

"You never heard of it?"

"No. Is it like… a story or something?"

Arjes leaned forward, his chains clinking softly. "*Sky City* ain't no bedtime tale. It's real. The last great haven. A floating fortress where the old world lives on. For those of us who still have hope."

Ahmed stared at him, mind racing. "But… that's not possible."

"You're right. Not for most. But that doesn't mean it ain't out there."

A siren wailed faintly overhead. Shift change.

Arjes straightened slowly, wincing at a pain buried deep. "You should go, kid. Before someone finds you."

"I want to know more!"

"Not tonight."

"Please."

"Alright, alright!" Arjes snapped. "Bring food next time. And maybe I'll give you a story worth sneaking in for."

I Am Dawn

I couldn't find the boy.

Again.

Ahmed had vanished from the berthing compartment like vapor bleeding through the seams of a rusted pipe. My chest tightens as I scan the rows of tightly packed bunks—each one a coffin-shaped cradle for the weary and displaced. His blanket is twisted, thrown aside in a way that speaks of haste, not rest.

"Not again," I whisper, but it comes out broken. "God... not again."

I shove off the cold alloy wall and burst into the main gangway. The lights above buzz, flickering with age, casting a sickly amber hue along the corridor's ribbed bulkheads. My boots clang against the steel decking, echoing between the walls like a war drum—too loud, too desperate.

The *Vesta* groans around me. Always groaning, as if resenting the burden of the broken world it carries on its spine. She was a vessel meant for salvation—once pristine, now corroded and aching. A floating relic of a time before the flood swallowed the Earth whole. One of the last of the Arc-Class ships, she cuts through the gray oceans with reluctant pride, her hull lined with algae scars and weld-patched wounds.

I pound past flickering security beacons and warning placards bolted to the walls:

RESTRICTED ACCESS — LEVEL 4 CLEARANCE ONLY

DECONTAMINATION REQUIRED BEYOND THIS POINT

DANGER: REACTOR COILS — AUTHORIZED PERSONNEL ONLY

I check them all. No sign of him.

My lungs burn—not just from exertion, but from something darker: the creeping terror clawing its way up my spine. It's not just sweat streaming down my face. It's the shame of knowing I let this happen again. And the weight of a broken promise that's haunted me since his mother's death.

Bootsteps—heavy, synchronized—echo from the rear of the ship. I spin around just in time to see the *Vesta* Commandos emerge from the lower deck, black-armored, helm-visors lit, moving with grim purpose. Their presence is never a good sign. They don't jog unless something serious has gone wrong.

"Commandos!" I call, falling into step beside them. "What's happening?"

The lead marine turns just enough to glance at me. His voice filters through the comm-grille of his helmet. "A boy went overboard, Council-woman."

My heart stops. Drops like ballast.

"No…" I breathe, my voice no longer mine. "Please, not him."

"We think it was that Fasil kid."

Of course it was.

My vision swims. My legs almost give out, but I force myself to stay upright, to breathe past the weight that's plummeted to the pit of my stomach. My hands tremble. I clench them until my nails dig into my palms.

I was supposed to be watching him. Protecting him. I made a vow as his mother lay in the infirmary, her blood thin and her voice thinner still. *Promise me; if something happens to me,* she rasped, *don't let him fade into the flood.*

And here I am—chasing echoes.

The crew hatch to the outer deck screeches as it opens. Cold air slaps me across the face, salt-rich and metallic, saturated with ocean vapor. The moan of the wind over the deck is almost human in its mourning. I follow the Commandos through, emerging into the blinding fog of early dawn—mist curling around the antennas and signal towers like ghost fingers.

There, near the stern, a cluster of Commandos stands pressed to the taffrails, peering over the edge of the *Vesta's* flank. Their shoulders are rigid. Silent. And silence means only one thing.

"No—No! NO!" I scream, shoving my way forward. "Where is he?!"

A gloved hand catches my arm before I can lunge over the side. "Councilwoman—!"

"Where is he?!"

None of them speak. They don't need to. Their helmets turn downward in unison, toward the gray, endless churn of the sea.

The water below is roiling—black, bottomless, and unforgiving. There's no shadow of a child. No shape, no splash. Just the hollow hiss of wind across a dead ocean and the dull clang of the *Vesta's* engines vibrating beneath my feet.

Their silence tells me everything.

Ahmed is gone.

* * *

A gracious descent tears me from the safety of the

deck.

No hesitation—just a breathless leap from the edge of the ark's hull.

I tuck my legs, point my toes, and cut through the frigid air like a harpoon loosed from divine hands. The wind roars past me, and for a breathless second, I feel weightless.

Then—impact.

The ocean strikes like iron.

A soundless implosion swallows me whole as I slice into the flooded graveyard that has become our world. The surface vanishes behind me, replaced by pressure, darkness, and cold that bites deep beneath the skin. The sea has no bottom, no mercy—only endless hunger.

Saltwater floods my ears, muffling the world above. The weight of the ocean clings to me like guilt. I open my eyes—the sting immediate, fierce, like fire inside my skull. But I force them wider. I have to.

And there he is.

Ahmed's small frame drifts downward, limbs slack, hair swirling like kelp. His body is suspended in the blue void, drifting deeper into oblivion, caught in the lullaby of the tide.

No.

I kick hard, muscles screaming as I cut through the drag. Bubbles dance around me like the spirits of the drowned. My fingers reach, then grip—his arm cold, limp, fragile in my grasp. I yank him close and twist upward, legs churning like twin screws against the abyss.

We break the surface.

The air is a violent thing—choking, wet, filled with distant shouting and the clang of rope against metal. The Commandos have already deployed safety rigs. A rope ladder slaps the hull beside me, and down the side of the ark, two suited figures descend on belay lines like descending angels of steel and carbon.

"I've got him!" I roar between heaving gasps.

Rough hands reach. I hold Ahmed to my chest as they secure lines to our harnesses. The winch groans, and we rise, swaying over the dark waters like fragile cargo. Spray lashes against my cheeks. Somewhere above, the sky cracks with thunder— whether from storm or stress fracture, I don't know. The world always sounds like it's ending.

The moment my boots strike the deck, I lay him down. Cold steel beneath him. The boy doesn't move. His skin has turned a ghastly shade of brownish-blue—like he's been carved from the ocean itself.

"Come on," I mutter, voice breaking. "Come on, dammit!"

I drop to my knees and begin compressions, my

palms pressing into his chest with every ounce of will I have left. One. Two. Three. Again. Again. The deck beneath us thuds with each thrust. Saltwater spills from his lips, but not enough.

"Don't do this," I hiss. "Don't you leave me!"

Tears blur my vision. I try to blink them away, but they come faster, heavier, as if every suppressed failure I've ever buried has come home to drown me.

My hands shake.

"Alana…" I whisper into the mist. "If you're watching—just give me one spark. One breath. You believed in him. You always believed in him."

The compressions blur into desperation. My rhythm falters. My mind screams.

And then—I break.

My sobs fall onto his chest. My hands clench at the edges of his soaked shirt as I howl into the wind like a wounded animal. Around me, the Commandos stand still. Helpless. Silent. The ocean groans against the hull, mourning with me.

I've failed him. I've failed her. I've failed the one promise I had no right to break.

"He's gone, Dawn," a Commando says softly, placing a hand on my shoulder.

"It's *Councilwoman Perry,*" I spit, jerking away from his touch.

I turn back to Ahmed and press again—harder

this time, reckless, furious with the world for thinking it could take him.

One last pump—

—and he coughs.

A violent, gurgling gasp erupts from his chest, water spraying from his mouth in a sick torrent. His body arches, lungs flaring as if remembering their purpose. He gasps again, wheezing, spitting, flailing weakly in the mist-slick air.

"Ahmed!" I cry, my voice raw, breaking open.

He blinks up at me, dazed, confused. "What… what happened?" he mumbles, reaching for the knot swelling on his temple.

"You tell me," I say, rising to my feet, wiping tears and seawater from my face in one trembling motion. I need to breathe. I need to get away before the rage takes over.

The moment shatters. Panic gives way to bitter fury. Compassion cracks beneath the weight of disappointment.

"You crossed the line this time," I say coldly. "You almost died."

Ahmed stares at me, unsure whether to cry or crack a joke.

And I'm not sure which would've made me angrier.

***

The silence after Ahmed's revival doesn't last. It never does.

The moment he's stable, the moment the adrenaline fades, the world rushes back in—cold, bureaucratic, and merciless. I barely have time to dry my face before the summons comes. A tribunal. Of course.

Now I sit rigid in the iron-backed chair, my shoulders tight with the tension I've swallowed whole since pulling Ahmed from the sea. The chamber stinks of old metal, recycled air, and sweat—an atmosphere of judgment clinging to every rivet in the walls. The kind of room designed to make you feel small.

I keep glancing down at him—my foster son. My responsibility. I give him another rub across his trembling shoulders, trying to channel some semblance of calm into the storm brewing behind his eyes.

Ahmed doesn't flinch.

Across the rust-patched chamber, Senior Councilman, Balthazar Dach looms behind the makeshift tribunal desk, which is nothing more than a gutted navigation console repurposed into something resembling order. The red emergency lights overhead cast deep shadows across his furrowed face, turning his scowl into something monstrous.

His fist slams the table with a boom, the sound echoing through the hollow bones of the ship.

"Is there something wrong with you, boy?!"

His voice hits like a gunshot—sharp, cold, unflinching. The kind of tone used on soldiers, not children.

Ahmed doesn't cower. His chin stays high. His small fists tighten at his sides. He locks eyes with the councilman, unblinking.

Balthazar leans forward, his silver beard bristling like wire. "Why in the name of this ship's keel would you pull something that reckless?"

Behind those words is more than anger. There's fear, desperation, fatigue. But like always, Balthazar buries it beneath authority.

"You could've exposed our position," he barks. "Do you have any idea what it means to fall overboard in these waters? Smugglers, scavengers, rogue vessels—we don't get second chances out here."

I straighten, my voice finally finding breath. "Maybe the fact that he almost died should carry a little more weight than—"

"Talk only when spoken to, Councilwoman," he snaps, jabbing a gnarled finger in my direction.

"You're not innocent in this. You vouched for him. His safety was your responsibility."

My fists clench tight enough to hurt. But I say nothing. Not yet. The heat is rising behind my ribs, but I bury it—deep.

Balthazar exhales slowly, then looks back at Ahmed. "Well? Anything to say for yourself?"

Silence.

I turn to Ahmed, watching his face carefully. His lip curls—not in fear, but in defiance. His eyes burn—not recklessly, but with pain he doesn't have the words to explain. And I recognize it. I've worn that look once too.

Then comes his voice. Low. Calm. Controlled.

"You never said why we weren't allowed up there."

His words strike the room like an unexpected swell—quiet, but undeniable.

I snap my gaze to him, a look sharp enough to pierce titanium.

Balthazar's eyes narrow. "You think that matters?" His fingers creep to the gavel beside him— an old piece of scrap fitted with a steel nut as a head. "That's the rule. It doesn't need explanation."

Ahmed's voice doesn't rise, but the defiance in it does. "Maybe it does. Maybe if someone explained things, people wouldn't go sneaking around."

I suck in a breath. His bravery—or maybe stupidity—is boiling over now.

"For gods' sake, kid," Balthazar snaps. "You nearly drowned!"

The hatch behind us hisses open with a groan. In steps Lawrence, a fellow councilman, drenched in ink and sweat, holding a stack of reports under one arm.

"You can't even swim, Ahmed," Lawrence says with a grim shake of his head. "What the hell were you thinking?"

Ahmed doesn't answer. He doesn't have to.

Balthazar grits his teeth and stands. The weight of his years leans hard into the desk as he levels a gaze that could bend steel.

"Two months' restriction," he says, voice low and final.

"Two months?!" Ahmed and I bark at the same time, our voices overlapping in shocked outrage.

He doesn't blink. "Next time, it'll be until your eighteenth birthday."

The silence that follows is thicker than the ocean fog outside. Ahmed storms from the chamber, boots stomping like cannon fire. His jaw is set like stone. His shoulders tremble not from fear—but from rage.

I sit still for a moment, staring at the doorway

long after he's disappeared.

A part of me wants to say Balthazar hadn't gone far enough. That Ahmed needs to learn what the world really is now—a graveyard dressed as a planet. That discipline is love, and pain is its messenger.

But another part of me—the mother in me—wants to tear the old man's desk apart and scream that he's gone too far.

The truth is somewhere between.

Balthazar is right.

And I'm not ready to admit it aloud.

If I want to honor the promise I made to Alana… if I want Ahmed to survive the kind of world that took her from him… then I'll have to be crueler than the sea. Not to break him. But to sharpen him.

Because love isn't softness anymore.

It's steel.

She Is Dawn

The chamber might've once been a perfect place for a captain to issue commands—broad, reinforced, and central to the vessel's inner hull—but there was no captain here. Not in name. Not in spirit. And certainly not in the mind of Balthazar Dach.

To him, captains were relics of a dead world—symbols of false superiority built on the bones of fading traditions. He had no interest in the pageantry of rank, nor the sentimental attachments that came with titles. Leadership, in Balthazar's worldview, was not about hierarchy. It was about control. And control did not tolerate shared power.

The walls of the Vesta's central command chamber were cold and damp with condensation. Metal beams groaned softly in the ceiling, and ancient rivets lined the edges of rust-darkened consoles. The Vesta herself sounded weary—her hull murmuring like a beast curled in on itself, tired from drifting too long through endless waters.

Balthazar stood at the head of the room, behind a table salvaged from the wreckage of the Demeter. He ran his hand over the worn surface absently, the grooves familiar to his touch. This was his table. His ship. His decisions, made in the vacuum left by drowning nations.

He didn't need anyone.

The entrance hatch creaked open with the guttural sigh of old steel. One by one, the council began to arrive.

First was Councilman Levy—loyal, methodical, and unflinchingly aligned with Balthazar's vision of brutal pragmatism. Levy was less a man than a ledger with legs, his presence marked by the scent of ink and antiseptic.

Next came Councilwoman Strauss, her boots sharp against the decking, posture stiff with self-importance. Of the two women on the council, Strauss carried herself like a scalpel—precise, cold, and sharp enough to cut with words alone. She slid into her seat without a glance to anyone, already prepared to dissect the agenda before it even started. After a few other members entered, Councilman Lawrence entered with an air of mild exasperation and damp shoulders, trailing mist from the sea spray outside. Alone.

Balthazar's eyes narrowed immediately.

"Once again," he said, voice dripping with disdain, "we're down a member."

His words hung in the air like fog—sour and heavy.

Lawrence didn't flinch. He loosened the collar of his weather-worn overcoat and replied evenly, "Give her a break, will you?"

"Breaks are for those who've earned them," Balthazar snapped. "Remind me again why she's on the council at all?"

Strauss smirked without looking up from her notes. "Some appointments were made out of pity. Others from desperation."

"Enough." Lawrence's voice cut through the growing tension like a blade. He took his seat, eyes flicking from face to face. "Perhaps we could wait until she arrives before gutting her name like a caught fish."

Levy raised an eyebrow. "And if she never shows, Lawrence? Will you defend her absence until we all drown waiting?"

Lawrence leaned forward, steepling his fingers. "Some would find it rude to badmouth a council member when she's not even present to defend herself."

He paused, letting that settle.

Balthazar's lip curled. "And some would find it naïve to expect accountability from the unaccountable."

"The woman saved a boy from drowning less than twenty-four hours ago," Lawrence said, voice sharper now. "You'd think that might earn her some delay."

"She endangered our secrecy doing so," Strauss muttered. "And she's too emotionally entangled with that boy to make clear decisions. Attachment weakens command."

"And yet here we are," Lawrence replied coolly, "barely holding this ship together with rust and rationing, and the only thing keeping our humanity intact is what little compassion we still allow ourselves."

Silence followed. A silence broken only by the steady, groaning breath of the Vesta herself.

Outside, the ocean heaved—a vast, moaning graveyard stretching to the ends of the world.

Inside, a different storm was brewing.

And Dawn Perry had not yet arrived.

I Follow Orders

The hatch groans open like the throat of some dying beast. I step in fast, breath still catching up to me, my boots slick with the damp from the misty passage outside. The air inside is heavier than the fog I left behind—thick with stale tension and the scent of rusted authority.

Every eye in the chamber turns toward me—some with irritation, some with quiet judgment. Balthazar's stare cuts through them all like ice. Of course, he doesn't bother to hide it.

I don't give him the satisfaction of flinching. I move with purpose, pull my notepad from my weather-worn satchel, and slide into my seat with a low creak of metal.

"Now that we've gotten that out of the way…"

Balthazar's voice slithers into the silence like a snake through a crack in the hull. "It's been brought to my attention that the weather patterns in the northeastern corridor have become increasingly erratic. If the *Vesta* is to remain seaworthy, it's critical we begin weighing the actual benefits of these humanitarian rescue efforts."

His gaze slides across the table, landing squarely on Lawrence.

There it is. The dagger tucked beneath the diplomat's tongue.

Lawrence stiffens beside me. "What exactly are you suggesting, Councilman?" His voice holds its usual restraint, but I can hear the offense simmering underneath. "We're not the only Ark sweeping wreck zones for survivors. Now you want to monitor my division like I'm bleeding the ship dry?"

Balthazar raises a hand—slow, calculated. "Easy, Councilman. I'm merely saying we weigh the benefits."

"You mean undermine them," Lawrence fires back. "You want the scales to tip where you've already decided they will."

"I don't pick sides," Balthazar says, feigning neutrality behind those stone-gray eyes. "I preserve order. I ensure survival. Your rescue missions may continue… for now."

Lawrence doesn't answer. But the stare he levels at Balthazar could bend steel.

The silence thickens like fog before a storm.

I have to break it. And I know I'll regret it before I even open my mouth.

"Senior Councilman."

Balthazar doesn't turn his head, but I see the corner of his lip twitch like he's just tasted something sour. "Yes, Councilwoman Perry?"

He never says my name without grinding it through his teeth.

"There have been new food complaints," I begin, voice steady, measured.

"Of course there have," he replies with a shrug that drips condescension. "The ship's on rations. We're all scraping crumbs and pretending they're meals."

"You didn't let me finish," I say, sharper now. "The reports are coming primarily from the children's quarters."

That lands. A pause flickers across the table. Even Strauss looks up.

"The children are starving."

Balthazar scoffs. "What I see are healthy bodies asking for more than what's needed. Hunger isn't famine. And they're still breathing."

I lean forward, eyes locked on him. "When do you see them, Balthazar?"

The room shifts. Faces turn. Even Levy blinks.

I don't stop.

"Do you ever step foot near the classroom berthings? I know the names of the kids who cry in their sleep. I know which ones pretend to be sick so they don't burn the energy of hunger."

He narrows his eyes.

"So I ask again," I say, voice lowering to a blade's edge. "When was the last time you saw what you're pretending to speak on?"

He bristles, rising slightly in his chair. "What would you have me do? Raid the regulator systems and feed everyone a fantasy? You think I don't know we're running thin? You think I haven't reviewed every schedule, every coolant cycle, every compression belt in those aging food synthesizers?"

"I'm saying if the projections were accurate, we'd have more left than we do."

"Well, we don't," he snaps, pounding the table with his gavel hand. "We're coming down to the bones now. The food regulators are failing—circuit degradation, panel fatigue, moisture rot. Machines age, Councilwoman. And sometimes, they die before we do."

My voice falters. For the briefest moment, I want to believe he's right. That we're all just chasing ghosts in a sinking hull.

But then I remember Ahmed's face after the rescue. Pale. Cold. And the look in his eyes when he thought he was dying.

"And what happens next?" I ask, quieter now, but louder in spirit. "What's the plan when the last protein spool runs out? When the last heater coil on the compost regulator melts down?"

Balthazar stares me down.

"You tell me," he says. "You've got all the empathy. Surely that comes with a backup plan?"

The chamber turns to me, the silence more violent than words.

I have none.

Not yet.

And he knows it.

"I thought so," he says, raising his gavel like a judge on judgment day. "This meeting is adjourned."

The gavel strikes. The sound echoes. But the argument… that's far from over.

The Truth

Ahmed did his best to pass the time, buried deep in the shadowed recess of his berthing rack—what the grown-ups called a "coffin bunk." Fitting, he often thought. The ceiling sat just inches above his nose when he lay flat, making each breath feel like it had to crawl through steel.

A stack of books lay half-concealed beneath the thin mattress, their corners dog-eared, spines cracked from repeated reads. He held one now, open and trembling slightly in his hands—*Peter and Wendy*—its old-world pages smudged with fingerprints and moisture stains. It was the only copy left in the classroom archive, and he'd taken it without asking. Not stolen, he told himself— borrowed until further notice.

He read the words as though they might lift him out of this place.

This Neverland wasn't the one in the book.

It had no flying children. No fairy dust. No mischief worth laughing at. The Neverland he lived in earned its name from absence. No land. Just water. Water and rust. Storms that never ended. And people who were slowly forgetting how to dream.

The *Vesta* groaned as it shifted with the swell of the sea, bulkheads creaking like old bones. Outside, the corridor lights flickered. The ship's heartbeat pulsed through the floor.

"Jeez, Ahmed."

He flinched. The voice cut through the silence like a snap of static.

Dawn stood in the hatchway, arms crossed, brow furrowed as she surveyed the chaos that had become his bunk.

Ahmed peered over the top of the book, eyes just visible above the yellowed pages. "What'd I do now? I'm stuck in here like you guys wanted."

"That doesn't mean you get to live like a sea rat," she muttered, stepping inside. She picked up a tangle of ragged shirts from the floor and held them at arm's length. "Are these clean or dirty?"

Ahmed shrugged.

Dawn gave him a look—one of those long, exhausted leers that made her cheek twitch with frustration. He knew the kind. He saw it often.

The kid had nearly drowned less than two days ago, and now here he was, sulking in a den of clutter and half-folded clothes like the world owed him something. But Dawn also knew he wasn't sulking out of laziness. Not really. This was armor. A mess was something to control when the rest of the world felt like it was spinning out of it.

"Get your butt up and clean this up," she snapped, her voice dropping that extra octave she reserved for when she was truly done.

Ahmed sighed dramatically, dragging himself out of the bunk like a prisoner being marched to the gallows. He moved with the sluggish shuffle of someone who'd already lost the argument. He picked up the scattered garments one by one, his bare feet brushing against the cold deck as he muttered under his breath.

"These still got time on 'em," he said, sniffing one of the shirts and shrugging as he folded it.

"Oh God, Ahmed," Dawn groaned. "Don't be gross."

"They do," he insisted, holding the shirt to his face again with a half-smile. "Smells like dreams and defeat."

"Is that how you put yourself to sleep? Inhaling week-old laundry fumes?"

"Can't sleep anyway."

She paused, letting that sit in the air. "Why not?"

He stopped folding. "Too much on my mind."

Dawn sat at the small desk in the corner, pulling her jacket tighter around her shoulders. The vent above the bunk hissed faintly. "Like what?"

"My mom."

The words came out soft. Vulnerable. Unprotected.

"I keep thinking… what if she couldn't deal with me anymore? What if she died on purpose?"

Dawn stood immediately. Her chair scraped the floor as she marched toward him. "Ahmed—don't ever say that."

His eyes darted down, unsure now.

"She risked her life to save yours," Dawn said, crouching down to his level, voice low but full of thunder. "She fought to get you on this ship. If there had been any way she could've made it… she'd be here. Don't twist her love into something it wasn't."

He didn't respond. His shoulders sagged.

"I knew your mother," she continued, placing a hand on his arm. "Heart to heart. She was stronger than anyone I ever met. And you—" her voice softened now, "—you were her world."

There was a pause.

"What about my dad?" he asked, almost a whisper. "Is he dead too?"

Dawn hesitated. Her eyes darkened, just a flicker.

"No," she said, carefully. "He's just… not here."

"Not here," Ahmed repeated, as if trying to taste

the meaning behind the words. "So he left?"

"He… made choices that didn't involve staying," she said, walking a tightrope between truth and protection. "That's all I'll say for now."

Ahmed's lip quivered, but he pressed it into a line.

Dawn didn't push further. Some truths couldn't be handed over all at once. Some had to be carried in pieces—one painful shard at a time.

She stood again, brushing her hands against her jacket. "You're not alone, Ahmed. Not now. Not ever. You hear me?"

He nodded, barely.

Outside, the sea groaned like a restless god. Inside, a boy folded old clothes with trembling fingers, and a woman stood watching, knowing there would never be enough words to make the world less broken.

I Demand Answers

The weight of the last conversation still clings to me like salt on skin.

Ahmed's voice—soft, uncertain—echoes in my mind as I step back into the round table chamber. His questions about his mother, his father, the ache behind them... they haven't left me. And now, here I am again, facing a different kind of ache. One that wears a uniform and speaks in decrees.

The chamber is suffocating—its steel walls sweating condensation from the cold bite of the sea outside, its air stale with the acrid tang of recycled fuel and too many bodies breathing the same tired breath. The overhead lamps flicker, powered by a grid we all know is dying, but no one says aloud.

We sit in silence, stunned into stillness. The Council, the officers, even the scribes—every eye fixed on Balthazar. His words still hang there like smoke, impossible to wave away.

"Two meals a day," he had said.

My own voice breaks that silence, though I half-hope he'll repeat himself, as if repetition will prove I misheard.

"Two meals… a day?"

Balthazar doesn't flinch. "Exactly what I said." He leans forward, placing his scarred hands on the rust-pocked table as though the weight of his decree might drive it through the deck plating. "If we don't act now, we won't have enough to last the month. Discipline is survival. Nothing less."

The words rattle in my chest like ballast stones. *Discipline. Survival.* Easy to preach when you stand over the rest of us with a plate always just a little fuller. My gaze drops to the corroded surface of the table, where rivet heads jut up like barnacles.

Lawrence speaks next, his voice quieter, breaking on the edges like a rope frayed against a cleat.

"Until when?"

"When ration levels stabilize," Balthazar says smoothly, as if the decision were not cruel but mathematical.

Lawrence presses again, his tone cracked open now, almost pleading. "Stabilize? Councilman, you're starving us in the meantime."

I stand before I realize I'm moving. The chair screeches across the deck, the sound harsh in the narrow chamber. My rage is hot, pulsing under my skin, and I can't cork it back.

"There are children on this ship," I snap. "Children who already eat less than they should."

Balthazar's reply comes like the strike of a whip.

"I know. More than there should be."

The air seems to drain from the room. That's it. The spark in the powder keg.

My voice drops low, the kind of quiet that only comes before a blade is drawn.

"What was that supposed to mean?"

His eyes glitter across the table, amused by my anger. He wants me to rise further. He wants me to break rank, to give him reason to cut me down. But I don't care. He can cast all the barbs he wants at me—I've endured worse. What I will not tolerate is the venom he's just spat toward the defenseless.

"Senior Councilman or not," I say, each word like a nail hammered into the deck, "this is cowardice dressed as command."

The room goes taut, silence stretched to the edge of breaking.

Then the alarm splits it apart.

The piercing klaxon erupts from the bulkhead speakers, a jagged shriek that sets my teeth on edge. The shipwreck alarm. It jolts me from the chair as though struck.

Lawrence is already halfway up, instinct carrying him. He's the one who swore to answer that alarm. His duty, his creed: that no soul adrift would be ignored.

But Balthazar's voice cuts across the din like a cleaver.

"Let it pass. We don't break course. Every rescue compromises our integrity and our position."

The alarm wails on, unanswered. Lawrence freezes, his back rigid, the muscles in his jaw clenching hard enough to crack teeth. His hand hovers over the brass speaking tube that would relay orders to the watch.

"We cannot just pass by and let them drown," Lawrence says, his voice hoarse with conviction. His eyes—honest, weathered eyes—lock on Balthazar. "Councilman, you ask us to murder by omission."

"I stand by my ruling," Balthazar replies, calm as the abyss. His stare fixes on Lawrence like a predator sizing the distance to strike.

For a moment I think Lawrence will move anyway, damn the consequences. But his shoulders drop, his eyes tear away from Balthazar's piercing glare. He shoves the chair back and storms out, boots pounding down the ladderwell until the echoes vanish in the ship's hollow bones.

I remain seated, nails biting into my palms, fury rattling in my chest. Balthazar has succeeded—

he's silenced us, reduced us to bitter compliance, left us stewing in the stench of our own impotence.

Yet I cannot silence the question burning through me.

What future does he see in this? A people whittled down to skin and bone, too weak to lift the lines or man the guns? A fleet that starves its children, its only continuity, to preserve a handful of ration crates?

The sea is already claiming the world. If we abandon those still afloat, if we cull our own from within, what will remain?

Extinction doesn't come only from hunger.

It comes from cowardice too.

A Selfish Sea

The clang of boots echoed through the docking chamber as the inner hatch yawned open, exposing the sea beyond. The *Vesta's* launch cradle hissed and groaned as its hydraulics strained, lowering a rescue craft toward the storm-lashed surface. Crewmen in soaked combat overalls and flak harnesses hurried along the grated catwalks, fastening safety lines, cinching helmets, and double-checking the launch cable locks.

The room reeked of diesel, rust, and brine. Red warning lamps rotated overhead, casting the space in a pulsing crimson gloom. Every sound—the creak of steel, the hammer of waves against the hull, the whine of the davits lowering—seemed sharpened, anxious.

The chamber doors slammed open.

Balthazar stormed in with a trio of his wardens at his back. His long coat, weather-stained and rimmed with salt, trailed behind him like a dark banner. His boots rang against the deck as he advanced, fury radiating from every step.

"Who in hell made this call?"

His voice boomed, guttural, a sound more suited for a tribunal than a rescue.

The men nearest froze. Only Lawrence—armor buckled, visor raised, life harness strapped across his chest—dared to answer. His gloved hands paused mid-adjustment of his shoulder plating, though his jaw stayed firm.

"There's a whole raft of children out there," Lawrence said, his words level but urgent, carrying over the mechanical din. "I saw them through the scope myself. One's already gone cold."

"And how's that a problem for this vessel?" Balthazar spat, stepping closer until he was almost nose-to-nose with him. His tone carried more venom than concern, the words sharpened like knives.

Lawrence didn't flinch. He gestured toward the hatch, where the launch skiff now hovered above the waves, straining against the lowering winch. "If we leave them, then we're no different than the bastards who shelled their ark. You know that. You'd have us turn our backs the same way?"

The docking crew fell into a silence thick enough to choke on, each man's eyes flicking between the two officers. Only the groan of the hull beneath the storm kept the moment from snapping.

Balthazar's face twisted into a scowl, teeth bared like a cornered animal. "You're blind if you think pity keeps ships afloat." He swept a hand toward the stacked crates of dwindling provisions lashed against the bulkhead. "The only thing that separates us from corpses in the water is the choices we make. Choices to survive."

"Choices like abandoning children?" Lawrence shot back, his voice hard, stripped of hesitation now.

Balthazar's glare could have cut steel. He stepped past him, turning to address the chamber at large. The red lights painted his features hellish, his voice rising above the storm's howl.

"You want to bring these strays aboard?" His tone dripped with disdain. "Fine. But every extra mouth costs us. You hear me?" He jabbed a finger toward the crew, sweeping the room like a commander delivering sentence. "As of now—effective immediately—we ration to one meal a day. For everyone. No exceptions."

Murmurs rippled across the chamber—shock, anger, a few curses barely swallowed. The thought of hunger sat heavy on every stomach, heavier than the storm outside.

Lawrence's voice came quieter now, but no less

firm. "You punish the entire crew for saving lives?"

"I preserve the crew by reminding them what survival costs," Balthazar snapped. "You want to play hero? Then you pay the price."

"You're not preserving anything," Lawrence said, stepping forward. "You're hollowing us out. You think fear will hold this ship together? It won't. It'll rot us from the inside."

Balthazar's lip curled. "Then let it rot. Better rot than drown."

Without waiting for a reply, he spun on his heel and stalked out, his wardens falling in behind him. The sound of the door slamming shut echoed like a verdict.

For a long moment, only the storm answered.

Lawrence stood rigid, his jaw tight, breath hard through his teeth. His hand lingered on the bulkhead rail, knuckles whitening. He could feel the eyes of every sailor in the chamber on him, weighing, waiting.

"Lower away!" he barked suddenly, his voice snapping through the silence like a whip.

The crew jolted back into motion, the winch engines whining as the rescue craft descended into the black maw of the sea.

Lawrence pulled his helmet down over his head. *Damn Balthazar,* he thought. *Some lines still have to be held, or there's nothing left of us worth saving.*

Not Enough

Kara sat hunched on the edge of the steel-framed bunk in the holding berthing, her body wrapped in a coarse gray towel that smelled faintly of rust and antiseptic. The metal walls around her sweated with condensation, groaning now and then with the deep, guttural strain of the *Vesta's* hull cutting through the storm-tossed seas.

Her hands trembled as she pulled the towel tighter—not from cold, though the chill was bone-deep—but from the residual echo of terror that refused to leave her veins. Every creak of the vessel reminded her of the splintering timbers of her own ship going under. The sound of death had a rhythm, and she could still hear it in the steel around her.

She had captained men, held command through fire and salt, but here she sat stripped of rank, another displaced soul in a ship too crowded with them already. She knew what came next. Questions. Suspicion. Judgment. No captain was ever rescued without her story being torn open and gutted in front of strangers.

The hatch groaned as it swung open.

Lawrence stepped in, his armored harness stripped away now, his fatigues damp with seawater. In his hand was a small tin container, steam whispering from the lid.

"You'll have to forgive me," he said quietly, offering it to her. "New ration protocols. This is all I could manage."

Kara accepted it without hesitation, her hunger overriding dignity. The rice inside was plain, sticky, little more than a half-portion, but she devoured it in shaking handfuls, shoveling it to her mouth as though afraid it might be taken back.

"Anything's fine right now," she said between gulps. "It's been… a long journey."

Lawrence watched her with a guarded expression, arms folded. "I can imagine. We get wrecks all the time."

Kara glanced up, swallowing hard. "Probably under… similar circumstances."

His jaw tightened, eyes lowering to the steel floor. "Sunken ships. Slaughtered dwellers. Yeah. We've seen too much of it."

Silence settled, broken only by the faint hum of ventilation ducts and the distant groan of the ship's hull. Kara lowered the container, her hunger sated only enough to let the weight of memory resurface. Her lips quivered before the words escaped her.

"I know his name."

Lawrence's gaze lifted sharply.

"He's not just some raider," she pressed on, her voice tremoring as though every word burned her throat. "He's deranged. A relentless maniac. And he commands a band of children."

Lawrence frowned, incredulous. "Children?"

"Not children," Kara whispered, shaking her head. "Assassins. Trained from the bone outward to kill. They slaughtered my crew in minutes. They… they didn't even hesitate." Her voice cracked, her nails digging into the tin until it squealed against her palm. "Please—inform your leadership before it's too late."

Lawrence straightened, his hand unconsciously brushing the sidearm at his belt. His tone softened, as if coaxing her back from hysteria. "Rest assured, Kara, you're safe here aboard the *Vesta*. We have steel in the water, blades in every corridor. Some of the best men alive sail with us."

Kara's head dropped, her damp hair shadowing her face. "Not against him."

The words struck colder than the sea itself.

Lawrence exhaled slowly, rubbing the bridge of his nose. For a moment, he almost dismissed her—

another survivor rattled by grief and hunger—but the weight in her voice anchored the warning. It wasn't just fear. It was certainty.

"What did you say his name was?" he asked quietly.

Kara hesitated. Memories clawed their way back—faces torn apart, the sound of steel on flesh, the laughter of children without innocence. Her chest rose and fell, shallow, frantic.

When she finally spoke, her voice was little more than a whisper, but it carried the gravity of a storm yet to break.

"War."

The name lingered in the stale air of the berthing like a curse, a word so sharp it cut through steel. Lawrence froze, the sound of it coiling around him like a tightening noose. The hum of the *Vesta* seemed louder now, more vulnerable.

He had seen the body. Or what was left of it. A drifting corpse, face half-gone, eyes wide open in the water. He had told himself it was just another casualty of the sea. But now, the pieces began to shift. The silence of the wreck. The precision of the damage. The absence of survivors.

And in that silence, Kara's dread became their own.

I Demand Reason

I nearly choke on my own breath when Lawrence stumbles into my berthing, his face drawn tight, his movements quick and restless. He doesn't even sit before blurting it out.

"One meal a day," he says, his voice carrying the weight of steel chains. "Effective immediately. I wish it wasn't true, Dawn. I really do."

The words land like a blow to my chest.

For a long moment, I can't speak. My eyes drift past him, to the little clay pot fixed to the corner shelf above my rack—the withering plant I've been tending since embarkation. Its leaves curled in on themselves days ago, brittle at the edges, clinging stubbornly to a life it no longer has the strength to hold. I stare at it as though it might offer some hidden wisdom, some whisper of hope.

But there's nothing. Only decay.

"He can't expect us to survive like this," I finally mutter, though my throat feels raw as I say it. A slicing pain churns in my gut, sharp enough that sweat dampens my brow. I press my hand against my abdomen, as if I can steady the storm inside. "Maybe the grown dwellers can endure it for a while. Maybe the hardened sailors too. But not the children, Lawrence. The children will starve."

Lawrence shifts uneasily in the narrow space, his shoulders nearly brushing the steel bulkhead. "We shouldn't go that drastic," he says carefully, his tone an attempt at reason—but it rings hollow.

"It *is* that drastic!" My voice cracks in the low-ceilinged compartment, sharper than I mean, but I don't rein it back. The thought claws its way into me before I can stop it.

What if that's the plan?

My breath hitches at the horror of it. And yet… in this world, where morality has been ground down to ash, is that thought really so unthinkable?

Lawrence flinches, as though I've struck him. "Don't be ridiculous, Councilwoman," he says quickly. "Not even Balthazar would sink that low."

I laugh, but it comes out bitter and broken, a sound that doesn't feel like it belongs to me. "He's yet to show me any reason to believe otherwise."

The silence that follows is worse than shouting. The low thrum of the ship's engines presses against my skull, a reminder of the machine we're all cogs inside. I lean back against the bulkhead, staring at the overhead pipes dripping condensation. Each drop echoes the ticking of time we no longer have.

How am I supposed to tell the children?

How do I walk into that mess hall, look Ahmed in the eyes, and explain that from now on the food they clung to as proof of our safety is being halved? That this isn't just scarcity—this is the beginning of the end.

That this is the last step before doom comes for us all.

Starving Old Man

A hmed's stomach tightened as the words replayed in his head—*one meal a day*. He had eavesdropped enough to know it wasn't rumor, but a decree. It pressed on him like a stormfront, heavy and suffocating.

He lingered outside the berthing door a moment longer, his bare feet silent on the cold deck plating, before slipping away down the corridor. His heart drummed against his ribs, louder than the faint groan of the hull. He knew he shouldn't be here, shouldn't be listening, shouldn't know. But ignorance burned worse. Would Dawn ever tell him the truth? Or would she keep shielding him with those careful half-answers, the way adults always did when they thought they were protecting you?

Secrets. Always secrets.

Ahmed padded down the passageway, the overhead lights flickering, dripping condensation from pipes that traced the ceiling like veins. The ship felt more like a dying animal than a vessel—its breath shallow, its bones creaking, its skin damp with fever.

When he reached the brig hatch, his breath caught—the steel door was cracked, open by the slimmest margin. Just enough. He pressed his thin fingers into the gap and slid himself through, careful not to let the hinges betray him with a squeal. He crept down the ladder into the shadowed space, his eyes adjusting to the dim yellow glow of a single swaying bulb. Rows of iron bars loomed on either side, cells empty save for one.

"Got you some rice," Ahmed whispered. He crouched near the bars, setting down a battered tin no larger than his palm. Inside was a thin layer of sticky grains—stolen from his own ration.

From the corner, Arjes shifted on the deck, bones jutting against his thin skin, his body sprawled like a broken marionette. His eyes, however, gleamed with a clarity that unsettled Ahmed.

"I don't know if I'll be able to keep doing this," Ahmed said quickly, panic tightening his voice. "They've put us on one meal a day."

Arjes blinked slowly, then let out a ragged laugh that rattled in his chest. "One meal," he repeated, his voice dry, cracked. "Why am I not surprised?"

"This is going to be bad for you," Ahmed pressed, his throat constricting at the thought of this withered man fading into nothing.

"Bad for me?" Arjes coughed out a chuckle, the sound dark, almost mocking. "Kid, it'll be bad for everyone. That's the part you don't understand yet." His lips curled into a thin, cynical smile.

Ahmed scowled, anger flaring. "What's so funny about starving?"

"I said I was not surprised," Arjes rasped, dragging himself closer to the bars, his voice low, almost conspiratorial. "Not worried. Worry is for those who still believe in tomorrow. Me? I've seen enough tomorrows to know better."

Ahmed swallowed hard, inching closer despite himself. "You still believe in Sky City, don't you?" The words tumbled out before he could stop them.

At the name, Arjes turned his head sharply, as if the syllables themselves carried weight. His gaze slid away from Ahmed, fixing instead on the small porthole high in the cell wall. Beyond the glass, endless blue swelled with stormclouds. He stretched a trembling arm through the bars, his hand opening into the rain that seeped in, letting it drench his skin. His fingers were so thin Ahmed thought he might slip right between the iron rods if he tried. But Arjes didn't try.

"You want to know something, boy?" Arjes

whispered, his face turned toward the storm outside. "The cruelest prison isn't made of steel. It's the one that tricks you into believing there's a way out. Hope is the worst kind of cage, when used against you. At least in nature's prison, there are no illusions. There is no escape."

He turned back, eyes hollow, meeting Ahmed's wide stare.

"I was there," Arjes continued, voice trembling, but not with fear. With memory. "When it happened. When the planet gave itself up."

Ahmed's lips parted. "But… you made it out, right?"

For a moment, silence filled the brig, broken only by the steady drip of seawater through corroded pipes. Arjes pulled his hand back through the bars, the rain dripping from his fingers. He closed it into a fist so tight his knuckles whitened.

"At least," he murmured.

The two words hung in the stale air, heavier than the sea pressing against the hull.

I Want You To Listen

The classroom berthing hums faintly with the *Vesta's* engines, the vibration running up through the deck plates into the soles of my boots. The children bend over their assignments, their small hands dragging pencils dull from overuse, their shoulders narrow and bony beneath their issued jumpers. They're quiet—not from discipline, but from exhaustion. Hunger has a way of silencing even the most restless.

I stand at the front of the compartment, watching them. And it hits me—these children carry something I never had.

Hope.

I was born in steel corridors like these, with bulkheads for walls and filtered air for sky. There was no *before* for me. No memory of dry earth or real sunlight. Hope never belonged to me. What I carried was obedience, survival, ration counts, and the endless creak of the hull as the ocean pressed against us like a weight that would never lift.

But these children—somehow, they believe in things unseen. They whisper about land. They draw pictures of cities not built on ships. They dream of rescue as if it were inevitable.

Ahmed leaps up from his seat, paper clutched in his hand, eyes burning with that restless energy he never seems to sit on for long. He practically shoves the sheet at me, words spilling out before I can even scan his work.

"I wanna ask you something."

"How did I know?" I mutter, half-exasperated, half-amused. He's got that tone—the one he always wears right before he lights a match and tosses it into a powder keg.

"How come we never talk about that closed-off boat room?" he asks, eyes gleaming with dangerous curiosity.

My chest tightens. "Because we're not supposed to talk about it. Any reason you are?"

"Well," he says, voice bouncing with conviction far too big for his thin frame, "you go through all the trouble teaching us about the past. Maybe you should teach us about what we have now."

The words sting. Because he's right. The ship itself is a lesson—an ark meant for survival, yes, but also a prison. And still, the knowledge locked behind those watertight doors is off-limits. Even to me.

"We just can't do that, Ahmed," I say finally, defaulting to the safe answer. The one drilled into every ranking crew member.

"Oh, come on! The boats are right there. It'd only be for a few minutes. We hear the alarms every time they go out!" His voice rises, sharp and defiant, catching the ears of the other students. Heads lift. Eyes flicker. The air grows restless.

"First of all," I snap, my tone cracking like a bosun's call, "keep your voice down. Your peers are studying. Second, I don't make the rules. Same as me, you follow them."

"I thought you were in charge."

"I *am!*" The word bursts from me, sharper than I mean. "I'm in charge of you as a crew member— and as your adoptive mother."

"You're *not* my mom!"

The words hit harder than he knows. Or maybe he does. Maybe that's the point.

He turns, shoulders stiff, walking off in the way only a child can—like defiance is armor, like it can shield him from the hurt he just threw.

I clench my jaw, biting back the words burning in my chest. Words I can't afford to say. Not here. Not now.

Before I can speak, a light knock echoes on the hatch.

Lawrence steps in, his broad frame filling the doorway. Beside him shuffle several younger children—smaller even than Ahmed, skin gray-pale, lips cracked from thirst, eyes ringed dark as bruises. Even after a scrub-down from the crew, they look half-dead already, their bodies wasted from too many days with too little food.

"Are they cleared to be here?" I ask, moving toward him, my heart sinking at the sight of them.

He gives a small nod, ushering the little ones to empty seats. Then he beckons me into the passageway, away from listening ears.

"They're hungry," he murmurs, voice low, eyes shadowed. "I mean *days* hungry. One ration isn't enough. Their bodies can't take it. They'll break."

"Don't you think I know that?" I whisper back, dragging a hand down my face. The recycled air stinks faintly of brine and rust, pressing heavy in my lungs. "They doomed themselves the second they boarded this ship."

"Doomed, yes," Lawrence admits, his jaw tight. "But compared to what's out there..." His gaze drifts to the bulkhead, as though seeing through it into the endless black ocean. "They've just bought themselves a little more time."

I look back at the classroom. At Ahmed, hunched over his desk now, pretending not to care. At the new children, too tired to even lift

their heads.
   Time.
   That's all we're buying anymore.
   And it's getting more expensive by the day.

Opportunity

The steel hatch groaned on its hinges as Lawrence eased it open, the sound carrying through the chambers like a warning bell. The room was dim, lit only by a single overhead red lamp that swung slightly with the ark's slow roll, painting the space in uneasy shadows. The air was stale with oil, sweat, and rust—the scent of confinement that clung to every bulkhead.

Balthazar sat alone at the long, makeshift meeting table, his posture sharp and unyielding, like the spine of the ship itself. His fingers tapped once, twice, then stilled against the tabletop. His eyes were already fixed on Lawrence, hard and piercing, as though the man had been expecting him all along.

Lawrence felt the sweat gathering in his palms, slicking the coarse seams of his trousers. Their last argument still weighed heavy in his chest—a storm unresolved, waiting to break. He closed the hatch behind him, the metallic clang louder than he intended, echoing like a gavel striking judgment. He walked forward but did not sit. Instead, he halted at the far side of the table, spine stiff, every step deliberate.

"You needed to see me," Lawrence said, his voice flat—more a declaration than a question. He tried to sound steady, but the nervous undercurrent slipped through, thin and brittle.

Balthazar did not move at first. Then his jaw flexed, his lips pressing into a grim line. His words cut the air like steel on steel.

"Direct orders were violated. You let those people on this ship knowing the restrictions I had implemented."

"I know... I know..." Lawrence replied too quickly, as if rushing to get past the lash of the rebuke, bracing for the punishment he knew was coming.

Balthazar leaned forward, the table creaking under the shift of his weight. His voice was low, cold—the tone of an officer who had long since forgotten mercy.

"Do you have the faintest idea what's at stake here?"

Lawrence bristled, his fists clenching at his sides. "You don't need to drag me down like I'm some schoolboy, Senior Councilman."

"Perhaps I do." Balthazar rose to his feet, his

shadow stretching long across the berthing wall, twisted by the red glow. His words came measured, each one heavy with condemnation. "Every decision you make jeopardizes every living soul aboard this ark. Every single one, Lawrence. You bring more mouths aboard, and it means rations must stretch thinner. Thinner until there's nothing left but bones."

"Senior Councilman..." Lawrence's voice faltered. He dropped his gaze to the deck, the weight of disappointment bearing down on him. "All of this... it's wrong. It shouldn't have to be like this."

"It isn't, but it is." Balthazar's reply was cold iron. He moved around the table with slow, deliberate steps, the scuff of his boots loud in the silence. "You want to break rules like a common dweller, then you'll work like one." He stopped close enough that Lawrence could smell the sharp tang of salt and sweat on his uniform. "Tonight, you will assess and feed the prisoners in the brig. You will see firsthand what breaking order costs. Down there lies a future darker than you've yet imagined. Get acquainted with it... or get in line."

With that, Balthazar turned, opened the hatch, and left. The clang of the steel reverberated long after he was gone, leaving Lawrence alone in the red-lit gloom—anger boiling in his chest, shame gnawing at his gut, and the taste of iron bitterness in his mouth.

The cart's steel wheels groaned against the grated ladderwell as Lawrence guided it down the steep companionway stairs, his boots clanging with each step. The deeper he descended, the heavier the air became — thick with rust, mildew, and the sour tang of confinement. The brig lay buried in the ark's lowest decks, a place where light and hope rarely reached. Flickering fluorescents buzzed overhead, casting jaundiced glows across sweating bulkheads.

On the tray before him sat the rations: pale, fist-sized lumps of processed starch — barely enough for sustenance. Lawrence kept his eyes on the portions, avoiding the stares of the prisoners behind the welded bars.

Cell by cell, he slid the lumps through the pass slots. Hands darted out, snatching the food with desperation. Then, from the farthest cell, a pair of eyes locked onto him — calm, calculating, and burning with something deeper than hunger.

Arjes.

The old man leaned forward, his wiry frame

barely outlined in the gloom. When Lawrence pushed the ration through, Arjes took it slowly, as if weighing its worth.

"Meals are shrinking," Arjes murmured, his voice gravelly but clear.

"I don't set the portions," Lawrence replied, his tone clipped.

"I know," Arjes said, tearing off a piece. "You just deliver them. Clean hands."

Lawrence's jaw tightened. "Watch it."

Arjes smiled faintly. "I'm just saying — it's easy to stay clean when you're not the one making choices."

"You're here because of your choices."

Arjes leaned in, eyes sharp. "And you're here because of yours."

Lawrence didn't answer.

"I raided to keep my people breathing," Arjes continued. "Not for glory. Not for power."

"Still theft," Lawrence said.

"Survival doesn't ask for permission," Arjes replied, finishing his meal. "It demands action."

Lawrence turned to leave, pushing the cart, when Arjes called out.

"Councilman."

He paused.

"My cot's off. Hurts my back. Can you help me fix it?"

Lawrence hesitated. "Why would I step into your cell?"

Arjes lifted his hands in mock surrender. "You afraid of me? Look at me — I'm eighty, half-starved, and locked up. You think I'm a threat?"

Lawrence frowned, pride nudging him forward. He unlocked the gate and stepped inside, motioning Arjes back. He knelt by the cot, inspecting the frame.

"There's nothing wrong with—"

A sharp shove knocked him sideways. His shoulder slammed into the bulkhead, pain flaring. Lawrence stumbled, catching himself against the wall.

The brig stirred — prisoners muttering, bars rattling.

Arjes stepped out of the cell, moving faster than expected. Lawrence lunged, grabbing his arm and dragging him back. They struggled, grappling more than striking, their movements clumsy and desperate.

Lawrence managed to pin Arjes against the deck, breath ragged. Arjes twisted, nearly slipping free, but a sudden voice cut through the noise.

"Enough!"

Dawn stood at the hatch, a dented baton in hand. Her eyes were wide, her voice steady. "I heard you were on this detail," she said. "Now I see why no one wants it."

She stepped in, helping Lawrence to his feet. He wiped his brow, bloodless but bruised.

"I'll get him back in the cell," he muttered.

Before they could move, boots thundered down the ladderwell. Balthazar burst in, his face stormy.

"What happened?" he barked.

Lawrence opened his mouth, but Dawn stepped forward.

"He was helping me," she said. "I followed him down. The prisoner tried to escape. Councilman Suarez stopped him."

Lawrence blinked, surprised, but nodded.

"That's right," he said.

Balthazar studied them both, then gave a curt nod. "Get him back in the cage."

Guards moved in, escorting Arjes without ceremony.

As Lawrence and Dawn climbed back toward the upper decks, the hatch clanged shut behind them.

"I owe you," Lawrence said quietly.

"You do," Dawn replied. "And I'll collect. I need a favor."

* * *

"Gather round!" the guard barked, his voice bouncing off the grated deck plates. He gestured toward the vessel resting in its hydraulic cradle — sleek, angular, and unmistakably built for speed.

Ahmed's breath caught. His eyes, wide and bright in the half-light, locked onto the boat as if it were sacred. While the others hesitated, murmuring among themselves, Ahmed stepped forward, drawn to the black hull, its sharp chine line, and the spear-like curve of its reinforced bow. Even dormant, the vessel seemed alive.

"The Wad-Wer LX," the guard announced, his tone practiced, "is a high-performance maritime craft. Designed for rapid-response evacuation, it can reach speeds up to three hundred and fifty knots."

The children whispered, but Ahmed mouthed the words to himself, memorizing them: *three hundred and fifty knots*. Not miles per hour. Knots. This wasn't just a boat — it was built for survival.

"With twin turbine drives," the guard continued, tapping the hull with a gloved knuckle, "and a reinforced composite frame, it can outrun storms and slice through swells that would crush lesser craft. In emergencies, this vessel is essential."

Ahmed's fingers twitched at his side, aching to touch the steel. His voice slipped out before he could stop it.

"Can we take it for a test run?"

The guard turned, his helmeted head tilting slightly. For a moment, his stern mouth softened into something almost kind.

"I know you're curious, lad, but this isn't for sightseeing. The Wad-Wer isn't a toy. It's reserved for emergencies."

Ahmed's brow furrowed. His gaze flicked from the guard to the vessel and back again. Then came the question — quiet, but heavy.

"Is Sky City an emergency?"

The chamber fell still. The hum of hydraulics, the distant groan of the ocean — all seemed to pause. The other children looked at Ahmed, their expressions a mix of wonder and unease.

The guard's face hardened. His reply came slow, deliberate.

"You know that's just a story, right?"

Ahmed didn't blink. "Says who?"

"Says the Council. The navigators. Everyone who's mapped these waters for decades."

"Maybe they didn't look hard enough," Ahmed said. His voice was soft, but it carried. There was something in it — not rebellion, but belief. A quiet, stubborn hope.

The guard stared at him, then let out a dry chuckle.

"Kid, we wouldn't be burning fuel and risking

lives on patrols if there was some floating city out there waiting to save us. That boat—" he gestured toward the Wad-Wer "—is here to keep real survivors alive. Not chase fairy tales."

Ahmed stepped closer to the vessel, his reflection warping across its dark hull.

"Maybe it's not here to save everyone," he said. "Maybe it's waiting for someone who won't stop looking."

The words lingered, echoing in the damp air. The guard opened his mouth, but no answer came. He glanced at the other children — now silent, watching Ahmed with wide eyes.

With a sigh, the guard turned away, signaling the group to follow. But Ahmed lingered, eyes locked on the Wad-Wer. The vessel seemed to regard him in return, like a dormant beast waiting for its rider.

And in that moment, deep in the rusting belly of the ark, Ahmed made a silent vow:

If Sky City was real, he would be the one to find it.

* * *

Ahmed lingered near the hatchway, palms damp

118

against the cold steel handrail. He had no business being here again. The brig was a place people avoided — where shadows stretched too long, and whispers clung to the walls like smoke. But something had gnawed at him since the tour of the drop bay, a quiet hook lodged deep in his thoughts.

Arjes was waiting.

The old man always seemed to know. He sat on the edge of his cot, eyes like dull lanterns glowing in the gloom, one corner of his mouth curled into that familiar smirk.

"Took you long enough," Arjes rasped, his voice tinged with satisfaction, as though Ahmed had confirmed something unspoken. "Been chewing on it, haven't you? Like a rat working at a line."

Ahmed stiffened but stayed silent, his thoughts locked behind clenched teeth.

"Talk to me, kid. You're standing there like a riveted bulkhead. Solid, sure — but useless."

The words burst out, raw and unfiltered.

"They've got a boat down there that can outrun storms. They've got everything they need to search for Sky City — and they just sit up here saying it's not real."

Arjes leaned forward, forearms resting on his knees, the dim light catching the creases of his weathered face. "Because it isn't," he said flatly.

Ahmed blinked, stung. "But you said—"

"Oh, I know it's real," Arjes cut in, eyes narrowing. "I've seen things these fools can't even imagine. But to them? If they can't chart it, anchor there, log it in a report — it doesn't exist. Same way luck doesn't exist. But I've sailed enough seas to know — luck decides more than law ever will."

Ahmed's shoulders sagged. His gaze dropped to the deck. "I don't want to die without trying to find it."

Arjes moved slowly, deliberately. From the torn lining of his coveralls, he pulled a small rectangle of laminated plastic — frayed at the edges, its holographic seal faintly glimmering. A keycard.

Ahmed's breath caught.

"So," Arjes murmured, turning the card over like a playing chip. "How badly do you want Sky City?"

Ahmed hesitated, eyes locked on the card. "I… I want to find it."

Arjes scoffed. "That's a galley answer. Hollow. Try again."

Ahmed clenched his fists. His voice steadied, rising past the weight in his chest.

"I want to find it more than I want to breathe. Because if I don't… if none of us do… we starve. We die."

Arjes grinned, satisfied. "Now that's the current I was waiting for."

He slid the keycard through the bars. Ahmed

stared at it, hesitant, as if it might burn.

"What is that?" he asked.

"This," Arjes said, almost reverently, "is a way out. It'll open the launch bay hatch. The Council think they own the sea. They don't. The sea belongs to anyone desperate enough to take it."

Ahmed swallowed. "How did you get it?"

"Took it off a Councilman too busy keeping his hands clean to notice mine were dirty," Arjes said with a shrug. "If I can't use it, someone else has to. Maybe it's you. Maybe it isn't. But you're the only one I've met on this rusting coffin who believes enough to even try."

The card hovered between them, waiting. Ahmed reached out, fingers brushing its rough edges. It felt heavier than it looked — like iron ballast.

"What if I can't do it?" he whispered.

Arjes chuckled, low and dry. "That's the beauty of it, kid. You're not afraid it doesn't exist — you're afraid you'll fail. That tells me you won't. Because you're the only one who still thinks the horizon's hiding something worth finding."

Ahmed clutched the card and slipped it into his pocket. Arjes leaned back, eyes drifting to the tiny porthole and the black waters beyond.

"Go on then," the old man said, voice barely above a whisper. "Go find Sky City — before this

Ark eats itself alive."

I Demand Answers

It can't get any worse.

That's the lie I keep telling myself. But aboard *The Vesta*, worse is always waiting. It lurks in the bulkheads, in the hum of the lights, in the silence between orders.

The air in the Council's's quarters is thick — not just with tension, but with something heavier. Like bilge water left to rot. The fluorescents overhead buzz with that high-pitched whine that crawls up my spine and nests behind my eyes.

Lawrence stands beside me, stiff as a mast, trying to look composed. But I see the twitch in his jaw, the way his fingers flex against his thigh. Across the table, Balthazar paces like a caged animal, boots clanging against the grated deck, each step a warning.

"We flushed the brig from stem to stern," Lawrence says, voice tight, almost pleading. "Security swept every detainee. Even Arjes. No sign of the key card."

Balthazar stops. His head turns slowly, like a turret locking onto a target.

"You understand the magnitude of this failure?" he says, voice sharp as a snapped cable. "A lost key card means unrestricted access to the drop bay. One swipe — one — and a vessel launches. No oversight. No failsafe. Do you grasp what that means, Councilman?"

"I understand, sir," Lawrence replies, trying to sound calm. "We're retracing steps."

Balthazar slams his hand on the table. The sound ricochets off the steel, a thunderclap in a coffin.

"You shouldn't be retracing anything! You should've locked it down! If that card lands in the wrong hands, it's not just the ship at risk. It's every soul aboard her."

The silence that follows is suffocating. I swear I can hear the Ark groaning through its frame — a deep, sickly vibration, like the sea pressing its ear to the hull.

Balthazar's eyes flick between us, cold and venomous. "You should be removed from the Council for this."

"Removing leadership in a crisis weakens us all," I say, cutting in before he can strike again. My voice is steadier than I expect. "It solves nothing."

He rounds on me, eyes flashing. "Then perhaps you shouldn't be here either, Councilwoman Perry."

His words hit like salt in an open wound. I clench my fist, fighting the urge to lash back.

"Perhaps," I say, voice flat, ice-cold, "I'll resign when you give me a reason to."

He stares at me, chest heaving, nostrils flared. Then he snaps.

"Search the ship again!" he roars. "Every compartment, every deck, every goddamn corner! Find that card before someone does something stupid!"

He gestures toward the hatch. We're dismissed. Thrown out like ballast.

Outside, the air feels no lighter. The tension clings to me, thick as storm humidity. Balthazar's fury still vibrates in my skull, sealed into the ship's metal.

"Check your berthing," Lawrence says beside me, voice low. "If it somehow got misplaced there, we can clear this up quickly."

I nod, but something coils in my gut — cold, tight, wrong. The Ark hums around me, engines rumbling below, air whispering through vents. But beneath it all is... absence.

By the time I reach my berthing, my pulse is hammering. The corridor stretches longer than it should. Red emergency lights strobe off steel walls. My boots echo in the hollow quiet.

I step inside.

Stillness hits me like a slap.

Everything looks normal — racks lined, lockers latched, the faint scent of machine oil and recycled air. But something's off. The void in the room gnaws at me. I scan every corner, waiting for my eyes to catch what my instincts already know.

Then it hits me.

Ahmed.

No sound. Not since the boat drop tour.

My chest tightens. My throat dries.

"No… no, no, no—" I whisper, panic blooming like fire. I break into a sprint, boots hammering against the deck, turning down narrow halls toward the lower berthing.

His rack is empty.

Blanket folded unevenly. Pillow still warm.

He's gone.

And the pieces crash together in my mind with horrific clarity. The missing key card. The silence. The timing.

Ahmed has it.

The child has the one thing that could open the drop bay — and unleash a disaster none of us can stop.

The lights flicker overhead as I grip the edge of his rack, knuckles whitening.

I don't think. I move.

If I'm right, every second we waste could be the one that gets us all killed.

The Drop

Ahmed pressed himself into the shadow of the corridor bulkhead, the cold steel biting through his shirt. A trio of Vesta guards marched past, their boots clanging in perfect unison against the grated deck. Each step vibrated through his ribs. He didn't dare breathe.

At his height, he was nearly invisible in the half-light. Small. Quick. Determined. For once, those traits worked in his favor.

The guards' voices faded, swallowed by the hum of the ventilation ducts.

Now or never.

Ahmed darted from the shadows and sprinted down the corridor. The overhead lights flickered, casting his shadow long and distorted across the bulkheads. His heartbeat thundered in his ears, syncing with the drone of the Ark's engines. The ship felt alive—breathing, watching, judging.

He reached the drop bay hatch: massive, reinforced, marked *AUTHORIZED PERSONNEL*

ONLY in faded yellow stencils. Rust scarred its surface. Welded patches spoke of years adrift on poisoned seas. His hands trembled as he pulled the stolen key card from his pocket.

"This is it," he whispered. "Please work…"

He swiped the card.

For a moment—nothing.

Then: a green flash. The scanner chirped. Hydraulic locks groaned. Gears clanked in deep, metallic rhythm. The central turnwheel spun on its own, accompanied by the hiss of depressurization.

"Come on…" Ahmed muttered, eyes darting down the hallway.

The hatch released with a heavy clang. He slipped through the gap and shoved it closed behind him, heart hammering. He yanked the card from the slot.

Inside, the drop bay yawned wide—half hangar, half cathedral to forgotten technology. Floodlights gleamed off the silver hull of the *Wad-Wer LX*, suspended above the ocean by massive clamps. The air smelled of ozone and machine oil. The hull groaned beneath them, the sea restless and hungry.

Ahmed's breath caught. The boat was magnificent—sleek, aerodynamic, lined with stabilizer fins and water-jet thrusters. It looked like it could fly.

For a heartbeat, awe overtook fear. He imagined himself at the helm, slicing through black waves, rising toward the sky no one believed in. *Sky City isn't a myth. It can't be.*

But there was no time to dream.

He ran to the control console. The metal floor rattled beneath his feet. He grabbed the lever and yanked it down.

The sound that followed was seismic.

A horn blared—a violent, mechanical roar that shook the decks. Red lights strobbed. The launch alarm.

"No!" Ahmed gasped, flinching. "No, no, no—quiet!"

Too late. The ship knew.

He turned to the vessel. The clamps retracted, pistons hissing. Floor panels split apart, revealing the churning sea below. Salt air flooded in, cold and wet.

Then—*BANG!*

A crash at the hatch. The door shuddered.

"OPEN THIS DAMNED DOOR!"

Balthazar's voice—furious, booming.

Ahmed froze, hands trembling on the rail. Another slam. Metal screeched.

"Ahmed!" Dawn's voice now—muffled, desperate. "Ahmed, open the door!"

"I'm going to find Sky City!" he shouted, voice cracking. "You'll see—it's real! We won't survive down here if I don't find it!"

Another blow. The steel moaned.

"Ahmed, listen to me!" Dawn pleaded, voice rising over the klaxon. "You can't go out there! The storms will tear you apart! Please—you're just a boy—"

"I'm not just a boy!" he screamed, gripping the railing. His body shook with adrenaline. "Someone has to try! Someone has to believe!"

The console flickered red. A synthetic voice echoed:

"Launch sequence initiated. Ten seconds to release."

"Ahmed!" Dawn slammed the door again. "Please—don't do this! We'll find it together. Just open the door and I'll help you. Please, sweetheart—"

Her voice cracked.

Ahmed's throat tightened. He turned toward the hatch. He could almost see her—hands pressed to the steel, tears streaking her face.

He wanted to open it. God, he wanted to.

But the sky called louder than fear. Louder than love.

"Maybe I won't make it," he whispered, staring at the gears rotating above. "But someone has to try!"

"**Five.**"

"Ahmed—!"

"**Four.**"

He looked once more at the hatch, tears burning his eyes.

"I love you… Mom."

Dawn's sob carried through the steel like a dying echo.

"**Three.**"

"**Two.**"

"**One.**"

The final clamp released.

The *Wad-Wer LX* dropped like a stone.

Chaos erupted—wind, water, sound. The vessel slammed into the black sea, the impact throwing Ahmed against the console. Spray drenched him, cold and sharp. The engines roared to life. The craft surged forward, slicing through the waves.

Behind him, *The Vesta* loomed—steel and light, fading into fog. Klaxons wailed, distant and dying.

Ahmed wiped saltwater from his eyes. Above the endless gray, faint streaks shimmered—ghostly cities in the mist.

He smiled, weak but certain.

"Time to prove it," he whispered.

And the *Wad-Wer LX* vanished into the storm.

IV

Vulcan

The Renegade Tide

Never shall one be left to drown,
This is the Renegade Tide.
Bound in battle, forged in flood,
We rise where others hide.
Faithful in the storm,
Fierce in the swell,
We take from none but the deep itself.
Brothers. Sisters.
Breath to breath,
We hold the line until the death.
This is the vow.
The Renegade Tide.

My Brother's Keeper

Sweat streaked down Gates' brow, warm and sour beneath the salt-heavy breeze. He didn't bother wiping it. His hand gripped the edge of the skiff like it was the only solid truth left in the world.

Behind him, the silhouette of the *Vulcan* loomed like a floating fortress—an angular steel monstrosity stitched together from the wreckage of older war arks. It was his home, if the word still meant anything. Home to him. Home to the lost. Home to the wicked.

It was packed to capacity with his kind.

And his kind were monsters.

The worst of them clung to the *Vulcan's* rust-flaked hull like barnacles—cutthroats, scavengers, traitors, and drifters—shaped by war, tempered by the ocean's wrath. They called themselves the Renegades. They didn't rescue. They didn't rebuild. They took. When the Renegades descended on a ship, they didn't leave survivors. Only empty holds and blood-streaked decks.

And yet Gates, just fourteen, was second-in-command of a platoon.

He was one of their smallest weapons, but also their sharpest.

Because Gates knew how to disappear.

Tonight, he was disappearing again—but this time, from them.

He took one last glance over his shoulder, his storm-gray eyes locking onto the *Vulcan*. A knot of guilt tightened in his throat. He swallowed hard. No one had noticed his absence yet, but when they did, hell would follow. He wasn't afraid of punishment—he was already past that. What gripped his heart now was the truth: that he might never come back.

And worse… that he might fail.

The sea stretched endlessly before him, black and vast. The waves rolled with slow menace, like something ancient and patient. Even in calmness, the ocean disapproved. Every current was a judgment. Every ripple whispered a warning.

But Gates was fluent in disobedience. It was his first language.

Flexibility when it mattered. Defiance when it didn't. That was how he survived. That's why the Gunny kept him close, and the rest of the Renegades kept their distance.

He had earned his scars. He'd killed. He'd lied. He'd followed orders.

But none of it mattered now.

Not compared to this.

His grip tightened on the rudder as he guided the tiny rescue boat through the mist. The hull creaked beneath him, cobbled together from scrap paneling and floatable steel drums, but it held. The engine was long dead—he relied on an improvised solar rig and paddle fins bolted to the sides. It was quiet. Low-profile. Built for stealth.

The kind of boat you used when you didn't want to be found.

He pulled his pack from behind him and adjusted the strap across his shoulder. It was too big for his frame—stuffed with gear, rations, and one precious object: a torn photograph sealed in hydrofilm. Two boys. One older, one younger. Both smiling before the separation.

Gates hadn't seen his brother in years.

Not since the Exodus fractured every family the sea didn't take.

Not since hope became a whispered myth traded for diesel and bullets.

He knew his brother probably thought he was dead. Worse—forgotten. But he wasn't. Not for a single day. That silence festered inside Gates like an infection. Every sleepless night. Every bloody skirmish. Every empty cargo hold. It was all background noise to the one thing screaming inside him:

Find him.

The moon pushed through the fog above, casting its silver eye across the dead sea. It made the water shimmer like obsidian glass and painted the sky with muted grief. The mist was thicker now, curling across the water's skin like breath over a coffin lid.

And there—there it was.

The *Callisto*.

She drifted in the distance, massive, proud, and half-lit like a sleeping beast. She wasn't the largest ark Gates had ever seen—but size wasn't everything. The *Callisto* had presence. Old-world armor plating. Weather-worn banners. Broad hull braced with tiered engine arrays. She looked like she'd survived more than storms. She looked like a secret.

Gates lifted the binoculars to his eyes—cracked, foggy, barely holding together. Through the distortion, he made out a small maintenance rig hanging off her portside, low to the waterline. No lights. No guards. Probably an old decon unit. A weak spot.

Perfect.

He exhaled slowly, fogging the eyepiece, then

wiped it on his sleeve. The chill of the mist kissed his face as he adjusted his course, inching toward the *Callisto's* belly.

His hand hovered over his belt—checked the blade. Still there.

His voice slipped from his lips, a whisper only the water could hear.

"Okay, Gates. Let's not die tonight."

But the dread didn't leave. It clung to him like the fog, thick and wet and full of teeth. He could feel the *Vulcan's* shadow behind him, even as it disappeared into the mist. He could feel the Renegades' breath on his neck, even as he fled.

And he could feel something else—something deeper.

The *Callisto* wasn't just another ark.

It was the beginning of something.

Or the end.

He braced himself. The ark drew closer, vast and indifferent.

And the hunt for answers began.

* * *

The rescue skiff drifted silently beneath the *Callisto's* immense shadow, swallowed whole by her colossal profile. Gates craned his neck skyward, breath catching in awe—and terror. From below, the Ark resembled a floating cathedral of steel, its hull etched with interlocking plating and power conduits that glowed faintly beneath a web of corrosion. She wasn't born of the old world. She was reborn from it. Reinforced bulkheads. Exo-skeletal ribs. A Titan of water navigation, forged not for comfort, but dominion.

Gates steadied himself, swallowing hard.

"All right… just don't die," he whispered.

He grabbed onto a grooved maintenance strut running along the starboard side, fingers finding purchase in the ridges worn by time and tide. Bit by bit, he climbed, boots scraping against blistered metal, muscles straining as he scaled the hull. A fall here wouldn't just break bones—it would erase him completely.

He reached the taffrail, slipped over like a shadow, and crouched low. The deck was slick with mist, glistening in the moonlight like oil on glass. Gates took a breath and moved swiftly, gliding toward the nearest hatch. Every movement was calculated. Every breath timed between gusts of sea wind. The *Callisto* felt asleep, but in places like this, stillness was never safe.

He gripped the latch and pulled gently—metal groaned. He flinched. Waited.

Silence.

He slipped inside, easing the hatch closed behind him with both hands, sealing out the outside world. Inside, the hall was dim—lit only by red emergency strips lining the baseboards. The air was thick with damp metal and recycled filtration, tinged with the distant stink of mildew and rust.

No footsteps. No voices.

Gates moved down the gangway, head on a swivel. He ducked under a broken pipe hissing faint steam and pressed deeper into the bowels of the ship, curving right past a junction bay. There, at last, a set of stairs.

He paused, hand on the rail. His breath hung in front of him in a pale cloud.

Dover... please be here.

No weapon, no order, no Renegade law had ever pushed him this far. It was his brother. Always his brother. The guilt clung to his ribs like barnacles. Years ago, he had left Dover behind—abandoned him on a crippled scavenger frigate during a mission gone wrong. His superior had barked the order: *"We move. Now."* And he had obeyed.

But Gates never forgot that scream. That small, blood-choked scream as the bulkhead sealed.

He descended into the dark.

The lower levels stank worse—raw sewage, oil,

something feral. The cells came into view, row after row of rusted bars and filthy hammocks. Prisoners lay half-conscious, their bodies gaunt, their eyes sunken like drowned sailors brought back from the abyss. No light here but the red haze of status strips blinking dimly.

He searched the faces. One by one. Hoping. Dreading.

But none of them were Dover.

His heart broke silently, a weight crushing his chest.

Another dead lead.

He swallowed the lump forming in his throat and backed away from the cells.

Get out. Before you're caught.

He climbed back up, retracing his path through the ship's half-lit veins. Night had fully fallen now. Beyond the bulkheads, the sea hissed and churned, cold and endless. Inside, the ship had grown quieter—too quiet. Every creak sounded like a scream. Every flicker of red light like an eye watching.

Then—footsteps.

Fast. Heavy.

Gates ducked behind a corner just as three figures emerged from the shadows, boots hammering the grated floor.

A voice barked behind him. "Hey!"

Gates turned sharply. A guard had spotted him.

"You're not authorized to be out of the berthings after hours," the man growled, tone suspicious and aggressive. He marched forward, baton already drawn. "Identify yourself. Now."

Gates swallowed and glanced at the baton in the guard's grip. His eyes narrowed.

"My name is—" he started, trying to summon a lie fast enough.

Too late.

Two more guards appeared behind the first, flanking the corridor like wolves closing in.

"Exactly what I thought," one of them snapped. "Kid's an intruder."

Gates raised his hands, voice even but tight. "I surrender."

The first guard stepped forward, circling him. "How'd you get on board, stowaway?"

"Better question," said another. "Why are you on board?"

"Trying to steal from us?" the last snarled. "We got punishments for that."

Gates didn't blink. "Punishment?" he said, tone flat. "You don't know what punishment looks like."

One of the guards snorted. "You're just a dumb kid with a death wish."

He grabbed Gates's arm, twisted it, and cinched

a zip tie tight around his wrists. Another guard moved in, reaching down to his thigh and yanking the dagger from its sheath.

"Don't touch that!" Gates shouted, jerking forward—too late.

The guard shoved him hard. Gates hit the wall with a metallic clang, breath knocked out of him.

"Been a while since I've seen one of these," the man said, admiring the dagger. The blade gleamed even under the red lights. It was old-world steel, curved and etched with strange markings.

"That's not yours," Gates growled, voice trembling with rage.

"You steal from us, we steal from you," another guard sneered, slamming him back against the wall, pressing his face into the cold, wet surface.

"I didn't steal anything!" Gates barked, trying to twist his body away. "You have no idea why I'm here."

"I know exactly what you are," one of them said. "A little rat playing pirate."

"Take him to the captain," said the lead guard, voice sharp. "Let's see what she wants done with him."

They dragged Gates forward, his feet scraping along the steel decking.

His head stayed high. His fists stayed clenched. He wouldn't cry.

Not again.

* * *

Chains clinked as the brig door groaned shut behind him, its locking mechanism wheezing like a tired lung. Rust crusted the corners of the cell, the floor slick with brine and rot. Red warning lights blinked overhead, casting long shadows across the grating like prison bars etched in blood.

Gates sat in silence, back against the wall, wrists bound with sea-cable. The cold bit through his soaked clothes, but he welcomed it. Cold meant he was still alive.

Footsteps approached. He didn't need to look up to know who it was.

The man who entered wore his authority like a weapon.

Captain Fletch.

Tall. Broad. Shoulders squared like a man who'd seen storms eat empires. His coat was patched with rank insignias from dead nations, and his boots thudded with deliberate power. A cutlass hung at his hip—not ornamental. Well-used. Well-honed.

He stopped outside the cell and leaned on the

door frame, eyes scanning Gates like a specimen under glass.

"What's your name, boy?" Fletch asked, voice gravel-thick with command.

Gates lifted his chin slowly. "Gates."

Fletch raised an eyebrow. "And?"

"I boarded your ship searching for someone. My brother—Dover."

There was a flicker. A pause in the captain's breathing. Then—disbelief.

"We know no one by that name," Fletch snapped, stepping closer. "And even if we did, what makes you think he'd still be alive?"

Gates didn't flinch. His jaw flexed, but his eyes stayed locked on the captain's.

Fletch leaned in, close enough for Gates to smell the salt-dried blood on his coat. "That patch on your shoulder. My crew recognizes it. You're one of those buccaneering scum from the *Vulcan*, aren't you?"

Gates clenched his fists.

"You lot have been tearing through these seas for years—raiding Arks, stripping them of supplies, leaving nothing but wreckage and corpses. Don't bother denying it."

"I don't know what you're talking about," Gates muttered, voice quieter, more guarded.

Fletch laughed—a sharp, humorless bark. "For

a thief, you're a terrible liar."

Gates tilted his head. "And for a captain, you're full of assumptions. You know, your guards welcomed me with a baton massage, a wall-hug, and a complimentary zip tie. Real hospitality. I was almost moved."

Fletch's smile vanished.

"I should toss you back into the water where you crawled from," he said coldly, pacing in front of the cell. "But as it happens… I have better uses for you."

He turned to go.

"You won't get away with this," Gates said, voice firmer now. "I have a crew. They'll come for me."

Fletch paused mid-step. He turned his head just enough to show the edge of a smirk.

"Oh? Is that a threat?"

Gates stared him down. "It's a fact."

Fletch's smirk curved into something darker. "One less pack of gutless raiders to pollute the sea. Once we find them… we'll eliminate them."

He stepped closer again, voice dropping to a growl. "And you'll be watching from the brig as your so-called crew sinks into the deep, screaming."

Gates leaned forward, eyes burning. "You think I'm afraid of drowning? I don't fear the sea. You think chains scare me? I've worn worse. You think you're the first captain to threaten me? You're not even the loudest."

Fletch studied him for a long moment, then straightened.

"You've got fire, I'll give you that," he said. "But fire goes out in the water."

He turned and walked away, boots echoing down the corridor.

The door slammed shut. The cell rattled. Silence returned.

But in these waters… Gates stayed burning… always.

Aye Gunny

F letch poured himself half a cup of coffee. The liquid trembled in the chipped ceramic mug, rich and bitter—over-brewed and barely warm, but still precious. Supplies like this were ghosts of a better time, clung to by those too stubborn to admit the sea had already taken more than it ever planned to give.

But Fletch helped himself freely, without hesitation.

Confidence—no, arrogance—poured out of him with every sip. No one aboard the *Callisto* would dare question the captain's use of dwindling rations. He believed the regulators would restock what was needed. They always did. That was the unspoken promise of men like Fletch—self-preservation, wrapped in ritual and myth.

And Gates? That scrawny teenage stowaway? The boy was a pawn at best. His threats—talk of someone coming for him—meant nothing.

Or so Fletch thought.

A flicker passed through the fog beyond the viewport. He leaned closer, narrowing his eyes. The mist, once idle and formless, now twisted like something alive. The horizon thickened. Shadows pulsed within it.

Then it broke.

An iron mass loomed from the gray veil—vast, silent, and monstrous. Steel plating the color of ash. Turrets like resting beasts. Three hulls layered atop one another, bristling with scavenged tech and makeshift weapons. It moved like it didn't fear the ocean—like the ocean feared it.

Fletch's blood ran cold.

The mug slipped from his fingers, shattering against the grated floor.

"Dillinger!" he shouted, stumbling backward.

Footsteps approached quickly, and a wiry teen emerged from the berth just off the bridge, uniform half-buttoned, eyes still blinking sleep.

"Sir?"

"Get the crew to alert stations. Now. And fetch the boy from the brig." Fletch turned away before the boy could respond. "Move!"

He stormed toward the weapons locker, yanked it open, and pulled out a hatchet. The blade was dull, but he held it like it could still carve fate. Panic simmered beneath his skin, boiling over in sweat as he barreled through the corridor, men falling in behind him in a rush of booted steps and shouted orders.

They stormed upward, brushing aside civilians—shipdwellers, wide-eyed and crying as they pressed their backs to the walls. Screams echoed behind them as the crew forced their way toward the top deck.

But the deck was already taken.

They emerged into cold air and chaos. The sea wind hit them hard, thick with diesel and brine. And across the deck stood figures—dozens. Young. Armed. Silent.

Children and teenagers. No older than seventeen. Uniformed in scavenged armor, reinforced with scrap plating and stitched leather. Some bore sabers stolen from military officers. Others carried serrated knives or repurposed harpoon rifles. Their faces were hardened with the kind of expression no child should know: the certainty of violence.

And at their center stood the man himself.

Massive. Broad-shouldered. Weathered by years of salt and blood. A beard grizzled with ash, a long coat swaying at his knees. He held a hooked sword in one hand, dragging it lightly against the steel deck with an ear-splitting screech.

Gunny War.

"You've illegally boarded the *Callisto*," Fletch

snapped, striding forward. He tried to hide the tremor in his voice with practiced bluster. "I order you and your…" He sneered at the group. "…your men to stand down and abandon this foolish raid."

Gunny didn't move. His expression remained unreadable. When he spoke, it was with the amused tone of someone who had already won.

"You haven't even let me introduce myself, Captain."

"I know exactly who you are," Fletch growled. "You're Gunny War. And these… rats you travel with? Feral thieves. That's all."

"Captain, O Captain," Gunny said, flashing a smile that didn't touch his eyes. "Introductions give context. Let you understand the shape of the blade before it's in your ribs."

"I don't need context," Fletch barked. "Take your little army and vanish, or we'll feed your bones to the black."

Gunny's smile vanished.

"These aren't an army," he said, softly. "They're citizens. And I didn't come here to trade threats."

"Then why?"

"You have something that belongs to us."

Fletch's grip tightened on his hatchet. "You mean the boy?"

"Let's call him a stowaway for now," Gunny said. "But he's more than you know. He's important to us."

"He attempted to steal from us," Fletch spat. "Punishable by death. That's the law on every vessel worth its salt."

Gunny twirled the hook-sword once. His voice lost all trace of warmth.

"Punishment for a crime he didn't commit? That's not law. That's desperation."

"You send children to do your stealing."

Gunny laughed—once, sharp and full of scorn. "These boys have never stolen a thing in their lives."

"You mock justice."

"No," Gunny said, stepping forward. "Because everything in these waters belongs to us."

And then he moved.

The headbutt was brutal. Bone crunched. Blood sprayed. Fletch reeled back, screaming, hands clasped over his shattered nose. Before he could stumble too far, Gunny drove a boot into his chest. The captain flew backward and crashed to the deck, gasping.

Fletch's men roared.

Blades were drawn.

The Renegades moved like lightning.

They didn't charge—they flowed. Coordinated. Measured. Each swing had purpose. Each step was part of a larger design. Where Fletch's men hacked wildly, the Renegades parried, disarmed, dropped them with bone-snapping precision. Every motion was trained. Every angle practiced.

These were not feral children.

They were weapons.

Fletch groaned, pushing himself up to his elbows, face soaked in red. His vision swam. He found Gunny again, standing still in the center of it all—watching. Studying.

"You bastard," Fletch hissed, and lunged forward.

Gunny sidestepped.

Fletch stumbled off balance toward the edge of the deck, catching himself on the taffrail just as a massive hand clamped around his throat.

Gunny lifted him—one arm, effortless.

Fletch's boots kicked against air, eyes wide as the sea rolled beneath him.

"A real captain," Gunny growled, "goes down with his ship."

But instead of throwing him, Gunny yanked him back and slammed him to the deck. Fletch crumpled like wet rope, choking on blood and bile.

Around him, the battle was done.

Fletch's crew had surrendered. They knelt with hands behind their heads, swords leveled at their throats. Renegades began zip-tying their wrists, some methodical, others smiling grimly.

Gunny stood over Fletch, looming like a storm-cloud.

"Run."

Fletch didn't think twice.

He scrambled to his feet and bolted through a nearby hatch, disappearing into the dark interior of the *Callisto*.

Gunny turned to one of his boys—a Renegade no older than thirteen, with a crimson sash tied tight across his chest.

"On my mark," Gunny said. "Disable the engine room. By the time I retrieve the boy, this place should be stripped to metal."

The boy nodded.

"Aye, Gunny."

* * *

Gunny War descended the stairwell slowly, each footstep echoing through the steel arteries of the *Callisto*. The ship groaned with age and defeat. Steam hissed from fractured pipes overhead, dripping moisture into rust-stained puddles on the grated floor. His eyes scanned every corner, every corridor branching into darkness—waiting for something to leap from the shadows.

But nothing did.

No guards. No posted sentries. No last lines of defense.

They hadn't been ready for him. They hadn't been ready for the Renegades.

The lower deck was desolate, drowned in low light and flickering emergency strobes. Faint screams of the ship's surrendering crew echoed somewhere distant, dulled by steel bulkheads and waterlogged silence. Ahead lay the brig—rows of reinforced cells bolted into the ship's spine like forgotten tombs.

Gunny's boots splashed through shallow pools of runoff as he moved forward.

"Gates! Status!" he barked, voice booming off the walls before he even rounded the final corner.

From the back of the brig came a rustle. A cough. Then a boy's voice—young, tense.

"Here. No injuries!"

Gunny's stride quickened. He moved with weight and purpose, cutting through the stillness like a coming storm. At the end of the row, behind a locked cell door, stood Gates—wide-eyed, pale beneath the flickering lights, hands tight on the bars.

Gunny stopped.

"I must've missed the briefing that appointed you in charge of my Renegades," he said, voice thick with reprimand. "Tell me, Gates—when was that briefing?"

The boy hesitated. Blue eyes wavered.

"There… wasn't one," he mumbled.

Gunny leaned forward.

"I didn't hear you."

With a sharp clang, he slammed the flat of his hook sword against the bars. The steel screeched.

"There wasn't one!" Gates snapped, louder this time—fear barely masked by defiance.

A smile tugged at the corners of Gunny's mouth. Not of amusement—something colder.

He reached down, unclipped a pouch from his belt, and drew out a ring of keys—taken from one of the ship's now-unconscious guards. One slid clean into the lock. With a dull click, the cell door creaked open.

Gunny stepped inside, his presence filling the space like a rising tide. Gates stood still as stone, his breath shallow.

"I've gotta admit," Gunny said, voice low now, controlled. "Takes guts to steal one of the *Vulcan's* boats… especially when you were under strict orders to let that trail go cold."

Gates didn't move.

"He's my brother," the boy said. "I have to find him."

Gunny's face darkened.

"And I am your commanding officer. The only reason you're not rotting at the bottom of the sea is because I made the call to come for you."

His voice thundered in the tiny cell.

Gates flinched.

"You defied direct orders. You took a Renegade skiff, burned through half our reserve fuel, exposed our position, and led me into a goddamn firefight—all for a ghost you can't save!"

Gunny stepped forward, towering over the boy.

"Make this the last time you disobey me, Gates… or next time, I'll personally carry you to the depths."

Silence.

Gates stared at the floor. His voice was a whisper.

"Yes."

Gunny growled. "Yes what?"

Gates met his eyes—scared, but no longer wavering.

"Yes, Gunny."

Gunny studied him for a long moment, then turned toward the door.

But Gates wasn't done.

"Oh, and Gunny?" he said, voice cracking with a mix of sarcasm and bruised pride. "I hope that's the last time these guards treat me like a piñata. I got zip-tied, face-slammed, and they stole my dagger. Pretty sure one of them tried to adopt it."

Gunny paused, half-turned, and raised an eyebrow.

"You're lucky they didn't adopt your lungs."

Gates shrugged. "Would've made it easier to breathe in here."

Gunny's expression didn't change, but something flickered behind his eyes—respect, maybe. Or recognition.

"Get your gear," he said. "We're not done here."

Gates nodded, rubbing his wrists where the cable had bitten deep.

He wasn't whole. But he was back.

A New Storm

Hours had passed, and the sea only grew angrier.

The horizon had vanished, swallowed by a storm-torn void—a horizonless sheet of black water and lightning. Night had fallen hard, heavy as iron. The *Wad-Wer LX* pitched and rolled like a wounded animal, its sleek frame reduced to a toy tossed between mountain-sized waves.

Ahmed clung to the controls, his small hands trembling, forearms screaming with exhaustion. The vessel groaned beneath him, its reinforced hull flexing with each impact. He hadn't slept. He hadn't eaten, not since that last ration square. It lay now in his palm, the foil wrapper fluttering with every jolt of the hull.

The smell of salt, rust, and oil mixed into something acrid—mechanical, humanless.

He hesitated before opening it. The tiny brick of protein and sugar was the last taste of home, the last trace of the *Vesta*. He thought of Dawn—her eyes filled with worry, her voice trembling with fear.

You can't go out there alone, Ahmed.

But he had.

And there was no going back.

He tore open the ration and ate it slowly, each grain of sugar a bitter reminder of everything he'd left behind.

The storm was building. He could feel it in his teeth—a low hum beneath the hull, deep as the Earth itself. The first blast of wind hit the *Wad-Wer* broadside, slamming Ahmed against the seat. The canopy was open; spray lashed through the cockpit in sheets. He scrambled to the control panel and hit the seal button. The canopy hissed shut, locking with a dull, metallic thunk.

Water streamed across the transparent surface as if he were inside the eye of some steel fish, diving deeper into hell.

Lightning arced across the sky—long, crooked veins of white fire that lit the sea for miles. Each flash revealed waves like walls, black and boiling. Thunder followed, cracking so loud it made Ahmed's ribs rattle. The *Wad-Wer* climbed one of those swells, engines screaming at full thrust, and for a breathless second he saw everything— the endless, violent sea below, and the suffocating darkness above.

Then gravity reclaimed him.

The boat plunged into the trough. The impact was brutal. His knees hit the console. His teeth bit his tongue. Blood sprayed the canopy.

"I can do this," he whispered. "I can do this, I can do this—"

Another wave came from the port side. It struck the hull like a hammer. The *Wad-Wer* heaved violently, rolling onto its starboard flank. Ahmed was thrown from the seat, his head cracking the plexiglass canopy. The reinforced glass spider-webbed, then shattered with a deafening burst. Shards exploded outward, slicing through the storm like razors.

Ahmed didn't scream—he didn't have time.

The force of the wave ripped him from the cockpit, hurling him into the open air. For one surreal heartbeat, he was weightless—suspended in the void between lightning flashes. Then the *Wad-Wer* fell away beneath him. The boy hit open air, then open water—a plunge into the freezing, black abyss.

The shock tore the breath from his lungs.

Saltwater filled his mouth and nose. His limbs flailed without rhythm or purpose. The storm owned him now. He tried to kick, to find the surface, but every direction felt the same—chaos and cold and darkness. Panic ripped through his chest. He screamed, but the sea swallowed it whole.

Then—something touched him.

A line. A wire. Then a dozen.

Something mechanical coiled around his torso, biting into his arms and ribs. He thought it was the sea itself pulling him under, until he felt the tension—the upward drag.

A net.

A machine-driven trawl, dragging him from the depths.

His body rose through the dark, through the current, through the cold. The last thing he saw before his vision dimmed was a massive shadow looming above him—a ship, but not like the *Vesta*. Bigger. Angrier. Armed.

Then everything went black.

* * *

When he woke, the world had changed again.

The air was thick with the stench of diesel and salt. The deck beneath him was cold metal, vibrating from deep engines. His head ached; blood crusted his forehead. He blinked hard, adjusting to the harsh light and the roar of machinery.

Above him loomed a ship built for war.

Enormous. A black steel beast cutting through the storm. Its hull was scarred, its plating welded over with mismatched armor. Gun turrets lined the deck, rusted but functional. Floodlights cut through the rain, swinging in slow arcs. The sound of chains clanking through winches echoed through the hull.

This was no ark. No refuge.

This was a predator.

A net hoist released him onto the deck with a wet thud. The impact jarred him fully awake. He coughed, spitting seawater, and blinked up into the face of the man who'd been watching him.

Gunny War.

He didn't need an introduction. The man's brutal features said everything—barrel-chested, beard streaked with gray, eyes like cold glass. His naval coat was reinforced with leather and scavenged armor plating. The hooksword strapped across his back looked like it had tasted blood more than once.

Standing just behind him was Gates—face gaunt, posture subdued, every muscle in him reading quiet obedience. The spark that had once made him seem unbreakable was gone. He looked smaller now, like something that had been trained not to flinch.

"He's alive," one of the crewmen grunted, kneeling to check Ahmed's pulse. "Just knocked cold."

Gunny War didn't kneel. He didn't even lean. He just stared at the boy for a long, unbearable moment, as if trying to decide if he was worth the air he was breathing.

"Then throw him in the brig until he wakes," Gunny said, voice deep and cold as ballast water. "If he's useful, we'll find out soon enough. If not, the sea can have him back."

Two deckhands obeyed without question. Big men—faces burned from salt, tattoos faded from years of exposure. They lifted Ahmed under the arms like a sack of gear, dragging him across the slick steel. His bare feet scraped the deck. He tried to speak, but only managed a ragged cough.

As they pulled him toward the interior hatches, Ahmed glanced one last time toward the edge of the deck. Through the haze of rain, he caught a glimpse of the *Wad-Wer*—half-submerged, distant, a dying light swallowed by the storm.

And for just a heartbeat, he thought he saw something else.

A shimmer on the horizon.

Shapes—tall, geometric, impossible.

Towers?

Then the lightning blinked, and it was gone.

They shoved him through a bulkhead and down

a narrow companionway. The air below deck was worse—a mix of mildew, sweat, and fuel. Steam hissed from pipes overhead; condensation dripped onto the rusted floor plates. The ship creaked and groaned with each swell. Commands were shouted somewhere deeper inside—rough accents, fractured English, like an army of ghosts.

They passed compartments labeled with stenciled words: *AFT STORAGE, ENGINE ROOM ACCESS, HOLD 3—RESTRICTED*. Somewhere beyond those doors, the engines throbbed like a heart. The deeper they went, the darker it got, the lights flickering, the shadows thick as smoke.

Finally, they stopped.

A small hatch. A cold, iron door.

One of the men spun the wheel lock and hauled it open. Inside was a tiny cell—little more than a metal box with a cot, a drain, and a rusted light swinging from the ceiling.

"Welcome aboard the *Vulcan*," one of them muttered with a sneer.

Then they threw him inside.

The door clanged shut. The sound echoed down the steel corridor like the toll of a bell.

Ahmed lay there for a long time, shaking from cold and exhaustion. Above, the storm raged on, waves hammering the hull. And beneath that chaos, in the stillness of the brig, the boy whispered to himself—words half dream, half prayer.

"I'll find it. I'll find Sky City."

* * *

Ahmed's mind spun in a haze of pain and hunger. His body ached as though it had been scraped raw by the storm itself, each breath a knife drawn against his ribs. He blinked hard, forcing his eyes open to the dull, red glow of emergency lighting. The world around him was swaying — metal groaning, pipes hissing, chains clattering like bones.

The air was thick with rust and salt, damp enough to taste. The smell of oil and iron filled his lungs. Slowly, he realized he was no longer at sea — at least, not in the same way. He was inside something vast, something alive. A ship.

The Vulcan.

It was enormous — far larger than the Vesta or anything he'd seen in his short, storm-torn life. From the hum beneath the deck to the distant, rhythmic boom of turbines, the entire vessel felt like a living beast — a predator cutting through the black waves. The steel walls vibrated with power,

167

and somewhere deep within, engines throbbed like a monstrous heart.

Ahmed sat up slowly. His body protested. His lip was split, his head throbbed, and his stomach screamed for food. He could barely remember how he'd ended up here — flashes of lightning, the violent drop of the Wad-Wer, then darkness. He wiped a smear of dried blood from his temple and took in his surroundings.

The brig cell was larger than the one he remembered on the Vesta, but rougher, crueler. The walls were jagged and scarred, as though someone had welded this prison together from the bones of other ships. The bars were thick and orange with corrosion, each one pitted with years of neglect. Water leaked from the ceiling in thin streams, pooling at his bare feet.

There was space, yes — but it was a trick. A cruel illusion of freedom. The kind of space that mocked you.

Ahmed climbed unsteadily to his feet, every movement echoing in the confined air. He pressed a hand against the wall to steady himself, then crept toward the bars, peering into the corridor beyond. The corridor was dark — almost completely black save for the distant pulse of a red alarm light somewhere far down the hall.

He swallowed. "Hello?"

For a long moment, there was only the sound of the ship. The deep churn of engines, the slow creak of metal, the steady drip of water from above. Then—

"No."

A whisper. Faint, like breath on the back of his neck.

Ahmed stiffened. His eyes darted through the dark, trying to place it. "Who's there?" he called out. "What is this place?"

"Get away from the bars," the voice hissed.

Ahmed didn't move. Curiosity wrestled with fear, and curiosity won. "Why?"

Silence. Then, almost inaudible — "War is coming."

Before Ahmed could ask what that meant, a blade slammed against the bars with a screeching clang. Sparks burst across the brig deck, showering his face with orange light. Ahmed flinched and stumbled back, heart hammering.

Gunny War stood outside the cell.

His shadow filled the corridor like a living storm. He was massive, his frame built like steel plating, his face half-lit by the dull red light. Rain still clung to the shoulders of his heavy coat; rivulets ran down the hooksword he held, sizzling as the blade met the damp air. His beard was a ragged map of salt and chew. The eyes that met

Ahmed's were gunmetal — small, cold, precise.

"Which ship sent you my way?" Gunny growled. His voice carried the depth of the ocean, each word a heavy stone dropped into a hull.

Ahmed froze, pulse pounding so loud he heard it in his teeth.

"Answer me, worm." Gunny's voice rose, shaking the air. "When I ask a question, I expect an answer."

"I— I wasn't sent by anyone," Ahmed stuttered.

Gunny stepped closer. The tip of the hooksword scraped the deck, a long metallic scream that left a thin black streak along the steel. "Then what makes a boy navigate the dead seas alone in a rescue craft built for a crew of ten?"

Ahmed's throat worked. He felt small, ridiculous, a child whose chest still held dreams too big for the world. He lifted his chin as best he could. "Sky City."

The name hit the corridor like an insult and a prayer. Gunny's expression shifted — first slow amusement, then a dangerous, calculating interest.

"Sky City," he echoed, tasting it. "You're a brave little fool, aren't you?"

"I'm not a fool," Ahmed said, trembling but stubborn.

Gunny's grin spread — all teeth, no warmth.

"Your half-witted mission is over, boy. Now that you're aboard the Vulcan, you'll follow orders and serve as instructed. You breathe because I allow it. You move because I say so. Understood?"

"...No."

The word slipped out before Ahmed could swallow it back.

Gunny's grin peeled away, replaced by a stare that pressed against the marrow of Ahmed's bones. "What did you say?"

Ahmed straightened as much as his wrists allowed. "I did this to find food. For my people. We're starving."

Gunny cocked his head, inspecting him like a deckhand checking rope for fray. "You think hunger makes you special? You think you're the only ones scraping life off these waves?" He lowered his voice until the words were a rasp. "That kind of thinking shows how little you know. Your disobedience shows even less. But don't worry."

He leaned in until Ahmed could see his own reflection in the man's iris — pale, frightened. "It will be corrected."

Gunny turned, his boots echoing, and the corridor swallowed him. "Gates!"

The call snapped like a lash. The name traveled down the spine of the Vulcan and back, and from the shadows Gates emerged — thin, a string of a man, all angles and old regrets. He moved without hurry, as if every step counted and none were wasted. There was a weary obedience in him that made Ahmed's skin prickle.

"Prepare our noble visitor for the walk," Gunny ordered, and his voice carried a grin that showed no mirth.

Gates hesitated, eyes flicking toward the cell. For a breath, Ahmed saw something in Gates' face — recognition, maybe, or pity — and then the mask snapped back into place. Gates unlatched the cell. The metal shrieked, the sound raw as a snapped hawser.

Ahmed stepped out. Chains clinked at his wrists as they were fitted. Cold metal bit into his skin. He felt naked despite the jacket that hung from his shoulders, wet with seawater and shame.

"Where's my boat?" Ahmed blurted, because if there was one thing he could still ask for it was an anchor he could name.

Gunny stopped, turning fully. The red light painted the hook of his jaw scarlet. "Has anything I've said registered in that fragile little skull of yours?" he asked.

Ahmed swallowed. "I don't care what you say. I'll find Sky City. I'll find it even if I have to tear through every ship to do it."

Gunny stared long enough that time stretched into a thin wire between them. Then he barked a laugh, not harsh but cold, and it cut the air. "Your choices make you who you are," he said, almost tenderly. "Remember that."

He motioned with a chin. Gates caught Ahmed's arm and led him up the grated stair. The ascent threw him into wind and salt. When they breached the deck, the Vulcan opened around them — vast, machinery everywhere: capstans groaning, vents bellowing steam, ropes and hawsers like coiled serpents. Crewmen moved in practiced lines, faces half-hidden beneath oilskins, eyes sharp and quick.

The deck smelled of hot metal, wet rope, and spilled diesel. The horizon bled iron and cloud. Waves slapped the hull in patient, murderous rhythm. Above them, the Vulcan's superstructure towered, gunports and observation slits like the eyes of a warship.

Gunny drew Ahmed past the crew as if showcasing a specimen. Men and women paused, their gazes appraising — some with hunger, some with a grudging respect that Ahmed could not yet parse. A young bosun spat to the lee side and muttered something that might have been a prayer or simply a curse.

"We'll see how long your courage lasts above

deck," Gunny said, voice raised enough for the line to hear. "The sea loves to test the brave."

Ahmed's feet dragged over oil-slick plating. The Vulcan rode the swell with the confidence of a thing that had weathered worse than weather — storms of men and storms of nature. Behind him, the brig door slammed shut like a verdict.

For a second, as the wind tore at his soaked clothes and the Vulcan's mast creaked overhead, Ahmed thought of Dawn — of cold hands and warmer promises — and of Alana's eyes, so tired and full of impossible trust. He felt the thin, hot ember of a vow he hadn't yet learned to keep.

He pulled his chin up. "No," he said, low this time — not for the ears of the guards, but for himself. "No, I won't stop."

Gunny's shadow fell over him like a verdict. "Then learn," the man said softly. "Or let the learning be painful."

Above them, the Vulcan pushed on, muscles and metal, a leviathan with a captain's appetite. The sea watched and waited.

War, the whisper had said. War was coming. The Vulcan was ready to teach the world what that meant.

* * *

Gunny War led the procession with slow, deliberate strides, the sound of his boots ringing off the grated deck like distant gunfire. Behind him, Ahmed stumbled forward, wrists bound in coarse rope that dug into his skin. Every tug from his captors sent fire through his arms, but he refused to make a sound.

The Renegades flanked him on both sides — silent, sharp-eyed, their movements crisp despite the storm. The air carried the smell of oil, seawater, and smoke; it clung to their skin like memory. The sound of the ship — the heartbeat of the Vulcan — was a constant undertone beneath everything.

The corridor opened into a blast hatch, and a gust of freezing air slammed into Ahmed's face. Diesel. Salt. Rain. The world outside was fury and chaos.

When they emerged onto the upper deck, the noise swallowed everything. The storm was still raging, clawing at the sky with fingers of lightning. The sea below writhed and thundered, black and bottomless. The Vulcan loomed like a moving fortress — its towers cutting through the storm, its floodlights sweeping the water in wide, merciless arcs. Every part of the ship shone slick with oil and rain, trembling under the weight of the wind.

Ahmed squinted against the gale, the sting of

rain biting into his eyes. He scanned the deck —
the cranes, the rigging, the rusted catwalks. Somewhere out there, he thought he might glimpse
the wreck of his rescue craft. The Wad-Wer. His
only connection to the world before this one. But
there was nothing. Just the sea — vast, silent,
indifferent.

Gunny War stopped and turned to face him.
His coat whipped in the wind, the hooksword
resting at his side. "Looking for something, boy?"
His voice carried easily, sharp and calm amid the
chaos.

Ahmed said nothing, jaw set, shoulders shaking
from cold and exhaustion.

Gunny smirked faintly. "Good. Because you
won't find it. Not your toy boat. Not your
home. Not your people. Out here, the sea eats
everything."

The words hit harder than the rain. Ahmed
looked down, lips pressed thin.

Two of the older crewmen approached, dragging a long, narrow beam of carbon and steel — a
makeshift plank, improvised but built to last. They
slammed it down beside the taffrail, the sound
cutting through the wind. Sparks flew as they
fastened the bolts.

The other end of the plank jutted out over the
ocean — hanging in the open air, trembling above

the black water. Lightning flashed, and for a heartbeat the sea turned white, the plank glowing like a blade suspended over the abyss.

Gunny clasped his hands behind his back, watching as the bolts were tightened. The storm's light flickered across his eyes — cold, unreadable, almost serene.

Ahmed's pulse quickened. "What... what is that for?"

No one answered.

Then Gates appeared — gaunt, pale, eyes shadowed. He carried a blindfold in one trembling hand. "Sir?"

Gunny gave a short nod.

Before Ahmed could move, Gates seized him by the hair, jerking his head back hard enough to make him gasp. The blindfold slid over his eyes, plunging the world into darkness.

"Walk onto the plank," Gates ordered. His voice cracked in the wind.

"What? No—wait!" Ahmed fought to keep his footing, but rough hands shoved him forward. His boots slipped against the rain-slick metal. The deck vibrated under him. He couldn't tell where the edge began — or where it ended.

"Walk, worm!" Gates snapped, pushing harder.

Gunny's voice boomed through the storm, low and resonant. "Do you know what's out there, boy? Do you know what waits below?"

Ahmed stopped, breath quick and shallow. He could feel the plank flex beneath his boots. The sound of the sea — the crash, the hiss, the churn — was deafening.

"Nothing but your fear," Gunny said. "That's what the sea is. Endless. Hungry. Waiting. It wants you to fall."

"I can't— I can't see where I'm going!" Ahmed shouted, his voice raw.

Gunny took a step closer, his tone turning hard. "And destiny doesn't require you to, boy. Neither do I."

Another shove. The plank bowed beneath Ahmed's weight. The ocean roared below — alive, breathing, patient.

"I'll fall!"

"Then fall!" Gunny barked, thunder cracking as if to punctuate his command. "The weak fall. The strong stand their ground. Which are you?"

Ahmed's pulse hammered in his skull. The rain was in his mouth, his eyes, his lungs. He felt the rope biting into his wrists, the storm tearing at his clothes — and somehow, he stayed standing.

Gunny's tone lowered, almost gentle now, and far more dangerous. "Tell me, Sky Boy — do you still believe in your city in the clouds?"

Ahmed hesitated. His whole body trembled.

But when he spoke, the word came from somewhere deeper than fear.

"Yes."

Gunny's grin widened. Lightning flashed, carving his face in white light. "Then maybe the sea will deliver you to it."

"Sir—" Gates began, uncertainty creeping into his tone.

Gunny raised a hand. "Enough."

He stepped forward. "Get him down."

Rough hands seized Ahmed. The blindfold was torn away, and the world exploded back into motion — lightning splitting the sky, rain slashing sideways, the deck alive with noise.

Gunny loomed above him, water running down his face, the hooksword gleaming like a live current in his hand. "Remember this feeling," he said. "This is what fear tastes like. You'll either learn to master it..." He leaned closer, his breath hot against the boy's ear. "...or drown in it."

He turned away, voice cutting through the storm. "Lock him below until I decide what to do with him."

The Renegades obeyed without hesitation, dragging Ahmed back toward the hatch. His boots scraped the steel deck, leaving dark streaks of water and dirt in his wake. He didn't fight. Didn't speak. He only looked back once — over his shoulder, toward the sea that seemed to watch him go.

When the hatch slammed shut, the roar of the storm vanished, replaced by the low hum of the Vulcan's heart.

But Gunny War's voice stayed with him, echoing in his skull long after the sound had gone.

This is what fear tastes like.

And somewhere deep below, the ship creaked — like it agreed.

* * *

The mess hall of the Vulcan was a cavern of cold metal and recycled breath. The hum of turbines shuddered through the ribbed ceiling, rattling the pipes until condensation dripped like rain from a steel sky. Rows of dented benches stretched the length of the chamber, their surfaces worn smooth by years of elbows and hunger. Children in frayed fatigues and torn coats sat shoulder to shoulder, eating with the silence of habit. The air reeked of iron, grease, and synthetic protein— an atmosphere brewed from desperation and recycled life.

Ahmed gripped his tray with both hands, every

step a balancing act. On it: a ration square of bread, a sliver of engineered meat, a scoop of reconstituted mash. Survival measured by grams. He moved carefully through the rows, eyes flicking for a place away from the noise and the stares. He found it — a corner table, dim, distant, half-swallowed by shadow.

He sat. The bench was cold, the metal biting through his thin trousers. For the first time since waking in the brig, he exhaled quietly and allowed himself the smallest illusion of peace. A heartbeat's worth of normal.

Then a voice cut through the din — sharp, mocking, and much too close.

"You're at the wrong table."

Ahmed froze. His shoulders tensed as he turned just enough to see the grin spreading across Gates's face. The older boy's insignia cap caught the dim light — DOVER stitched across it in faded thread.

Ahmed didn't speak. His jaw locked.

"You deaf, Peter Pan!?" Gates barked, loud enough to draw glances from the next row.

The nickname scraped across Ahmed's nerves. His fists clenched beneath the table.

"Stop calling me that," he muttered, his voice low but trembling with heat.

"Until you tell us your name, you'll be assigned

one." Gates leaned in, his grin widening. "Now move."

Ahmed didn't move. Instead, he slid his tray slightly closer, a small, dangerous rebellion.

The nearby Renegades stopped chewing. Eyes turned, not to intervene — but to watch.

Gates exhaled through his nose, amused. "Fine. Sit there then."

Ahmed lowered himself, muscles tight, every motion deliberate. He tore a piece of bread from the loaf, quick and discreet, and slipped it beneath the table into his lap.

The motion didn't go unnoticed. A girl sitting opposite — thin, dark-haired, her sleeves rolled to the elbow — caught his wrist in an instant. Her grip was iron.

"You trying to get us all put out on the beam?!" she hissed, voice sharp enough to cut through the background hum.

Ahmed's eyes widened. "I wasn't—"

Before he could finish, the clang of Gates's boots rang out like a verdict. He loomed behind her.

"Let him take it," Gates said flatly.

The girl looked up, her eyes darting between them. She hesitated — then dropped Ahmed's wrist as if it had burned her.

"He can feed the old rat in the brig," Gates added, grinning as he sat down across from him.

The tension at the table tightened like wire. Ahmed's hand trembled slightly as he set the bread back on his tray.

Gates bit into a synth-apple — a rarity on the Vulcan — with a sharp, echoing crunch. The scent of artificial sweetness filled the air between them. His gaze never left Ahmed's face.

"There's a bright lad," he said through the bite, his tone half-taunt, half-measured.

Ahmed frowned. "Why do you eat in the morning?" he asked softly.

The girl snorted. "So we don't die."

Ahmed's eyes flicked toward her, then back to Gates. "If you wait till mid-day, you won't be as hungry at night."

Gates chewed slowly, his smirk never fading. "And why's that, then?"

"Because it's easier to sleep through hunger," Ahmed said.

Gates wiped his mouth with the back of his hand, leaning back on the bench. "Why eat one meal a day when the rations are infinite?"

Ahmed blinked, confused. "Infinite?"

"Triple R's, Pan," Gates said. "Renewable ration resources. Synthesizers can print food for a century if we keep the lines clear."

Ahmed stared at his tray, at the beige mash congealing in the recycled light. "No one ever told me that," he murmured.

"Then you've been living under a rock," Gates said, chuckling. "Or whatever's left of one."

Ahmed looked up, meeting his eyes. "My colony's running out of food."

Gates's laughter erupted, bright and cruel. The others joined in — even the girl cracked a reluctant smile.

"You're a dense bloke, Peter Pan," Gates said. "The sea's full of idiots starving on broken ships, and you come floating in here thinking the world's still ending."

Ahmed's brow furrowed. "It is ending," he said quietly.

The laughter dimmed — not gone, just quieter. A flicker of something passed across Gates's face, but it was gone as soon as it came.

Then Ahmed said it:

"Sky City."

The name landed like a hammer. The laughter stopped entirely.

"You believe that?" Gates asked, the humor bleeding from his tone.

"Yes."

Gates leaned forward, elbows on the table. "Big into fairy tales, huh?"

Ahmed didn't answer. His silence was sharper than words.

The air changed — and everyone felt it.

Heavy footsteps, rhythmic and deliberate, echoed through the hall. Gates's expression snapped to alert. He sprang to his feet so fast his tray clattered over.

"ATTENTION ON DECK!"

Every Renegade in the room rose instantly, trays and utensils forgotten. The noise cut to absolute silence. Ahmed hesitated a heartbeat too long, then scrambled up, his tray sliding off the table with a dull clang.

Gunny War entered.

The mess seemed to shrink around him. His presence pulled the air tighter, colder. The man's coat was soaked from the rain above deck, streaked with oil and salt. His steps were measured, precise, and the sound of them was enough to make the walls vibrate.

"At ease," he said.

The word rumbled through the chamber like distant thunder.

The Renegades obeyed, sitting as one. Ahmed followed, slower, uncertain.

Gunny's gaze moved across the tables, assessing — not people, but assets. His eyes stopped on Gates.

"Is John Doe briefed on his duties," he asked, voice low and dangerous, "or is he still in the dark?"

Gates shot to his feet. "Still dark, Gunny."

Gunny's jaw flexed. "What are you waiting for, a land sighting? Should I assume you'd prefer to lead from the brig?"

"Negative, sir!" Gates barked, spine straight as a mast. "I'll ensure Peter Pan is up to speed and trained."

Gunny's gaze lingered. A faint smile tugged at one corner of his mouth.

"Peter Pan," he repeated. The name rolled out like a threat.

"Yes, Gunny."

Gunny chuckled — a single low sound that contained no warmth. "Carry on."

He turned, his boots striking the deck in sharp rhythm, and disappeared through the hatch.

The air released, all at once. The room filled with the sound of breathing again.

Ahmed sank back into his seat, his pulse still hammering. He looked at the empty doorway, then at the faces around him — all turned back to their trays as if nothing had happened.

He swallowed hard. "What do you guys do?" he asked quietly.

"Enough with the questions, Pan," Gates said without looking up. "Eat."

Ahmed lowered his gaze to his tray. The bread

had gone hard. He chewed slowly, tasting iron and salt and silence.

Then his eyes drifted to the patch on Gates's cap again — DOVER — the thread frayed, the letters almost erased.

"Is that a nickname?" Ahmed asked.

The sound that followed was a gunshot in the room's quiet.

Gates's fist slammed the table — hard enough to rattle every tray around them. The entire mess hall went still. Ahmed's heart jumped into his throat.

But he didn't look away.

He just stared down at the dull reflection in the steel surface — his own face, hollow-eyed and defiant — and waited.

Sink or Swim

Night bled across the Vulcan like an ink stain, swallowing light, swallowing warmth. The storm outside had quieted, but the silence it left behind was worse. It pressed in on the hull — dense, endless, suffocating.

Deep below the main decks, in the narrow belly of the berthing compartment, Ahmed lay on his rack, eyes wide and unfocused. Every sound — the hum of generators, the rattle of pipes, the distant groan of the hull — sank into his chest like a heartbeat not his own.

Sleep had long abandoned him. The Vulcan never truly slept — it just shifted, groaned, and endured. Around him, the others were shadows beneath thin blankets, their bodies twitching in uneasy dreams. Some mumbled names. Some whimpered. Some didn't move at all.

Ahmed rolled over and stared at the ceiling just inches above his face. The paint was peeling in long gray flakes. He reached up, brushing his fingertips against the cold metal, feeling the vibration of the engines running through it — constant, relentless. The ship felt alive, and not in a way that comforted him.

His fingers twitched restlessly, rubbing the salt from his palms, then the rope burns still faint on his wrists. His thoughts circled like vultures — Sky City, the starving faces of his people, the thin line of horizon he'd once believed led to salvation. Now it led only to steel.

Then —

POUND.

A sudden, jarring blow against the side of his rack. The steel quivered. Dust and condensation rained down on him.

Ahmed flinched upright, yanking the thin curtain closed in reflex. His pulse thudded in his ears.

"Can't sleep?" a voice sneered. "Good. Get up, mate."

The curtain was yanked aside, and the dim red light from the corridor spilled over Gates's frame. He was fully geared — armored in his usual patchwork plating of rubber, steel mesh, and weathered Kevlar. His face gleamed with sweat, his hair slicked back beneath his cap. He looked like he hadn't slept in days, and maybe he hadn't.

Ahmed blinked up at him, eyes narrowing. "Why me?"

Gates smirked — that same crooked half-smile that never reached his eyes. "Because you've been invited."

"Invited to what?"

"To the deep," Gates said simply, turning on his heel. The light from the corridor caught on the scratched plate at his shoulder, casting a flash like a signal flare. "Come on, Pan. Don't make me drag you."

He started down the passageway, boots scraping against the grating with hollow finality.

Ahmed hesitated. He could hear the others breathing — shallow, rhythmic — pretending to be asleep. No one spoke. No one warned him.

He swung his legs off the rack, the metal freezing against his bare feet. The floor vibrated under him, humming with the slow pulse of the engines. The corridor beyond his berth was a throat of shadows, lined with pipes and dangling wires that dripped condensation like veins leaking cold sweat.

He followed, slow at first. "Where are we going?"

"You'll see."

Ahmed's heart thudded. "If it's training, it's the middle of the night. Shouldn't it wait until—"

"Until what?" Gates glanced back, his grin barely visible in the dim light. "Until Gunny thinks you're ready?"

Ahmed's stomach tightened. "He doesn't— he didn't—"

"—Tell you much?" Gates interrupted, stepping through a narrow hatch and motioning for him to follow. "Yeah, that's how it works around here. The sea doesn't give warnings either. You learn fast or you sink."

They passed through another corridor — narrower, darker. The walls here were slick, glistening with a thin sheen of condensation. The hum of the ship was louder, like a whisper directly behind Ahmed's ear. Somewhere deep below, he could hear the churn of turbines.

Gates slowed near a ladder leading down into darkness. He rested a hand on the rung and looked over his shoulder. "You're not afraid of the dark, are you?"

Ahmed's throat went dry. "No."

"Good," Gates said, his smirk returning. "Because you'll see plenty of it before morning."

He started down.

Ahmed followed, the metal rungs cold beneath his hands, slick with oil. The deeper they descended, the thicker the air became — hot, damp, humming. The noise of the ship's belly surrounded him, echoing off the bulkheads like distant thunder trapped in a cage.

At the bottom, a faint blue glow flickered through the mist — the reflection of water. The compartment smelled of brine and machine grease.

Ahmed stopped, his breath catching. "Where are we?"

Gates turned toward him, eyes gleaming in the low light. "The ballast hold."

"Why?"

Gates's grin widened. "Because Gunny says every man on this ship needs to learn what it means to fear the sea. You've had your lesson above deck. Now you get the rest."

He moved to a set of levers mounted on the wall. With a sharp pull, one of the ballast hatches ground open, and seawater began to spill in through a grated vent, slow but deliberate. The sound was deafening — a rush, a growl, a living thing entering the space.

Ahmed's breath came faster. "What are you doing?"

"Training," Gates said simply. He grabbed a small, rusted pipe wrench from a nearby crate and tossed it to him. "Plug the leak before the water reaches your knees."

Ahmed stared at the wrench, then at the growing pool beneath his feet. "Are you serious?"

Gates leaned back against the bulkhead, arms

folded. "Deadly."

The cold water surged around Ahmed's ankles, biting through his skin. The level rose fast. His hands shook as he knelt by the vent, trying to see where the flow came from. The wrench slipped once, clanging against the steel.

"Faster," Gates barked. "You'll drown slow if you don't hurry."

"I can't see the—"

"Then *feel it!*"

Ahmed fumbled in the dark, his heartbeat pounding in rhythm with the rushing water. The wrench hit something solid. He twisted hard, the metal squealing under strain. The flow slowed — then stopped.

He sat back, chest heaving, soaked to the knees.

Gates studied him in silence for a long moment. Then — a slow, satisfied nod. "Not bad, Sky Boy."

Ahmed looked up at him, trembling. "Was this a test?"

Gates smiled faintly. "Everything's a test on the Vulcan."

The hum of the engines returned to dominance, and above it, the faint, rhythmic drip of water echoed like the ticking of a clock.

Ahmed's pulse refused to slow. He didn't know whether to feel relief or terror. He only knew this — he was still breathing. For now.

* * *

By the time Gates led him topside, the ship had gone silent again.

No alarms, no chatter — only the deep, rhythmic pulse of the Vulcan's engines echoing through the steel. Ahmed's breath clouded in the cold as they climbed the last ladder, the air thinning with every rung. The metallic taste of salt thickened in his mouth, and for the first time, he realized how high above the waterline they'd come. Each step away from the warmth of the decks below felt like stepping closer to judgment.

When the hatch swung open, the wind hit like a blade.

The night air above the Vulcan was cruel — sharp enough to cut, heavy enough to choke. The wind came in bursts that stung the skin and carried the metallic scent of the ocean's endless hunger. The deck was slick with rain and oil; the floodlights cast long, trembling shadows across the steel.

Below, the sea writhed like a living thing.

Black. Boundless.

It breathed in waves, rising and falling as though the ocean itself were waiting — patient, hungry.

Ahmed clung to the taffrails, his fingers pale and

rigid against the rusted bars. Each gust of wind tore through his clothes, cutting him open with cold. His breath came in gasps, thin and desperate. He looked down and saw nothing but darkness — a pit of moving ink.

"Gates, please!" he shouted, his voice nearly swallowed by the storm. "Please!"

Gates stood several paces behind him, arms folded, the dim floodlight gleaming across the patched armor that wrapped his chest. His silhouette looked carved from the ship itself — jagged, hard, unrelenting.

"If you want to stay on this ship," he said, his voice low but clear over the wind, "prove your worth."

Ahmed turned, eyes wide, drenched in sweat and sea spray. "Prove my worth? How?!"

"By doing what I tell you," Gates replied, pacing lazily toward him. His boots made slow, deliberate thuds against the deck plates. "That's how we all did it."

Ahmed's voice cracked. "What did you have to do?"

Gates's grin returned, faint and humorless. "Prove my flexibility. Show Gunny I could adapt. You'll do the same."

Ahmed's pulse pounded so hard it blurred his vision. "This isn't even my ship!" he shouted. "I just want to go home!"

Gates's laughter rolled through the air — loud, wild, and utterly without warmth. "You are home, mate."

The words struck harder than the wind. Ahmed's hands shook where they gripped the rail. He stared down at the shifting black beneath him. The sea seemed closer now — alive, whispering.

"This is higher than I've ever been," he whispered.

Gates grinned. "No squat! The Vulcan's the largest ark on these seas. You're standing on a floating city, Sky Boy!"

Ahmed's voice cracked again. "Please— can we do something else?"

Gates tilted his head, feigning thought. "Okay," he said slowly, stepping closer. The deck vibrated beneath his boots. "Maybe we send you back out to sea without any rations, no gear, no raft. Let's see how long you last out there."

Ahmed's stomach turned to stone. "You'd do that?"

Gates's grin flattened into something cold. "Dead weight can't carry itself."

Ahmed shook his head. His voice came out small. "No."

"That's the spirit!" Gates barked, eyes flashing with cruel amusement. His hand clapped down on Ahmed's shoulder.

The shove came a second later. Not hard — just enough.

Enough to end balance.

Enough to start the fall.

The world lurched. Ahmed's boots slipped from the slick steel, his stomach dropping with him. For one suspended heartbeat, he hung between ship and sky — caught in the violent glow of the floodlights — and then gravity claimed him.

The Vulcan vanished above as he plummeted into the dark. Wind tore at his clothes, his scream lost to the storm. The sea rushed up to meet him, not like water, but like stone.

Impact.

The ocean hit him like a wall. His body folded, spun, his lungs emptying in an explosion of salt. There was no up or down — only pressure, blackness, cold. He kicked wildly, but the cold was a thief, stealing strength from his limbs faster than he could summon it. The surface was nowhere. His lungs burned. His heartbeat roared in his skull.

Then — a hand.

Hard fingers gripped his collar, jerking him upward.

Through the chaos, through the bubbles and pain and noise — Gates. His armor gleamed faintly in the blue darkness.

The surface broke open above them like shattered glass. They erupted into the air, gasping. Ahmed sucked in a lungful of night and salt and pain. He coughed, choking between ragged breaths. "Are you crazy?!" he screamed, voice hoarse.

Gates only laughed, water streaming down his face. "You're alive!"

"That's not funny!" Ahmed shouted, flailing to stay afloat.

"Lay back!" Gates barked, treading easily in the heaving waves. "Let the water carry you!"

Ahmed coughed, eyes burning from salt. "It'll carry me?"

"Yes," Gates said, still grinning, water dripping from his chin.

"Promise?" Ahmed demanded, his voice cracking between anger and disbelief.

"Yeah, sure," Gates said casually, and before Ahmed could protest —

He shoved him under.

The sea closed over him again, colder this time, heavier. Ahmed kicked, thrashed, screamed into the water. His limbs burned, his chest felt like fire trapped in ice. The ocean pressed down, relentless, until sound and light began to fade.

Somewhere above, the faint ripple of laughter

bled through the water — distant, distorted — and then even that was gone.

The dark swallowed him whole.

* * *

By the time they hauled him back aboard, Ahmed's limbs felt like stone. His skin was pale, his lips trembling as he clutched the soaked rope ladder. His arms burned, each motion a small act of defiance against exhaustion.

He dragged himself over the edge of the deck and collapsed, gasping on the steel floor, coughing seawater.

A half-circle of Renegades surrounded him, their faces blank and judgmental in the pale light of dawn. They stood like soldiers watching a failed recruit, the cold in their eyes sharper than the wind.

Then the boots came—heavy, rhythmic, unmistakable.

Gunny War emerged from the fog rolling across the deck, his massive frame blotting out the gray light. His eyes locked onto Ahmed, still sprawled on the floor like a drowned rat.

"Formation!" he barked, voice like thunder.

"Move!"

The Renegades snapped to attention as Ahmed lay trembling at their feet, his breath shallow, his mind spiraling between terror and disbelief.

Fight for your Night

Ahmed's arms ached from the night before. Every muscle screamed as he hauled himself up the rope ladder, fingers raw and slick with seawater. The deck loomed above like the surface of another world. When he finally pulled himself over the edge, he collapsed onto the planks, gasping for breath.

Around him, the Renegades stood in formation, their shadows long and unmoving. A dozen pairs of eyes bore into him — judgmental, unimpressed. He felt like a castaway crawling ashore.

Pounding boots broke the silence. Gunny War emerged from the haze, armor glinting beneath the overcast light, his expression carved from stone.

"Formation!" Gunny barked. "Move!"

The Renegades snapped to attention. Ahmed stayed down, chest heaving. Gates stepped up behind him and kicked the back of his leg.

"You're not finished," Gates growled. "Up.

Now."

Ahmed groaned, forcing himself to his knees. Gunny War motioned to the ranks.

"Jaxon!"

A small figure broke formation — Jaxon, fourteen at most, with cropped hair and a spark of overconfidence. He looked like he had something to prove.

Gunny tossed Ahmed a wooden sword. It landed beside him with a dull *thud*.

"Go ahead, Peter Pan," Gunny said. "Show us what you're worth."

Ahmed stared at the blade. His voice was ragged. "That's not my name."

"It is until I say otherwise." Gunny's tone left no room for argument. "You want me to help your ship, right?"

Ahmed swallowed hard. "Yes."

"Then tell me what it's called."

There was hesitation — a quiet pause before he answered. "The Vesta."

Gunny's gaze softened just slightly. "While you're on *The Vulcan*, prove your worth… and we'll help your people."

Ahmed nodded, gripping the sword tighter. A faint tremor ran through his hand.

Jaxon stepped forward, grinning. "Let's see what you've got, Peter Pan."

Ahmed barely had time to react before Jaxon lunged. Their swords clashed, wood smacking wood in a hollow rhythm. Sparks of fear shot through Ahmed's chest as he stumbled back, blocking one strike — but the next came faster.

Jaxon kicked him square in the stomach, knocking him flat.

Gunny's voice cut through the air. "Get up!"

Ahmed wheezed, forcing himself to his feet, legs shaking.

"I'd hate for your colony to starve," Gunny added coldly.

Rage flickered across Ahmed's face. He swung again, wild, desperate. Jaxon parried easily, sidestepped, and slammed the butt of his sword across Ahmed's jaw. The impact dropped him.

He hit the deck hard — world spinning, blood in his mouth.

"Come on!" Gates barked. "Get up!"

Ahmed groaned, clutching his face.

"Say something!" Gates yelled.

"No…" Ahmed whispered through his teeth.

Gunny crossed his arms. "Let him quit."

Gates blinked, unsure.

"Go get his pathetic raft ready," Gunny continued.

The words cut deep.

Ahmed's chest rose and fell rapidly. Blood

dripped from his lip onto the deck. He forced himself up again, every movement a war between will and pain.

"Go tell your people you failed to save them," Gunny said. "I'm sure your mother would be proud."

That struck something raw.

Ahmed's glare turned sharp as glass. "Don't talk about her. You don't know her."

Gunny's expression froze. The air between them thickened — a silent current of anger and defiance.

"Well then," Gunny said slowly. "If you want to save her… keep up."

Ahmed raised his fists, no longer relying on the wooden blade. Gates circled him, eyes sharp, waiting to see if he'd swing again.

Then —

"Gunny!" Jaxon shouted, voice urgent. "There's an emergency in the core room!"

"Not now."

"Gunny, it's—"

"I said not now!" Gunny snapped.

Before Jaxon could respond, the deck trembled beneath their feet. A deep rumble rolled through the ship's hull — a sound that didn't belong to the sea. The vibrations grew, shaking loose the bolts along the railing.

Then came the silence — brief, breathless — before the next tremor hit, violent enough to throw everyone off balance.

Ahmed stumbled back, bracing against a bulkhead as Gates grabbed a support beam.

Gunny's hardened composure faltered for the first time. His eyes widened, not in anger — but disbelief.

The Thing That Makes Us Go

T he engine room of the *Vulcan Ark* was alive — breathing, grinding, and pulsing like a metallic heart on the edge of arrest.

A thousand gears turned in hypnotic sequence, teeth locking with teeth, pistons firing in mechanical rhythm. Steam hissed from copper arteries that snaked along the ceiling and walls. Beneath the grated deck, coolant lines shivered and sang, glowing faintly blue as fluid pumped through the Ark's veins like liquid fire. The air itself seemed to hum with fatigue — a deep, trembling bass that sank into the bones.

At the center of it all hung the **Core** — a circular orb encased in reinforced glass, suspended by electromagnetic clamps that hissed and sparked with erratic pulses. Its glow was a sickly, fading green, uneven and broken, like a candle guttering in its final breath. Each flicker sent a rippling shimmer across the engine room's walls — light and shadow fighting for dominance.

Jaxon stood before it, drenched in sweat. His coveralls were smeared with soot and rust, sleeves rolled to his elbows. Every muscle in his jaw was tight as he stared at the diagnostics dancing across the cracked console screen. Rows of numbers poured down the glass like rain — pressure, temperature, magnetic alignment, fusion output — all dipping deeper into red.

"It's failing," he murmured, barely audible over the noise. "If we wait any longer, it'll shut down completely."

The sound of Gunny War's boots on the steel deck was unmistakable — slow, heavy, deliberate. He moved through the haze of steam like an iron specter, his coat brushing against the railings, his breath steady as a drumbeat.

He loomed beside Jaxon, eyes locked on the readout. His reflection flickered in the green glow — a face carved in shadow, sweat glinting off the scar that split his cheek.

"How long?" Gunny asked, his voice low and resonant, the kind that made the air vibrate.

Jaxon swallowed. "Three days, maybe less. Depends if the plasma ring keeps its magnetic hold."

Gunny's hand flexed on the console. "And if it doesn't?"

Jaxon hesitated. "Then the singularity collapses."

Gunny turned his head slowly, fixing him with a stare. "Speak plain, engineer."

Jaxon exhaled. "Then it eats the ship from the inside out."

The silence that followed wasn't quiet. It was filled with the *heartbeat* of the Core — thrum, thrum, thrum — uneven now, slower, as though even the machine was listening.

Gunny's jaw tightened. "A storm will flush us under easily if it goes cold."

Around them, the Renegades stood frozen — a handful of grease-smeared boys and girls pretending not to be terrified. One of them whispered something about "the Curse of the Core," but fell silent when Gunny's gaze turned toward him.

The engine room was their cathedral, and the Core was their god. The heat was suffocating, the air thick with burnt ozone and the bitter tang of oil. Every vibration through the floorplates was a reminder that this ship was not just metal — it was a creature kept alive by faith and force of will.

But the god at its center was dying.

"It's alien," Jaxon muttered, almost to himself. "Never meant for human hands. I keep thinking… maybe we weren't supposed to have it."

Gunny shot him a look that could have shattered glass. "And yet here we are, kept alive by what you don't understand."

Jaxon's hands trembled. "Sir, the containment fields are degrading. The coolant's running hot. If it breaches—"

Gunny slammed his fist into the bulkhead beside him. The impact echoed through the chamber, a sharp metallic crack that silenced every breath in the room. Steam hissed from the pipes like the ship itself recoiling.

"You should have told me the moment it started!" Gunny roared.

Jaxon flinched, eyes wide. "We tried to patch it— we thought—"

"You *thought*?" Gunny snarled. "You don't *think* with a Core like this. You react. You move."

The flickering light deepened to a sickly emerald, casting jagged shadows across their faces. The Core gave a shudder, a long, low groan like a living thing in pain.

"We could..." Jaxon began, licking the salt from his lips, "we could abandon ship. Split to the other Arks. There's still time."

Gunny's head turned slowly, his eyes burning cold. "Abandon ship?" He said it like a curse.

"Yes," Jaxon said. "We can't fix something we don't understand. We barely keep it running. Maybe someone else—"

Gunny took one slow step toward him. Then

another. The floor rang with every impact of his boots. When he stopped, he was close enough for Jaxon to see the fury twitching beneath his skin.

"No one," Gunny said, voice sharp and deliberate, "abandons *The Vulcan.*"

Jaxon opened his mouth, but Gunny cut him off, his voice rising with every word.

"This ship is our blood. Our bones. Our memory. It's all we've got left that still moves. You think we drift away like rats the moment the engine coughs?" He leaned in, eyes inches from Jaxon's. "I *rise* with it. And I *fall* with it."

The words hung in the steam, heavy and final.

Jaxon looked away, chest heaving. "Then what do we do, sir?"

Gunny turned back toward the Core, his reflection fractured in its dying light. "We hold it together," he said. "Until it burns us, or the sea does."

He raised his hand, pointing toward the catwalk above. "Get sentries on the upper deck. Double patrols. I want eyes on the horizon — if this thing's going to die, I'll see the storm coming before it hits."

The Renegades snapped to motion, boots clattering on steel. The hum of the ship deepened, echoing up through the bulkheads like the growl of something ancient and uneasy.

Jaxon lingered a moment longer, watching Gunny's silhouette in front of the Core. For the first time, the man looked *small.* Not in size — but in the way his shadow no longer reached the walls.

When Jaxon finally turned to leave, the last flicker of green sputtered against his back.

Gunny War stayed where he was — a statue before his dying god, the glow of the Core reflected in his eyes like distant lightning.

And for the first time since the Ark's birth, *The Vulcan* didn't sound invincible.

It sounded afraid.

Rise and Shine, It's Renegade Time

The nights bled into days, and the days bled back into nights until time itself collapsed — a formless tide swallowed by the ship's grinding rhythm.

Sleep came in fragments, meals in silence, and pain in constancy.

On *The Vulcan Ark*, the sun and moon meant nothing. The only cycle that mattered was survival.

The showers hissed with the sound of rain imprisoned in steel. Ahmed stood beneath the rusted pipes, head bowed, shoulders trembling beneath the weight of the water. It wasn't warm. It wasn't even clean. It was desalinated runoff recycled so many times it stung the skin.

Blood — his blood — swirled with grit and salt down the drain, a thin red spiral fading into the grate like a ritual offering to the sea. His hands shook as he scrubbed his face, but the bruises remained — blue and purple constellations across his ribs and jaw.

He looked up at the fogged mirror. The boy staring back was hollow-eyed, the softness gone from his face. The reflection blinked — just once — and he wondered if it was even him anymore.

When he finally collapsed into his rack, the mattress felt like cold iron, thin as regret. The hum of the engines rocked him like a heartbeat — steady, cruel.

He'd almost drifted when the *bang* came.

"Get up! Get up! Get up!"

Gates's voice tore through the berthing compartment like gunfire. Ahmed's body moved before thought — jerking upright, bare feet hitting the deck, heart slamming in his chest.

And so began the cycle.

Every dawn was the same. Every night was worse.

They dragged him to the lower deck — to the open platform above the ocean's black mouth. The storm never really stopped out here; it just changed moods.

"Overboard, fish boy!" Gates barked, rain slicing across his face.

Ahmed stood trembling on the slick rail, the sea below roaring like a living beast. He could barely breathe before Gates's shove came. The air vanished. The cold swallowed him.

The water was a knife that cut from every direction at once. He kicked, gasped, choked — his arms thrashing against an enemy that had no shape, no mercy.

"Swim or sink!" Gates shouted from above, laughing.

Ahmed always sank.

But every time, Gates's hand came down like a hook — seizing his collar, dragging him up by the neck, hauling him onto the platform where he collapsed, coughing seawater and blood.

"Better," Gates would mutter, crouching beside him. "Still pathetic. But better."

The next day, it happened again.

And again.

Until the fear of drowning became as familiar as breath.

The deck by daylight became another kind of ocean — one of fists, sweat, and bruised egos.

Combat drills turned the open air into a furnace.

"On your feet!"

"Faster!"

"Don't think — move!"

Wooden training blades cracked against his ribs, his knuckles, his back. Every impact sent lightning up his spine. The Renegades circled him — lean, sunburned, vicious — shouting insults that cut deeper than the blows.

Gates prowled along the edge, shouting corrections that sounded more like challenges.

"Hit harder, Pan! You want to live? Then fight like you mean it!"

Ahmed's arms felt like they were filled with stone. His lungs burned. But he kept swinging. Even when the blade slipped from his hand, even when his knees buckled, he reached for it again.

Once, during a sparring rotation, Jaxon stepped in. His strikes came faster, cleaner, the kind that didn't need to land to hurt. When one finally connected, a boot to Ahmed's ribs, the sound echoed off the deck plating.

Ahmed hit the bulkhead with a grunt.

"Stay down, Peter Pan," Jaxon said. His smirk was practiced, but his eyes weren't cruel — just tired. Maybe even sorry.

Ahmed spat a mix of blood and seawater, wiped his mouth with the back of his hand, and pushed himself up again. "No," he whispered.

Jaxon stared at him for a long second before turning away. "Suit yourself."

The days blurred into one another, a loop of training, bruises, and brief meals eaten in silence.

In the showers, he watched his body change. The bruises stayed, but the trembling stopped. His breath steadied. The pain dulled. The ship's hum began to sync with his pulse.

The boy who had once trembled at the sound of waves was gone — replaced by something harder, quieter.

Then came night again.

The air in the berthing compartment was cold and metallic. Ahmed lay in his rack, half-awake, staring up at the ceiling just inches from his face. His hands twitched unconsciously, as though still fighting some unseen current.

He thought of Sky City — the way he used to imagine it shining above the clouds, untouched by hunger, by storms. But the image flickered now, weaker each time he tried to summon it.

"Up, fish boy!"

The voice again. The same boot against the same frame.

Ahmed swung his legs over the side before Gates could bark a second order.

Outside, the deck wind screamed, tearing across the Ark like it wanted to peel the metal apart. The drills began before dawn and ended after it — if dawn even meant anything here.

Every motion hurt. Every order grated. But Ahmed no longer moved like prey. He had learned the rhythm — breathe, strike, fall, rise.

And somewhere between the noise and pain, he began to anticipate the next blow before it came.

"Not bad, Sky Boy," Gates muttered one night, catching Ahmed's arm mid-swing. "You're starting to look like one of us."

Ahmed stared back, panting, salt stinging his eyes. "I'm not like you," he said, the words coming out hoarse but steady.

Gates smirked. "Keep telling yourself that."

The days dragged on. The bruises turned to scars. The scars to calluses.

The sea no longer terrified him.

The ship no longer felt like a cage.

It was brutal, yes. It was merciless.

But it was *alive.*

And so was he.

By the end of that unseen stretch of time — days, weeks, or months, no one could say — Ahmed stood beneath the showers again, the water hissing across his shoulders.

This time, there was no blood. No trembling.

He looked up at the ceiling, listening to the hum of the engines through the pipes.

He didn't know it yet, but the boy from the Vesta — the one who'd once dreamed of Sky City — was gone.

What remained was something the sea had forged —

and *The Vulcan* had claimed.

No Longer Just a Boy

By dawn, the ship shuddered under the relentless assault of the waves. The horizon bled a dull silver into the black clouds, the storm's remnants licking the edges of the sky like cold fingers. Ahmed stood at the edge of the deck, boots planted against slick steel, knuckles white around the railing. Every gust of wind tugged at him, every wave pounded like a drum beneath the hull.

Gates leaned casually on the rail behind him, arms crossed, a smirk masking what could have been concern. "Ready?" he asked, voice deceptively light.

Ahmed inhaled, feeling the icy slap of wind and salt sting his lungs. He thought of the hollow corridor, of Gunny War's words, and of the storm itself — of everything he'd tried to outrun. And then he leapt.

The water hit like a shockwave, numbing his body, knocking the air from his lungs. Cold as death, sharp as glass. But he didn't falter. He sliced through the waves, every stroke precise, every kick deliberate. No panic. No flailing. The boy who had once been carried by fear was gone; in his place was something harder — determination tempered by pain.

When he broke the surface again, the Renegades awaited him on the Vesta's deck. Shadows in the morning haze, silent, expectant. Gunny War stood among them, arms crossed, unreadable. Ahmed's fingers closed on the wet wood of a training sword left carelessly on the deck.

Jaxon stood opposite him, smirking, spinning his own blade with casual arrogance.

Gunny gave a single nod.

Jaxon charged, reckless and fast. Ahmed pivoted, letting the swing pass him, then swept Jaxon's legs out with a clean, practiced motion. The boy hit the deck with a hollow thud that echoed across the steel.

Jaxon struggled to rise, eyes blazing with fury, and attacked again. Ahmed met every strike, block after block, his arms shaking but precise, his breath steady. A heel smashed against Jaxon's jaw, and he crumpled unconscious, a heap on the deck.

A ripple of murmurs ran through the Renegades. Even the shadows seemed to lean in.

Gates blinked, impressed despite himself. "He's got fight in him," he muttered under his breath.

Gunny War said nothing. His gaze stayed fixed on Ahmed like steel on fire.

"Gates," he said finally, voice low.

Gates turned, uncertain. "He's not ready."

"If he's not ready," Gunny said, tone flat and heavy, "then you failed him."

The words struck like a lash. Gates' grip tightened on his own wooden sword, and the fight began again — more brutal, more urgent. The clash of wood, the slam of boots on wet steel, the hiss of spray rising from the deck — it became a storm within a storm.

Gates lunged, a low sweep aimed at Ahmed's knee. Ahmed twisted, rose with a sharp headbutt, sending Gates staggering back, gasping. The Renegades circled closer, anticipation crackling in the air like static.

Gates swung wide. Ahmed ducked, rolled, and drove a kick into Gates' chest. He flew back, landing hard against the railing. For a moment, the deck was silent except for the hiss of the waves and the ragged intake of breaths.

Gunny War started to clap. Slowly. Deliberately. Each echo of his hands carried weight, finality, approval.

The Renegades followed, at first hesitant, then

louder, until the deck rang with the rhythm of recognition.

Ahmed stood in the center, chest heaving, hair slick with seawater, the taste of salt in his mouth. His body shook, exhausted, alive, trembling with the knowledge that he had passed the trial — that he had *beaten* them.

Gunny's voice cut through the applause. "You're ready."

Ahmed looked up at him, disbelief and pride warring with exhaustion. Gunny's eyes softened for a fraction of a second, almost human.

Then Gunny turned toward the horizon, sharp as a hawk. A gray ship emerged through the mist, silent, foreboding, a shadow cutting across the silver morning. The wind caught the sails, or perhaps it was engines — Ahmed couldn't tell yet. All he knew was that whatever came next, the trial had ended… and the war was about to begin.

Ahmed clenched the sword, water dripping from the tip like blood. The deck beneath him was slippery, his muscles screaming, but the storm in his chest had never felt more alive.

And for the first time, he understood the full weight of Gunny War's lesson: fight, or drown.

The Truth About War

The sea lay restless beneath a moonless sky. Waves pitched against the narrow hull of the small, armored vessel as it sped through the water, engines humming a steady mechanical growl. Spray lashed the deck, cool and briny, carrying the scent of rusted iron and oil.

Ahmed sat toward the stern, his hands gripping the edge of the seat as the boat cut through the dark. The salt stung the cuts on his knuckles — quiet reminders of Gunny War's "lessons." Around him, the Renegades moved with disciplined calm, their armor patched and mismatched, their weapons silent and sheathed.

Ahead, through rolling fog, a distant glow appeared — faint amber lights cutting through the mist. The silhouette of a ship materialized: *The Wilusa Ark*.

Ahmed leaned forward. "So this ship… they're friendly?"

Gates, standing beside the helm, didn't answer

immediately. His eyes stayed on the horizon. "Friendly enough."

Gunny War stood at the bow, the faint red of the instrument lights brushing across his scarred face. His voice broke the wind like gravel.

"Our contact on the *Wilusa* owes us a favor," he said. "They've got supplies, maybe even a working core unit. If this goes right, we're one step closer to getting the *Vulcan* back in the water."

Ahmed nodded, hopeful. "Then this is just a negotiation?"

Gunny smirked faintly. "You could call it that."

Jaxon appeared beside them, brandishing a makeshift flag from a window — white, frayed at the edges. It flapped wildly in the gusts. Ahmed squinted. "White? Isn't that surrender?"

"Depends on who's holding it," Jaxon muttered.

From above the fog, the dim lights of the *Wilusa* brightened. A voice echoed down through a megaphone, distorted by distance.

"State your business!"

"Survivors from the *Vulcan Ark*," Gates called back. "We were hit by raiders. Need aid and fuel."

A tense pause followed — long enough for the chill to sink in. Then came the response:

"Hold position. We'll send a ladder."

Gunny smiled, faintly satisfied. "That's our invitation."

* * *

The *Wilusa's* galley was alive with motion and sound — the hum of power conduits overhead, the hiss of steam vents, the metallic clang of pots. Warmth and the scent of cooked meat filled the air, so thick and comforting it almost felt like home.

Ahmed sat at a crowded table among his new crew, quietly eating, still trying to make sense of his place among them. Around him, the Renegades laughed easily, passing plates and joking with the sailors of the *Wilusa Ark*.

Gunny War sat opposite Captain Pryor, a broad-shouldered man with sun-cracked skin and weary eyes. Between them, a half-empty bottle of grain liquor and the bones of a shared meal.

Gunny raised his glass. "You've done well for your people, Captain," he said, voice calm and low. "Not many arks still run this smooth."

Pryor grinned, slicing through his chop. "Smooth's not how I'd put it. Patchwork, maybe. But we stay afloat."

Gunny nodded. "That's all that matters anymore."

Ahmed ate slowly, watching the two men. The conversation didn't sound like training. It sounded… too careful.

Gunny leaned forward, dropping his voice just enough for Ahmed to strain to hear. "You've seen the raiders, then?"

Pryor's jaw stiffened. "Enough to know not to go looking for them. Most just vanish."

Gunny's eyes glimmered under the overhead light. "You believe they're still out there?"

Pryor gave a dry laugh. "I don't have to believe it. I've seen the smoke."

Gates, sitting nearby, kept his gaze on his plate but his shoulders were tense, his hands never far from the knife at his side.

The laughter around the table died down. A faint tremor passed through the deck — the engine's rhythm shifting. The ship's internal hum seemed to deepen, as though the *Wilusa's* heart had skipped a beat.

Gunny raised a brow. "That vibration — your core housing stable?"

Pryor hesitated. "Stable enough. The old reactor still holds, but it's been running hot."

Gunny smiled thinly. "Heat can be useful. Pressure, too. Sometimes it shows us who can endure."

Ahmed frowned. "Sir?"

Gunny didn't look at him. "Finish your meal, cadet. Long night ahead."

* * *

The hum of the reactor grew louder, almost a pulse beneath their feet. A faint alarm blinked amber over the galley door — routine pressure fluctuation.

Captain Pryor stood, stretching. "Apologies, gentlemen. I'll check with engineering—"

Gunny rose with him, almost casually. "No need. My crew's trained for diagnostics. We can take a look."

Pryor's brow furrowed. "That won't be necessary."

Gunny's smile thinned. "It wasn't a request."

Before Ahmed could process the shift in tone, the tension in the room snapped taut. The Renegades stood almost in unison — chairs scraping back. Hands hovered near weapons.

Ahmed blinked, confused. "Gunny?"

The overhead lights flickered once. Then again.

A sailor's hand twitched toward his radio.

Gunny moved first.

The butt of his rifle caught the man square in the jaw. Chaos erupted. Tables crashed. Steam pipes burst. The air filled with shouts and alarms as red emergency lights snapped to life.

CORE STATUS: COMPROMISED.

Ahmed stumbled back, horror spreading across his face. Gunny War didn't hesitate — his commands were sharp, drilled, efficient. The Renegades stormed the galley, subduing sailors, wrenching open storage crates.

"Secure the bridge!" Gunny barked. "Get that core online and isolate engineering!"

Ahmed grabbed the edge of a table, disoriented. "Gunny—what are you doing?! This isn't training!"

Gunny turned, his face lit by the crimson glow. "It's the only kind of training that matters."

"You said we were here to get help!"

Gunny's voice hardened. "We were. We're taking it."

Captain Pryor tried to rise, but Gunny shoved him back into his seat, pressing the barrel of his weapon against the man's chest. "Your aid's been received, Captain. In full."

"Wait," Pryor gasped, "there are families aboard—"

Gunny's expression barely flickered. "There are families everywhere."

Ahmed's stomach turned. "You lied to me."

Gunny glanced at him, his tone almost paternal. "No, cadet. I prepared you."

Ahmed's hands trembled. "Prepared me for

what?"

Gunny stepped closer, voice lowering to a near whisper. "For truth. The world doesn't owe you mercy. It only owes you the chance to survive."

Ahmed's jaw set. "Then I don't want it."

Gunny's glare cut sharp through the red light. "Then you're already dead."

Before Ahmed could react, a sailor lunged from behind him — and the butt of Jaxon's rifle cracked against Ahmed's skull.

The world went red, then black.

* * *

When consciousness returned, Ahmed felt motion beneath him — the roll and sway of a vessel in rough water. The rhythmic pulse of the engine vibrated through the deck plates.

He opened his eyes to the dim interior of the small cutter again — the Renegades' vessel. His head throbbed where he'd been struck. The others sat in silence, their faces grim and cold in the glow of the console lights.

Boxes marked **RATIONS** lined the floor.

Gunny War stood near the prow, wind howling around him, his coat snapping against his legs. Far behind them, the *Wilusa Ark* burned against the dark — a silent inferno spilling smoke into the night.

Ahmed turned his face away. He didn't want to see.

Gunny's eyes stayed on the horizon. The fog ahead swallowed them whole.

And Ahmed, for the first time since joining the Renegades, understood the truth he'd been too afraid to face:

He wasn't on a rescue ship.

He was on a warship.

The Bigger Picture

Ahmed lay motionless against the cold deck plating, half asleep, half trapped in the memory of the burning *Wilusa*. The image clung to him — the orange bloom of fire reflected in the sea, the crack of steel collapsing, the screams fading beneath the roar of water.

A sudden clang jolted him awake.

A metal tray skidded through the bars and struck his face, scattering its contents — pale broth, two pieces of dried bread, and a dented tin cup of water.

Ahmed blinked through the sting, adjusting to the flickering light. The air smelled of rust and brine.

Gates stood outside the cell, canteen in hand, his silhouette cast by the dull yellow glow above the corridor. He took a long drink, wiped his mouth with the back of his hand, and said flatly,

"You really are that dense."

Ahmed pushed the tray back through the bars.

"That food doesn't belong to you."

Gates scoffed. "I forgot I was talking to the biggest saint in the seas."

"You lied to me," Ahmed shot back, voice low, but trembling.

"I told you everything you needed to know."

Gates kicked the tray back inside, the sound clanging sharp against the silence.

"Now eat."

Ahmed stared at the food, jaw tight. "I want to go home."

"Home?" Gates snorted. "You've got a bed, food, and a roof — that's more than most get out here."

Ahmed didn't answer. He kept his eyes on the tray, as if staring long enough might turn it into something else — something that didn't taste of pity.

"Why did you save me?" he asked quietly.

Gates's tone softened, but only slightly. "Renegades don't leave each other, mate."

Ahmed looked up. "Is that what happened to Dover?"

The question froze the air. Gates stiffened — his jaw locked, his gaze fixed somewhere beyond Ahmed.

"I'd shut it if I were you," he said darkly, his accent thickening. "Or I'll throw you off the beam myself."

Ahmed rose to his knees, gripping the bars. "I've lost people too, Gates. That's not a threat. It's the truth."

The metal canteen struck the bars with a sudden *clang*, splattering water across Ahmed's face. Gates didn't wait to see it hit. He turned and stormed down the corridor, boots slamming against the grated floor.

For a long time, there was only silence — the hum of the engine, the occasional drip from above. Ahmed stood still, hands trembling against the cold metal.

Then, faintly — a cough.

He turned, peering into the darkness stretching down the length of the brig. The flickering light barely reached the far cells.

"I know you're in here," he said cautiously.

Another cough, weaker this time. Then a voice — dry, thin, and oddly calm.

"I wish I could go home too."

Ahmed's breath caught. "Who said that?"

"Down here." The voice came from the shadowed end of the row. "Don't bother looking. The lights don't reach."

"What's your name?"

A pause. Then, quietly: "I don't have one. They call me Wrat."

"Why?" Ahmed asked, his voice almost a whisper.

Another long pause. The sound of water dripping between them.

"Because I am beneath them."

The answer hung heavy in the air. Ahmed swallowed hard, gripping the bars tighter.

"No one's beneath anyone," he said softly.

From the dark, a dry laugh — brittle, almost hollow.

"That's what we all say before the sea teaches us otherwise."

Ahmed lowered his head, staring at the tray again. The bread had already soaked through with water, dissolving into pale mush.

He took a deep breath.

"Everyone sleeps on top of water," he murmured, almost to himself. "Not below."

Silence.

Then — faintly — Wrat's voice again, softer now, fading into the sound of the ship's breathing.

"Not for long."

Ahmed sat down against the wall, pulling his knees close to his chest. The light flickered once more, dimming into near darkness.

* * *

The ship's core was coughing itself to death.

The *Vulcan Ark's* engine room shuddered with every breath the machine took — grinding, wheezing, the metallic rhythm of something vast and angry. The air was thick with heat and the sour tang of oil. Red indicator lights pulsed across the bulkheads, bleeding against the shadows.

Gunny War stood motionless at the center of it, his face lit by the flicker of warning lamps. His reflection trembled in the core's steel casing — warped and multiplied.

The hatch behind him rattled under a heavy pounding.

"Permission to speak openly!" Gates shouted from outside.

Gunny's voice boomed over the din. "Granted."

The hatch clanged open, and Gates stepped in, his uniform soaked with sweat, his eyes darting from the sparking consoles to the vibrating machinery.

"There's talk of a possible ship sighting, Gunny," Gates said, raising his voice over the noise.

Gunny didn't turn. "Destiny marches forward, Squad Leader."

The engine coughed again — a violent tremor shaking loose a shower of dust from the ceiling. Gates braced himself, steadying on the bulkhead.

"Once we secure the core," Gates pressed on,

"the next challenge will be installing it. We'll need time. And hands."

"I'm aware," Gunny said flatly. Then, finally turning, he fixed Gates with that unblinking stare that always felt like a blade against the soul. "But there's more to your visit, isn't there?"

Gates hesitated. The noise of the room filled the space between them — the grind of gears, the churn of pipes. Then he spoke.

"It's about the search for Dover," he said. "My brother."

Gunny's jaw tensed. "You're clinging to a memory," he replied, voice low, dangerous. "Neglecting your duty."

"My duty *is* to family."

"Your duty is survival, you inane ass!" Gunny roared, stepping forward. The sound of his boots against the grating floor cracked like gunfire.

Gates stood his ground. "Sir, with all due respect—justifying abandonment to excuse your other moral failures is hypocrisy."

Gunny's eyes narrowed — two sparks under heavy brows. "Dover's fate was of his own making. He was a liability."

"He was a *child!*" Gates shouted, the word ripping from him like something torn loose.

Gunny slammed his palm against the core casing, the entire chamber ringing from the impact.

"And a liability for eight years!"

The machine answered with a violent shudder. Steam hissed from a fractured valve, curling up between them like smoke from a fuse.

Gates's breathing grew ragged. "You promised we'd find him," he said, his voice trembling between fury and grief.

Gunny stepped closer — his expression unreadable, his words sharp and cold.

"Fall in line, boy."

Gates didn't move. The ship groaned again beneath them.

Gunny's fist came without warning — a heavy, disciplined strike to the jaw. Gates hit the deck hard, the clang echoing through the room like a gunshot.

Gunny loomed over him, his breathing measured. "Discipline saves men. Emotion buries them."

Gates stared up at him, blood dripping from his nose. "Then maybe you're already buried," he muttered.

For a long, brittle moment, neither man spoke. The core behind them growled, shaking the deck plates as if the ship itself were listening.

Finally, Gates pushed himself up, wiped his face, and turned for the hatch. His boots left a faint trail of blood as he left the engine room without another word.

Gunny watched him go — his reflection in the trembling core fractured into a dozen warped versions of himself.

He turned back to the console, laying a gloved hand on the overheating surface. "Destiny," he whispered, "doesn't wait for the sentimental."

* * *

Ahmed sat with his back to the bars, rolling a biscuit across the floor until it vanished into the darkest corner of the cell.

"Ever tried getting out of here?" he asked quietly.

From the far end of the block, a faint, rasping voice answered.

"Many times."

Ahmed tilted his head toward the sound. The voice was familiar somehow — soft, but scraped raw by years of damp and silence.

"Think you can help?" he asked.

A pause. Then, with a brittle honesty:

"No."

He exhaled sharply, resting his head against the cold iron. "Figures."

The silence that followed was heavy — not the still kind, but a living quiet that seemed to breathe between the walls.

"What did you do?" he asked finally.

"I took something from Gunny."

"What?"

"It doesn't matter," the voice said. "He found me."

Ahmed clenched his fists. "He'll find my colony next. Will he sink them?"

"Yes."

"You're sure?"

"I'm sure," she whispered. "He sank the ship I was on."

Before Ahmed could respond, the hatch at the end of the corridor creaked open. Light flooded the block, glinting off the puddles on the floor. Gates appeared, carrying a tin tray. He slid it under the bars.

"I already ate," Ahmed muttered.

"Eat again."

"I don't want—"

"I helped you for Dover," Gates cut in, voice low but trembling. "He just wanted to be like me. He got hurt... and Gunny left him."

Ahmed looked up. Gates wasn't his usual self — no swagger, no armor of humor or cruelty. Just a man barely holding together.

"Dover dreamed of flying," Gates said softly. "Said he'd fly us both away from this rust bucket. Guess he almost did."

He looked toward the dim ceiling, exhaled sharply through his nose.

"Can't see where I'm going if someone's always covering my eyes."

He pushed the tray closer. "I know he's alive."

Ahmed frowned, startled by the certainty in Gates's tone.

Gates turned away, the light catching the deep bruise on his jaw. "Your boat's ready," he said quietly, and left the brig without another word.

The hatch slammed shut, leaving Ahmed alone with the dim buzz of the lights. He unwrapped the tray, frowning at the stale biscuit. When he tore it open, something small and metallic dropped into his palm.

A key.

His pulse quickened. He glanced toward the shadows at the far end — no guards, no footsteps.

He slid the key into the lock. The gate groaned softly as it opened.

Ahmed slipped into the corridor, bare feet splashing through the puddles. He stopped, glancing toward the farthest cell — the one half-swallowed by darkness.

"Hey!" he whispered.

No reply.

He moved closer, the damp air growing colder, the smell of rust and salt thick in his lungs. He reached the cell door and peered inside. A shape sat slumped in the corner, thin as shadow.

"Come on," he said. "I'm getting out of here."

A faint voice answered. "I'll only slow you down."

"How?"

"I can't see where I'm going."

Ahmed froze. That voice—he knew that voice. The tone was fragile but warm beneath the years, a melody from another life.

A pale foot shifted into the light.

"Don't even know your name," the voice murmured.

He swallowed hard. "It's Ahmed."

The figure stirred. The chains rattled. Then slowly, painfully, she lifted her head.

"Ahmed?"

The sound of her saying his name broke something open inside him. He stepped closer, his knees weak. Her hair was matted, streaked with silver. Her eyes, clouded and unfocused, searched for him in the dark.

"Mom," he breathed.

Her breath hitched. "No… it can't—"

But when he spoke again, the truth trembled in

his voice. "It's me."

Alana rose on unsteady feet, her hand reaching out into the void. Ahmed caught it and pressed it to his cheek. Her fingers were cold, trembling, but the touch was the same — the gentle, circling motion she used when he was a child, tracing his face to know he was safe.

Tears welled in her sightless eyes. "You're alive," she whispered.

"So are you," he said, voice breaking.

She smiled faintly through the tears, her face hollow from years of captivity. "Not in the ways that matter."

Ahmed pulled her into his arms. She felt weightless, fragile, like she might vanish if he let go. Her tears soaked into his shoulder, and his own fell freely, washing away the years of believing she was gone.

The ship groaned somewhere above, and the lights flickered. But in that moment, the noise of the world faded — nothing but the sound of her heartbeat, frail but steady, beneath his hand.

For the first time in a long time, Ahmed felt whole — and terrified of what that might cost.

V

The Break of Dawn

Find me on the edge of the world.
I look and feel nothing.
I've seen pain.
The pain of others.
Take it away so that I can smile.
Push it away, so that I can pull in light...

- Captain Dawn Perry

Still My Son

The cold air bites at my wrists where the restraints cut into my skin. My hands are bound behind my back, palms slick with sweat, but I refuse to let them see me flinch.

The wardroom of the *Vesta Ark* feels colder than usual tonight — not from temperature, but from judgment.

Seven of them sit before me, lined up like executioners in uniform. Their polished buttons catch the light, and every reflection seems to mock me.

Balthazar sits at the head of the council table, back straight as a pike, while Lawrence lingers beside him, looking like he'd rather be anywhere else.

The engines hum beneath the floor — steady, low — the ship's faint pulse that somehow feels more alive than anyone in this room.

Balthazar speaks first. His voice, sharp and mechanical, echoes off the steel walls.

"Not only did he violate every rule of personnel safety," he says, each syllable measured, "he endangered the integrity of this vessel."

My stomach tightens. He's talking about Ahmed — my son — the boy they've already condemned before they ever tried to understand him.

I open my mouth to defend him, but my voice catches somewhere between my chest and my fear.

Lawrence leans forward, tone more restrained. "And exile is the best course of action for his mother?"

There's a tremor in his voice. He doesn't agree with this. He just doesn't have the courage to stand against it.

Balthazar doesn't answer. Instead, he slams the gavel onto the table. The sound cracks through the room like thunder. Papers slide across the polished surface, pushed toward him by a silent aide.

"As decided by the vote," Balthazar says, his tone final, unshakable. "Dawn S. Perry — you are hereby relieved of your council duties and placed under close watch. I trust you comprehend the gravity of the situation?"

I force the words out through a throat that feels too small to breathe.

"Yes, Councilman."

He studies me for a moment, almost satisfied

with my compliance. Then:

"Do you have anything else to say?"

I lift my head. My voice shakes, but I don't care anymore.

"Please… for my son's sake, can we send just one more rescue party?"

The silence that follows presses down on me like gravity itself. No one moves. No one blinks. Even the lights seem to hum quieter.

All seven pairs of eyes turn toward Balthazar.

He leans forward, resting his elbows on the table, his expression void of compassion.

"Given Ahmed's rather precarious choices," he says, drawing out every word, "we can't entertain that request."

The words hit harder than any physical blow. I stare at him — at all of them — the same faces that once called my son a prodigy, a promise. Now they speak of him as if he were a contagion to be contained.

The guards step in beside me. Their hands are firm but not cruel as they lead me toward the exit. I don't fight them. Not yet.

At the threshold, I look back one last time. Seven silent figures in pressed uniforms. Seven people who have already buried my son in their minds.

They don't understand. They never will.

Ahmed isn't gone. I *feel* it — somewhere beyond these walls, beyond the rules and orders that strangle us all, he's still out there.

And if the council won't send a rescue party, then I'll find him myself.

Even if it means becoming everything they already believe I am.

* * *

I move through the berthing like a woman walking through memory. The racks are too clean in the weak light — beds made with the efficiency of a crew that has learned to fold order out of chaos. I smooth the blanket on Ahmed's bunk with hands that still smell of oil and engine grease from the bridge. My fingers find the small notebook where he sketches his foolish, wonderful things; I open the cover and the world narrows to the slim pencil lines he's left: the crooked hook, the jagged edge of a hull, a rough map of stars and a child's handwriting that declares Sky City in a single hopeful scrawl.

Lawrence stands at the foot of the bunk, the notebook open in both his hands. He reads as if the pictures might explain the vanishing. The overhead bulkhead lamp throws a hard line across his face; there are new cuts in his expression, like the ship itself has carved him older by a shade. He looks up.

"He had quite the imagination," he says, not an accusation but a fact that hurts him.

"Has," I correct him, the present tense like a small defiance. I won't let the past tense claim him.

He closes the notebook slowly, as if shutting a hatch that might never open again. "Dawn… there's nothing out there but death."

The sentence is meant as caution; it lands on me like an accusation. I feel the thin vibration of the Ark's engines through the deck beneath my boots and let the lie fall away.

"It's in here too," I say, thumbing the sketch of the hook. There is more than hunger on these floating islands of metal — there are choices no one speaks aloud, things that grow like rot behind the planks.

Lawrence's jaw tightens. "Look — we've got an inspection in the morning."

My grip on the notebook becomes a white-knuckled clasp. "Still can't find the access key?"

He looks away. The truth moves in the air like steam. "When I scuffled with the prisoner earlier, I think it was snatched."

"Ahmed was feeding a prisoner, wasn't he?" I ask. My voice is steady even though my hands shake. In the mattress seam I can still feel the faint indentation where he stowed ration bars.

"Yeah," Lawrence says. "He was close to somebody down there. Arjes."

The name lands with all the wrong familiarity. I stand before the bunk as if the wood could give me the boy back. The restraint on my wrists from the wardroom feels criminal now; sitting still while Ahmed drifts on the black tide would have been a worse crime.

"Fine." I rise too fast; the seat scrapes the deck and the light in the corridor flares. "I'm going. I need to know."

"What are you doing?" Lawrence's voice breaks as he reaches for the door lever. "You're under watch."

"So watch me," I snap. The words surprise me with their steadiness.

The brig smells of damp metal and old breath when we descend. The corridor lights throw long bands on the grating; bilge water stains the seams. Arjes lies half-rolled on his cot, ribs rising and falling like a bellows that takes too little air. When I enter he lifts his head with a familiar, snake-like smile — the grin of a man who has seen worse months than I have names for.

"Lie to me," I tell him without preamble. The promise in the sentence is a blade. "And I'll strangle you."

His laugh is not a laugh at all. It rasped through the cell like a broken winch. "Oy," he says, as if I'd proposed a joke. "Don't promise favors you can't come by."

"The boy is gone," I say plain. "He fled on one of the boats."

Arjes props himself up, a little more energy than his gaunt frame should have. "Ah," he croaks. There's warmth in the way he says it that turns bile in my throat. "That's a good lad, that one."

My patience snaps thin. "Lawrence! Open the cell!" I bellow.

He hesitates — he knows the politics well enough to understand what a wrong move looks like. He steps forward, fingers steady even if his face is not. The hatch clangs. The brig's air rushes in full: salt, stale bread, the iron tang of old injuries.

"He's ten, you asshole!" I shout, voice fracturing into the hold. Arjes watches me as if he's been granted a private spectacle.

Lawrence's voice drops. "He won't survive out there."

"How would you know?" Arjes spits, trying reason when I want rage. "Your pale skin could use a little sun," he says casually, the insult meant to wound: you are sheltered, you are preserved.

"Where is he going?" I demand.

"To find his path to the truth," Arjes answers, as though reciting a line from a ledger. His cadence has the tired certainty of men who have watched empires sink without flinching.

"You're about to find your teeth," I warn, raw edges and sleepless nights turned to tinder.

Arjes makes a sound somewhere between a chuckle and a cough, like a man amused by inevitability. "You want answers?" he asks, and then listens, hand cupped at his ear as though tuning to some far-off frequency.

"You hear it?" he asks after breath.

I wait.

"Nothing is ever what it seems," he says. Lawrence's eyes flick from him to me. For a second panic and politics cross his face.

"Look," Arjes says, "these vessels were stocked with enough supplies to last a century. Yet here we are, starving ourselves for fifty-five years."

The assertion settles in the brig like a stone. It smells of rot and administration: not an accusation as much as a reckoning.

"You of all people should've known that," Arjes says. The words push, not gentle.

Lawrence swallows; diplomacy snaps back into

place like a muscle. "Let's go before someone catches you down here," he urges, the urgency in his voice a rope pulling me toward the hatch.

Arjes makes a sound that isn't laughter and isn't resignation. It slides along me like oil. As we climb the ladder back toward the berthing the rung vibrates under my palms. I think of Ahmed on the wet black, of him drawing a crooked hook in a notebook that still smells faintly of pencil and salt. I think of all the things we pretend not to see.

If the council will not look, if the fleet will not act, then someone must. I press the rough page of his drawing into my palm and taste salt in my mouth. The line has been drawn; we are walking across it.

Lies and Deception

I wake with the taste of salt in my mouth and a weight in my chest I can't name. For a moment I lie still, listening to the ship breathe — that low, mechanical heartbeat I once trusted. The berthing hatch shudders each time the engines flex; that small, dependable sound steadies me like a metronome.

Then I sit up, and the metronome becomes a call I can't ignore.

The hatch stares back at me like an accusation. I slide from the bunk, the blanket whispering against my calves, and cross the narrow berth on bare feet. My hands move on their own, practiced and precise — the collar of my coat, the coil of my hair, the small flashlight I keep where the light can't find it.

I have no right to what I'm about to do. That's the point.

Down the spiral stairwell the metal tastes cooler, each step a careful sound meant not to wake the wardroom. I approach the hatch that leads to the council wings — the brass wheel I've watched them spin a hundred times, the padded seal that once reassured me there were places aboard I couldn't touch.

Tonight, I treat it like a safe: a combination I know by heart, a movement learned in the hours when I pretended to sleep during late meetings. When the latch gives with a soft pop, my throat closes around a small, private victory.

The door says **STATEROOM** on a strip of golden tape. The letters were printed neat and official long before scarcity taught us to disguise theft as austerity. I move inside, the flashlight's edge cutting through the gloom. Cupboards line the wall like silent witnesses.

I open one. Empty shelves. Another. Vacuum.

The first few are rehearsals; my pulse keeps time with a mounting certainty.

Then my hand hits something that has weight. The back of one cupboard folds inward like a false book in a child's tale. A seam I hadn't known to look for gives way like a secret admitting me. Cold air breathes out of the hollow.

I step into the gap and sweep my light across the belly of the ship.

Rows upon rows of sealed bags stare back at me — powdered proteins, tins stamped with dates from a decade ago, sacks of nutrient paste. Each one bears the label I've heard whispered about but never believed: **COUNCIL ONLY.**

The labels are crisp. The bags are thick and many. The room is an embarrassment of plenty.

I stand there a long time, the beam of my flashlight trembling against the plastic. The absurdity of it strikes deeper than any blade. These are the supplies they told us were gone — the reason we rationed, the reason children cried at the mess line.

The betrayal is physical. A cold that spreads from my hands to my chest. I press a pack against my heart as if it could warm me.

Light flares behind me.

I spin.

Balthazar stands in the doorway, silhouette edged in corridor light, his scowl carved so precisely it could've been etched in metal. He doesn't shout. He doesn't need to. The door snaps shut behind him like a trap.

I don't pretend surprise. I fold my hands in front of me, the frozen bag pressed hard enough to smear frost across my palm.

"You keep this hidden," I say, my voice steadier than I feel. "You keep it while people—children—starve."

He crosses the room in three strides and rests

his palm against the stacked sacks with the casual cruelty of a man confident he'll never answer for it. He doesn't touch me. He only looks, like a judge inspecting evidence.

Behind him, the rest of the council steps into view, faces schooled into calm.

It isn't a trial. It's theater. I see it clearly now — they've rehearsed this moment the same way they rehearsed rationing: clean, precise, inevitable.

They bring me back to the wardroom bound at the wrists. The restraints bite into my skin, reminding me this isn't dignity — it's spectacle.

Seven faces circle me. Polished. Practiced. Small.

Balthazar raps the gavel. The sound cracks like a pistol.

"The members of the council have reached a verdict," he says, voice cool as coolant. "Six of seven."

He lets the pause sit like a lid. Lawrence shifts in his chair, hands trembling.

"Guilty."

Anger rises, then empties into something hollow. "May I speak?" I ask. Each word is a light against the dark.

"Given it may be the last you utter on this vessel," Balthazar says smoothly.

The politeness stings worse than the chains.

I breathe in once, steady. "There's no excuse I can give for sneaking in," I say. "I know the laws. But I can't fathom how you sit here and decide that your lives are worth more than theirs. How you—"

My voice catches. "How you let them starve while food rots in your cupboards."

Someone makes a small sound — shame breaking loose.

"That's enough," Balthazar snaps.

"You were going to let them die."

He slams the gavel. "Order!"

"Pathetic, gutless cowards!"

Only Lawrence flinches. His eyes betray him.

"You knew about this?" I ask him quietly.

He doesn't answer right away. Then, softly: "Yes. Some of us thought… to ration it differently. We thought—"

"You thought of yourselves," I finish.

He looks away.

Balthazar folds his hands. "Eventually, scarcity reaches all. Hard choices must be made."

"Which is why you hoard?" I ask. My voice has gone low and dangerous.

He doesn't blink. "You have a choice, Dawn. Stay silent and remain aboard… or face exile."

I feel something inside me click into place — not surrender, but clarity.

"I'd rather die with my ship than live as a coward."

Balthazar's lips twitch. "Seems you already missed that chance," he says. "Throw her in a cell. She'll be cast off in three days."

They move efficiently, like clerks signing death warrants. As they drag me from the room, the corridor lights dim — deliberate, ceremonial.

Three days.

The number catches in my throat like grit. I taste salt again, but this time it's sharper.

They think they've broken me. They're wrong.

The word *exile* sounds like a sentence. But to me, it feels like a beginning.

* * *

Arjes's cell smells of damp and old iron. The light in the brig flickers dull and jaundiced, making everyone look older than they are. When I push the bolt and peer through the bars, he's propped against the far wall like a rag someone forgot to fold. He blinks at me with eyes that have seen too much — bloodshot, glassy, the skin around them raw and papery.

"You okay?" I ask, because not asking feels like

259

shirking my last responsibilities — as Council-woman, and as a mother.

He lifts one hand in a weak nod. The motion is small, almost embarrassed, and then his knees give way. He folds to the floor in a heap, trembling. His breath comes ragged, like someone trying to suck air through a straw.

"Somebody—help!" My voice cracks in the hollow room.

Footsteps pound down the corridor, and Lawrence is there before I can count three. He pries the cell open and eases Arjes onto a blanket, his hands practiced, economical. I watch him check pulse and pupils, the way his jaw clenches when he finds what he's looking for. The way doctors become judges in the dark.

"Looks like some kind of infection," Lawrence says, draping the blanket over Arjes's ribs. His voice carries that weary cadence of a man forced to issue bad news with the same breath he uses to breathe.

"Help him," I say — almost a plea. "All that medicine and food in there—the Council-only stores. Use it. If people are sick, we treat them."

Lawrence's reply comes slow, like he's tasting it to make sure it's still safe. "He's a raider."

"He's a human being," I snap back before I can stop myself. The cell feels smaller now, like the ship itself is closing in around us.

"So we defend thieves now?" Lawrence asks. There's an edge in his tone that makes my hands curl into fists.

"Who should I defend then? You?" I fire back, sharper than I mean to. The words hang heavy in the wet air between us. He doesn't answer. He can't. He's still the man who voted to seal my fate — and everyone else's.

He stares at Arjes for a long moment, his finger tracing a worn seam on the blanket. When he finally speaks, his voice fractures. "Survival comes at a cost, Dawn. It isn't as simple as charity."

"It's never simple for you," I say, and the words taste bitter. "It's never simple when it's not your children starving at the edge of a plate."

Lawrence rubs his forehead — that gesture he makes when he's trying to balance the man his office demands with the one his conscience remembers. "Look," he says quietly. "I'm choosing to live."

The statement lands between us like a thrown stone. I think of the council's vote. Of Balthazar's calm. Of the cupboards I opened and the labels stamped **COUNCIL ONLY.** I feel the weight of that discovery sitting in my gut like iron.

"You have to see it differently," Lawrence says, softer now. He wants me to translate his cold math into human terms.

"You know what I see?" My voice drops until it's only for him. "I see time running out for everyone, Lawrence. Council or no council." I grip the bars until my knuckles whiten. The metal vibrates with the ship's slow crawl through the water. "You can hide food. You can hide decisions. You can ration and declare. But when the tide comes, all your accounting won't hold back the water."

He shifts, and for a second the man I used to trust — the one who judged fairly, who believed in mercy — flickers through. "Dawn," he says, voice low, "you can't keep breaking every rule because you feel wronged."

"Do you know what it's like to watch someone die?" I ask. I need to hear him say it — need to know he's looked that truth in the eye. My throat feels raw.

Lawrence bows his head. He's silent long enough that I can almost see him replaying the memory of a dying face. Finally, he murmurs, "I've seen it. More than I wanted."

"Have you watched someone raise a white flag," I say, "and not have the courage to answer it?"

He flinches, the color draining from his face. There's no defense left in him. Only silence — and in it, the sound of the ship: the hiss of coolant, the slow pulse of machinery, steady and indifferent.

Arjes coughs — small, wet, desperate — his fingers clutching the blanket like it's the last thing tethering him to life. His eyes flutter open and find mine.

Lawrence straightens, brushing his palms as if to wipe off compromise itself. "We should move him to med," he says at last. "Isolate him, get antibiotics if we can bring them online."

"Do it," I tell him. My voice comes out thin, a small thing flung against a gale. "Use whatever's needed. Tell the Council if you have to. I don't care."

He hesitates, then nods and gets to work. As he leaves the brig, I watch him go and feel the line between us shift. The lights flicker overhead, throwing the bars across the floor like long black teeth.

Alone with Arjes, I lean down so my face is close to his. His skin is cold. "Stay with me," I whisper, the words more prayer than command.

He smiles — a small, knowing thing, worn at the edges. "You fight like your son," he rasps. "That boy of yours will take the sea by the hand and demand the truth."

I press my forehead to the cool metal. I've already begun to chart a course that puts me against every rule the council ever made. If protecting him means breaking those rules, then

I'll break them.

Outside the brig, the ship sails on through black water, and in that endless motion I feel the fragile thread that ties each of us to life — and how easily it frays when someone in charge decides what counts as survival.

It's Real!

When you've captained a ship long enough, you start to believe the ocean remembers you. Every course, every storm, every name you whisper into its endless dark—some part of it always comes back.

I used to think that was comforting. Now, sitting behind cold steel bars, I'm not so sure.

The hum of the Vesta is steady but thin, like it's straining to hold itself together. Across from me, Arjes lies half-conscious on the floor, his breathing shallow and uneven. His skin has gone grey, his eyes red-rimmed and unfocused.

I kneel near the bars. "Hey," I say quietly. "You still with me?"

He mumbles something, little more than air.

Moments later, the hatch creaks open and Lawrence appears, silhouette framed by corridor light. He carries a small med-kit under his arm and a canteen slung over his shoulder.

"Found something," he says, crouching beside

Arjes. He flips open the case—small vials, a few syringes, two sealed packets labeled Antiviral/An tibiotic.

I raise an eyebrow. "Since when do you play medic?"

"Since nobody else wants to." He gives a humorless half-smile. "Council doesn't waste medicine on raiders."

"And yet here you are," I say softly.

He doesn't answer. He just fills a syringe, checks the dosage, and injects Arjes with a precision that surprises me. The man twitches, a low groan slipping out, but the tension in his body eases slightly.

Lawrence sits back on his heels, wiping sweat from his brow. "That's all I've got. The rest of it's rationed for officers."

I lean against the wall, watching him work. My voice comes low. "I used to ration too. Food. Water. Hope."

His head turns. "You're talking about your old ship."

"Yeah." I let out a bitter laugh. "We called her *The Demeter*. Fitting name for something that didn't live up to it."

Lawrence stays quiet, letting me fill the silence.

"They come out of the fog one night—thieves. Fast boats, white flags, no reason. We fight until the deck burns. I can still smell the oil and blood when I close my eyes." I draw a sharp breath, feeling my chest tighten. "We lose everything. Everyone. A few of us drift for days. When the Vesta finds us, I think it's salvation."

He looks down, fingers idly tracing the edge of the med-kit. "You blame yourself."

"I command that ship," I say. "It's my call to fight. My call to stay. Every time I close my eyes, I still see their faces. And Ahmed—" My throat tightens. "He's just a boy when the fire starts. I think saving him means something. That maybe it will make all of it mean something."

Lawrence sets the kit aside and leans against the bars beside me. "You can't carry all of it, Dawn. No captain could."

"Maybe," I say, "but I'm the only one who's supposed to."

We fall silent. The faint hum of the engines pulses through the walls, steady as a heartbeat. Then, somewhere deep in the ship, a low, resonant swish reverberates—so deep it passes through my bones.

The walls tremble. A canteen rolls across the floor and clangs to a stop.

We freeze.

"That isn't a ship," I whisper.

Lawrence's eyes shoot to the ceiling. "Stay here."

"Like hell," I snap, stepping closer to the bars. "Don't leave me down here!"

"I have to see what that is!"

"And what if we're under attack?!"

He hesitates. The corridor lights flicker. Then, with a resigned sigh, he reaches into his pocket and pulls out a ring of keys. The lock clicks, and the cell door swings open.

"Stay close," he mutters.

We climb through the narrow gangways, the ship shuddering beneath our feet. When we burst onto the deck, the night air hits like ice. Crew members stand frozen, all staring upward.

I follow their gaze—and feel my breath leave me.

Above the clouds hangs a massive pyramid of light, suspended in the sky like a judgment from the heavens. Its surface shimmers with shifting colors—gold, violet, and white—while arcs of lightning crawl silently along its edges.

For a moment, I can't move.

"Oh my God..."

Lawrence takes a step forward, voice barely a whisper. "Unbelievable."

The light from the structure bathes his face, painting him in gold. Around us, the crew murmurs prayers, curses, disbelief.

I can only stare, heart pounding against my

ribs. Whatever that thing is—it isn't ours. It isn't human.

And somewhere deep down, I feel the truth settle like a stone in my stomach.

Whatever we've been running from... it has finally found us.

The Arrival

Balthazar bursts through the hatch like a storm given shape. His voice is the first thing I hear—sharp, commanding, full of venom.

"Why is she up here?"

Every head on the deck turns toward me. For a moment, I feel the weight of their stares pressing against my skin.

Lawrence steps forward, calm as ever. "We're seeing beyond that, Councilman."

Balthazar's eyes cut to him, then to the horizon—where the faint shimmer of that impossible structure still lingers among the clouds—before snapping back to me.

"Regardless," he snaps, "her presence makes us vulnerable. She belongs in a cell."

I've had enough of being silenced, enough of the shadows they try to bury me in. I step forward, wind whipping my hair across my face. "If you're quite finished with your tantrum," I say, "maybe you can tell everyone where the surplus rations went."

A murmur ripples through the deck. Faces turn. Doubt flickers in eyes that have long since learned to obey.

Balthazar freezes. For once, his authority falters.

"Careful, Captain," he growls.

"Oh, I'm well past careful." I hear my own heartbeat now. "Tell them how you and the council have been hoarding food synthesizers while the rest of us scrape the bottom of empty trays."

The murmurs turn to gasps. Someone shouts, "Is that true?"

Balthazar's jaw tightens. "You worthless wretch!"

"Some of us wouldn't survive another month!" I shout back.

"Arrest her!" His voice cracks. "Remove her from the ship at once!"

The commandos move—but the people move faster. They form a barrier around me, shoulder to shoulder, faces set in defiance.

"Stand down!" Lawrence barks, voice booming over the chaos.

And then—everything goes silent.

A sound tears through the sky, low and thunderous, like the heavens splitting open. The clouds roll black above us, and the air feels electric. I look up—and my stomach drops.

"There it is again," I whisper.

The mist peels apart, revealing something enormous descending through it—metallic, elegant, silent. It isn't a ship. It's something beyond ships. A ramp unfolds from its belly, glowing blue.

Everyone stares. Even Balthazar.

The figure who descends moves like he owns the air itself—tall, armored, his presence commanding in a way no council gavel could ever be.

"I demand to speak to the leader of this vessel," he says. His voice resonates, deep and unwavering.

Balthazar puffs his chest. "I am Balthazar Dach, leader of the Vesta Ark. State your purpose."

The man's eyes glint. "I am Royal Allegiant Remy, of the City of Azur."

For a heartbeat, I can't breathe. "It's real," I whisper. "It's been real the whole time."

Remy inclines his head. "We have come to prepare your people for exodus. But your leader must first meet with the Royal Order."

"Don't trust him," I say, stepping forward. "He's no leader."

Balthazar turns on me, red with rage. "And you're a reckless agitator!"

"She's exposing the truth," Lawrence says, stepping between us.

Balthazar's voice breaks. "Enough!"

"No," Lawrence says. "It ends now, Councilman."

Remy raises a hand, silencing us all. "Then let's make it simple," he says. "Will anyone join us in Azur—or shall we depart without you?"

The deck erupts into chaos—shouts, arguments, fear. The wind carries their desperation like wildfire.

Lawrence's voice cuts through it. "If he goes, she goes."

Remy turns his gaze to me. "And who is she?"

I straighten my shoulders. "Captain Dawn Perry," I say. "Former Captain of *The Demeter Ark*."

Remy's expression softens with recognition—or pity, I can't tell. "Where is your vessel?"

My throat tightens. "Destroyed," I say quietly. "Sunk."

Lawrence speaks before the silence can swallow us. "Dawn represents the best of us. If anyone deserves to speak for our survivors—it's her."

Remy regards me for a long moment before nodding. "Prepare for departure. Let's put an end to this chaos."

As his troopers ascend the ramp, I turn to Lawrence. Our hands meet, fingers gripping tight, like we're holding back everything that could still break.

"I want to see the world through your eyes," he says.

I swallow hard. "Then take care of our people," I tell him. "I trust you."

He nods once, firm and resolute.

And as I step toward the ramp, toward that blinding blue light that hums with destiny, I feel the weight of everything—loss, defiance, and a fragile, dangerous hope.

For the first time in a long while, I'm not walking into exile. I'm walking toward the truth.

* * *

The jumper breaks through the last veil of clouds, and there it is—Azur.

I've imagined it a thousand different ways during the long, hollow nights aboard the *Vesta Ark,* but nothing—absolutely nothing—prepares me for what I see.

It isn't just a city. It's a miracle carved from the bones of the heavens.

The air shimmers around it, thick with ionized light and mist that glows faintly gold in the sun. Massive pyramids of glass and alloy hang suspended in perfect harmony, their mirrored surfaces scattering light in cascading patterns across the clouds below. Each structure connects to the next by shimmering bridges that look too delicate to hold the weight of a single human—yet entire transport vessels glide along them, sleek and silent.

Below the city, colossal propellers churn the air like slow, eternal hearts, keeping the impossible afloat. Between them, great channels of light pulse rhythmically, blue and white, like veins of energy feeding the city's core. It's both mechanical and divine—alive and eternal.

I press my hand against the window, unable to breathe. "Dear God..." I whisper, though I'm not sure I believe in Him anymore.

The jumper's glass canopy fills with reflections—pyramids within pyramids, towers rising higher than anything man should ever build. Gardens spill from the terraces like green waterfalls, their leaves shimmering with dew that glitters in the thin sunlight. Below them, mist curls and dances between the gaps, turning the sky itself into a living ocean.

It's beautiful—and terrifying.

Balthazar steps up beside me, his reflection flickering in the glass like a ghost. His face tightens, jaw set hard. He looks at Azur as if staring into the mouth of judgment itself. When his eyes meet mine, the anger is still there—burning, fragile, and small against the vastness of what waits ahead.

"Magnificent, isn't it?" I say softly, my voice barely above a whisper.

He doesn't answer. He doesn't have to.

Because in that moment, as the jumper glides toward the gleaming spires and the sound of the engines softens into a steady hum, I know we're both thinking the same thing.

* * *

The jumper hisses and slows as it enters a massive chamber of light and motion. Below us stretches a metallic field of landing pads, gleaming like mirrors under the blue glow of Azur's sky. Hundreds—no, thousands—of people move with precision and purpose. Mechanics in glistening uniforms guide other jumpers into formation. Drones zip overhead, their movements so synchronized it's as if the city itself breathes in rhythm.

I've never seen so many people alive in one place since *The Demeter.* My chest tightens at the thought. The *Vesta* has grown silent over the years—a ghost ship of whispers and fear. But here, life pulses through every corner.

The ramp extends, and light pours in like liquid gold. The air smells clean—sharp, almost electric—and when my boots touch the polished surface, I feel as though I've stepped into a dream I'm not sure I belong in.

"Welcome to the Royal City of Azur," Remy says, his voice proud but even.

"There are so many people," I whisper.

"Indeed," he replies. "The Royal Order awaits your presence. Right this way."

Balthazar strides ahead as if the place already belongs to him. I follow, my eyes unable to rest on one thing for more than a moment—walls made of glass that ripple like water, silver walkways suspended by light, banners of deep indigo shimmering in the artificial breeze. Everything about this city hums with life and intention.

We enter what Remy calls *the Terrarium*. I gasp before I can stop myself.

A vast transparent tunnel stretches before us, encased within a dome teeming with life. Vines curl up crystalline pillars, birds dart through beams of light, and rabbits hop along a carpet of impossibly green grass. I press my palm to the glass as we walk, staring at the lush world breathing just inches away.

"Magnificent, isn't it?" Remy says.

"It's alive," I murmur. "Everything here… feeds everything else. It's beautiful."

Balthazar snorts behind me. "Plants," he says, his tone flat, dismissive.

Remy turns to him, patient but sharp. "A self-sustaining ecosystem," he replies. "Vegetation. Wildlife. Balance. The very things your kind once lost."

Balthazar's only answer is silence.

Ahead, enormous golden doors loom—carved with symbols I don't recognize, glowing faintly along their edges. They open without a sound, and we step into another world entirely.

The chamber beyond is majestic.

The ceilings soar higher than I can follow with my eyes. Curtains of deep crimson frame massive windows that look out upon the endless sky. Light spills across marble floors veined with silver. At the far end of a vast table sit two figures—their presence commanding enough to still the air.

"Your Excellencies," Remy announces, bowing deeply. "May I present the leaders of the *Vesta*."

The man—Lord Leveth—regards us with quiet scrutiny, smoke curling lazily from the cigar between his fingers. Beside him sits Sovereign Kit, younger, yet no less composed. Their eyes are sharp and measuring.

Leveth leans back. "So," he says, voice like gravel. "You wish to become citizens?"

Balthazar steps forward, hands clasped behind his back. "Yes, my lord. With the inclusion of our entire colony."

Sovereign Kit nods slowly. "Then it's imperative your people understand the bylaws of Azur."

Before Balthazar can respond, I step forward. "I have a question," I say, my voice steadier than I feel. "Followed by a request."

Kit tilts her head. "Proceed."

"Why is this the first time we've seen you?" I ask. "We've been sending signals for years. We nearly starved waiting for proof this place even existed. The only ones who believed were a dying prisoner and a ten-year-old boy."

Leveth's eyes narrow. "Where is this boy?"

My throat tightens. "Missing. He went looking for this place."

"You know this?"

"I know he went in search of hope," I say. "The kind that's been buried and forgotten down below."

Leveth exhales a long stream of smoke. "Maintaining balance here requires secrecy. Difficult decisions are the price of survival."

I feel my anger flare, but I force myself to

breathe. "We made difficult decisions too," I say. "We gave away our food to keep others alive."

"Commendable," Leveth replies. "But misguided."

Sovereign Kit's voice softens. "Concealment has kept Azur safe since the Great Flood."

"Then…" I whisper, the realization striking deep. "Then he was right. My son. He knew you'd come."

"The boy?" Kit asks.

"Yes," I say. "And I want your help finding him. Please. He's my son."

Balthazar's voice cuts in, cold and dismissive. "Assuming he's even alive."

I turn on him, the fury in me boiling over. "Maybe you should tell them what you've done before you start doubting others, you coward."

"Enough!" Leveth's voice thunders across the chamber. The sound echoes through the walls, leaving a sharp silence in its wake.

He leans forward, eyes like stone. "Permission is granted for your colony to board Azur," he says slowly. "But a search for one child is… impractical."

I step closer, meeting his gaze head-on. "Then consider this not as a leader's plea, but as a mother's. I didn't choose motherhood. It found me. I've failed as a captain, but I will not fail as a mother."

For the first time, Leveth's expression softens. The flame in his cigar dims slightly. "Your devotion is admirable," he says quietly. "And as a father, I understand your pain. But understand this—faith offers no guarantees. And in Azur..." He pauses, his eyes cold again. "...risk is the one thing we cannot afford."

And with that, the great room falls silent.

I stand there—trembling, furious, and small beneath the weight of their judgment—knowing I will not leave this city without my son.

VI

Azur

**The Constitution of Azur — Chapter I,
Verses 1–9
Quoted by Aurora, Keeper of the Blue
Flame**

*Behold, our home; a city crowned in light,
where the clouds part in reverence and the
firmament bends low to bless her name —*
Azur.
*Blessed it is, high in the heavens, raised not
by conquest but by covenant, by the hands
of dreamers who refused the silence below.
Here, the winds carry the songs of our
forebears, and the stones remember the
weight of their hope.*

Done With It All

The brig was suffocatingly still—**thick** with the metallic scent of rust, sweat, and something else Lawrence couldn't name. The kind of smell that clung to you, that got under your nails and into your lungs until you felt tainted by it. The dim overhead light flickered with a nervous pulse, casting long, shivering shadows that crawled across the walls like restless ghosts.

He shoved the cell door open with a clang that echoed down the empty corridor, a sound too loud, too final. The hinges shrieked as if protesting the intrusion.

Arjes lay motionless on the cot, cocooned in a tattered blanket, drenched in sweat. His skin had gone the color of old parchment—thin, almost translucent beneath the trembling light. His breathing came in shallow bursts, each one shorter than the last, like his body had forgotten how to keep going.

"Come on, man," Lawrence muttered, voice raw,

cracking halfway through. He dropped to one knee beside him, pulling a small vial from his pocket with shaking hands. The antibiotic sloshed inside, uselessly alive in his grip. "You've got to take this. It'll help."

He pried Arjes' jaw open and tipped the vial toward his lips. The bitter liquid ran down his chin as he coughed—weakly, pitifully—spitting most of it back up. The sound tore through the silence, wet and broken, like something dying in the dark.

Lawrence swallowed hard, his throat burning. "You hear me? You're not dying down here."

Arjes stirred, barely. His eyes fluttered open— bloodshot, unfocused—and found Lawrence's face with a faint flicker of recognition. It wasn't relief, or fear. Just resignation.

"I'm done with it all," he whispered.

The words floated out of him like breath itself— thin, final, dissolving into the heavy air. His gaze drifted, then emptied. His chest rose once more, a trembling effort… then fell. And didn't rise again.

Lawrence froze. For a heartbeat, he refused to believe it. The light above them buzzed, stuttered, went dark for a second—long enough to make the silence absolute.

Then it came back on, too bright, too cruel.

"No…" Lawrence whispered. He grabbed Arjes

by the shoulders, shaking him once, twice. "No, no, no, don't you quit on me! Not now!"

Arjes' head lolled to the side, limp. His hair stuck to his damp forehead. His lips were still parted, as if he might speak again.

Lawrence's breath came in sharp bursts. He pressed his hand against Arjes' neck, searching for a pulse he already knew wasn't there. His fingers trembled. His jaw clenched so tight it hurt.

"Damn it…" he breathed. "You weren't supposed to go like this."

The weight of it settled over him slowly—first in his chest, then his gut, until it filled the entire room. The cell seemed smaller now, the air heavier, pressing down on him from every direction. He sat there for a long moment, staring at the still form before him, feeling the guilt seep into his bones.

He thought about Dawn—how she'd trusted him to look after the others. About Ahmed, and the way the boy had looked up to Arjes like a brother. He thought about all the promises he'd made that he hadn't kept.

The silence swallowed everything.

And then, faintly—almost too faint to notice— came a sound from above. A deep, distant groan of metal shifting under strain. The hull trembled, dust falling from the ceiling in soft, lazy spirals.

Then came another sound—low, thunderous, like something vast turning in the dark.

Lawrence's head snapped upward, heart hammering. The noise lingered, a hollow echo that rolled through the brig and faded into nothing.

But the unease it left behind did not fade. It rooted itself deep inside him, spreading like a sickness of its own.

He looked back at Arjes one last time, the flickering light casting long shadows across the man's still face. And for a moment—just a moment—Lawrence thought he saw him breathe again.

But it was only the light.

Rough Seas

The sun hung low, a pale coin bleeding light across the gray expanse of sea. The wind had turned restless, rippling the tattered banners strung along *The Vesta Ark's* railings. Lawrence stood at the bow, binoculars pressed to his face, the metal cool and trembling in his hands.

Through the shifting glare, he saw it—a massive vessel carving toward them with unsettling speed. Its dark hull threw waves aside like a predator parting water. He frowned. The ship bore no markings, no signal flags. Just silence and intent.

He lowered the binoculars, jaw tight. Something about it felt wrong.

"Prepare for defensive positions," he ordered. His voice rang across the deck, sharp enough to cut through the wind.

The Vesta Commandos snapped to life, their boots thudding on the metal planks as they moved to ready stations. The hum of charging plasma rifles and the click of locking safeties filled the tense air.

Lawrence glanced toward the horizon again. The vessel was closer now—too close. Its engines roared like something feral. He searched for a comm ping, a hail, a signal—anything—but the radios remained dead.

Then, before he could process the silence, thick ropes flew over the side of *The Vesta Ark,* coiling across the deck with heavy thuds. Figures in gray tactical suits descended from above, sliding down in swift, practiced motions.

They moved like soldiers, but there was something off about them. No insignias. No callsigns. No coordination with Vesta Command.

Lawrence's hand fell to the hilt of his blade. "Identify yourselves!" he shouted.

The intruders said nothing. They hit the deck and spread out with eerie precision, weapons drawn. Their helmets reflected the dying light of afternoon, hiding their faces.

"By order of The Vesta," Lawrence continued, stepping forward, "you are commanded to depart this vessel immediately—or face arrest."

One of the men advanced. He was tall, broad-shouldered, his gait unhurried, confident. A jagged metal hook gleamed at his belt, catching the sunlight. His eyes—dark and unreadable—met Lawrence's with quiet challenge.

"There aren't enough men here to arrest me," the stranger said, his voice low and gravel-thick.

Lawrence felt the hair rise on his neck. "It takes only one determined man to dismantle an entire fleet of arrogance," he replied evenly. "You're outnumbered."

The man gave a slow, humorless grin. "Outnumbered isn't the same as outmatched."

He drew the hook-sword from his belt, the steel curving like a predator's tooth. The deck seemed to still around them—the sea's rhythm pausing in anticipation.

"Your authority means nothing out here," the stranger said.

Lawrence steadied his stance. "Leave. We have nothing to offer you."

The stranger tilted his head. "Then you'll give us what you have."

He lunged.

The sword came fast, cutting through the light in a silver arc. Lawrence barely managed to sidestep, drawing his own blade in one swift motion. Steel met steel with a shriek that echoed across the open sea.

All at once, the deck erupted into chaos. The Vesta Commandos surged forward, engaging the intruders in a storm of flashing blades and shouts. The clash of metal drowned out the pounding surf below.

Lawrence and the stranger fought at the center of it all, circling, each testing the other's strength. A sudden blow from the man's fist caught Lawrence across the jaw—sharp, punishing. His vision blurred as he hit the deck, his sword skidding out of reach.

The stranger loomed above him, the hook-sword raised, gleaming with sunlight and salt.

"Get to the engine room!" he barked to his men.

And just like that, the invaders moved with purpose—storming deeper into *The Vesta Ark*, leaving behind the sounds of battle and the crackle of fear in their wake.

Lawrence wiped the blood from his mouth, breath ragged, realization dawning like a shadow stretching across the sea—

whoever these men were, they hadn't come by accident.

* * *

The dim corridor pulsed with a flickering amber glow, the emergency lights struggling to pierce the heavy fog of steam that leaked from cracked vents above. The air smelled of rust, oil, and something faintly metallic—blood, maybe, or fear.

Ahmed moved quickly but carefully, one arm wrapped around his mother's. His hand guided hers along the cold wall as they advanced, step by step, through the trembling passage.

"Careful here," he murmured, steadying her as the deck pitched beneath their feet.

Alana's milky eyes glimmered faintly in the low light. She tilted her head, listening—not to the ship's creaks, but to something deeper. "The hull… it's shaking," she said softly.

Ahmed glanced upward. Distant echoes reverberated through the ship—shouting, metal striking metal, the unmistakable sound of boots pounding steel.

"Stay close to me," he said. His tone was calm, but a tremor threaded through it.

They turned a corner—and froze.

From the far end of the gangway, shadows detached themselves from the walls. A group of figures emerged—lean, fast, armed. Their ragged uniforms marked them as *Renegades*, though their faces were half-hidden beneath scarves and helmets.

One of them—a boy no older than sixteen, his grin too wild for his years—lifted his blade in recognition.

"Peter Pan!" he called out, voice cracking with

mockery and something like respect.

Alana's head turned sharply toward her son. "Why are they calling you Peter Pan?"

Ahmed's jaw tightened. "It's a long story," he said under his breath. "One I'll tell when we're not about to die."

The Renegades didn't wait. They charged, their footsteps clanging down the corridor like war drums.

"Get back," Ahmed said, pushing his mother gently behind him.

The first attacker lunged, blade flashing. Ahmed caught the strike with a snap of his wrist, metal ringing out in the narrow hall. He pivoted, twisting the man's arm and sending the sword clattering to the floor. Before the Renegade could recover, Ahmed slammed him against the bulkhead—one clean motion—and the man dropped, gasping.

Another came from the side. Ahmed ducked low, his elbow driving into the attacker's ribs, then kicked his legs out from under him. The man's breath left him in a choked groan as he hit the deck.

"Let's talk this out," Ahmed said between breaths, his tone almost playful.

The third Renegade swung wildly, panic setting in. Ahmed caught his wrist mid-arc, spun, and used the man's momentum to hurl him into the opposite wall. He slumped, unconscious before he hit the floor.

Silence fell—broken only by the hiss of the failing lights above.

Ahmed exhaled slowly, glancing at the three motionless forms. He turned to Alana, reaching for her hand again, his touch softer now. "Come on, Mom," he said gently. "We're good."

Alana's brows knit, her blind gaze searching his face as if she could see through the calm he was trying to wear. "What happened?"

Ahmed gave a faint smile, the corner of his lip bleeding from a cut he hadn't noticed. "I think we talked it out," he said.

* * *

The sky split open with a sound like the world tearing in two.

Engines roared overhead, and the heavens themselves seemed to tremble. Silver jumpers screamed through the clouds, their underbellies aglow with the insignia of Azur. The sunlight fractured off their hulls and scattered across the sea in ribbons of gold.

295

Gunny War lifted his head, squinting into the light. His face—scarred and salt-streaked—was carved from stone, the shadow of his helm casting deep lines across his weathered features. Around him, the Renegades scrambled to arm themselves, shouting orders drowned by the thunder of propellers. Yet Gunny did not move. He only stared upward, lips curling into something between a sneer and a smirk.

A mechanical voice boomed from the sky. "Surrender now!"

The command echoed across the ship, reverberating through the steel beneath their boots. The jumpers shifted formation and hissed open, releasing cables that fell like silver serpents from the clouds. One by one, Azur troopers descended—sleek armor glinting in the light, their arrival as precise as clockwork.

And then she appeared.

For a moment, she was just a silhouette framed by blinding light. Then she stepped forward through the haze, her form taking shape—dark, purposeful, resolute.

Dawn.

Her armor shimmered with rain and light, her saber catching fire with every reflection. Each step she took down the ramp was deliberate, echoing with quiet authority. When her boots struck the deck, the air itself seemed to draw taut.

Gunny War turned to face her. His hook-blade rested lazily against his shoulder, eyes glinting like black glass. The two locked gazes, and for a heartbeat, the world held its breath.

"Oh," Gunny said at last, voice low and rough with memory. "You. Long time."

Dawn met his stare, unwavering. "I'll die before I let you harm these people."

Gunny smiled, all teeth and venom. "Good. I'll finish what I started."

He lunged.

The hook-sword came down with a metallic shriek, cutting the air between them. Dawn met it head-on, the clash erupting in a storm of sparks. The sound rang across the deck—metal on metal, fury against resolve.

They moved like echoes of a shared past—his strikes heavy and brutal, hers fast and sharp, every motion measured and desperate. Rain began to fall, a cold drizzle that slicked the deck beneath their boots and painted their armor in silver. Around them, chaos unfolded—Renegades and Azur troopers clashed in a storm of shouting, gunfire, and steel—but Dawn heard only the rhythm of their duel.

Gunny's voice cut through the storm. "You think they'll remember you as a savior?"

Dawn pivoted, driving her blade upward. "They'll remember who stood between them and you."

He lunged again, their faces inches apart, eyes locked in defiance. "Then die like one."

Their swords met once more with a shriek that tore through the wind. Dawn's muscles trembled from the strain, her breath ragged, her heart pounding. But her gaze never wavered.

She shifted her footing, caught his next swing, and turned his strength against him—forcing him back with a surge of will and fury.

The jumpers above flared with light, casting the deck in gold and shadow. For a single breath, time stood still. Then the storm returned—rain hammering steel, thunder roaring overhead, and the echo of their blades singing through it all.

The battle raged on.

But the tide had shifted.

* * *

The tower trembled with the sound of chaos below—shouting, gunfire, the faint clash of steel. Somewhere down there, Dawn was locked in battle, the Azur troopers were swarming, and the

Renegades were falling apart.

But Gates?

Gates had other priorities.

He yanked open a storage locker and began shoving ration packs into his satchel like a man possessed. "Never know when a guy might need emergency snacks," he muttered, sweat beading on his forehead. The tower walls shook again, dust sprinkling down from the rafters. "Or… second lunch. Or morale food."

He glanced around—nobody watching. Good. He tossed in a few water pouches for good measure, then spotted something shiny on a nearby shelf. "Ooh! Fruit gel. Premium." He added it to the pile, nodding approvingly as though he were curating fine art instead of looting a ship mid-crisis.

From below, the unmistakable crack of blaster fire echoed upward. Gates froze, then looked toward the door. "Okay. Time to go."

He zipped the bag, slung it over his shoulder with a heroic flourish—and then the door burst open.

Three Azur troopers stormed in, sabers drawn and gleaming.

"Surrender!" one barked.

For a split second, Gates just stood there, blinking. Then, with theatrical grandeur, he unsheathed his sword in a single, dramatic motion. "Gentlemen," he declared, his grin spreading wide. "First—we must dance."

He twirled the blade like he'd practiced in front of a mirror. It was almost impressive. Almost.

Then—*WHACK.*

A trooper's gauntleted fist connected squarely with his jaw.

The world spun. Gates stumbled backward, his sword clattering to the floor as he collapsed in a heap of armor and ego.

Flat on his back, he groaned. "Okay. No dance."

The troopers stood over him, unimpressed. One of them glanced at the bag of rations and sighed. "What were you even doing?"

Gates, still dazed, looked up with a weak grin. "…Meal prepping."

The trooper shook his head. "Unbelievable."

As they dragged him to his feet, Gates winced but managed to keep talking, because of course he did. "Just so you know, I *was* going to win that dance."

"Sure you were," one muttered.

And with that, they hauled him out of the tower—his bag of snacks dangling from one hand, his dignity left somewhere on the floor behind him.

The deck was a storm of noise and light—metal clashing, engines roaring, the sea itself raging beneath them as if it could sense the violence above. Ahmed burst through the upper gangway, Alana clinging to his arm as the world around them came undone.

Smoke and salt filled the air. Jumpers circled overhead like vultures of war, their thrusters scattering waves of heat across the deck. From the taffrails, he saw them—Dawn and Gunny War—locked in brutal combat. Sparks leapt from each collision of their blades, a deadly rhythm of fury and defiance.

Ahmed froze, heart pounding, transfixed by the sheer ferocity of the duel. Dawn moved like lightning, every swing an act of defiance, every step a statement of control. Gunny countered with savage precision, his face twisted with a fury that felt centuries old.

Then Alana's trembling hand tightened around his arm. "Ahmed… what's happening?"

He looked down at her, saw the fear in her sightless eyes—and made a choice.

"It's okay," he said softly. "Stay here."

He pulled free, sprinted to the taffrail, and

seized a dangling rope. For one impossible second, he felt weightless as he swung out into the storm of wind and smoke—then landed hard on the Vesta deck below. The impact rattled his bones.

"**Dawn!**"

She turned at the sound of his voice—just for a fraction of a second. Her eyes widened in surprise, in relief. And in that heartbeat of distraction, fate struck.

Gunny War's blade lunged forward. Dawn twisted aside—too late. The curved hook of his sword caught her as it retracted, slicing deep into her abdomen.

The sound tore through Ahmed's soul. *SLIT!*

Her gasp was soft, almost confused, as blood darkened her armor. She staggered back, the saber slipping from her hand.

"**No!**" Ahmed's scream ripped through the chaos. He lunged forward, but she was already falling.

Gunny War wrenched his blade free, the motion cruelly casual. Dawn crumpled to the deck, her knees buckling beneath her, a streak of red marking her descent.

For an endless moment, the world stopped. The roar of engines, the shouting of men—all drowned out by the silence in Ahmed's chest.

He hit the ground beside her, hands shaking as

he pressed against the wound, desperate, useless. "Stay with me. Dawn—look at me!"

Her hand found his face, trembling and wet with her own blood. Her lips quirked upward in a faint, fragile smile.

"You're okay," she whispered.

"*No.* Don't—don't you say that. You're okay, not me. Please—"

Her eyes fluttered. Her breath came shallow. "I told you… not to follow me."

And then… nothing.

Her hand went still against his cheek. Her eyes, once fierce and alive, stared past him into the storming sky.

Ahmed sat there, motionless, the world crashing around him. Azur troopers stormed the deck, weapons raised. Gunny War—his face suddenly calm, resigned—dropped his sword and lifted his hands in surrender. But Ahmed barely saw him.

The troopers shouted, engines blared, and the sea howled, but all Ahmed could hear was the faint echo of her voice—*you're okay.*

He wasn't.

He gathered her against him, cradling her as if the warmth of his body could pull her back. The blood soaked into his hands, his clothes, everything.

And as the sun sank low on the horizon, the light

glinted off the still blade that had ended her—cold, unfeeling, and final.

Ahmed bowed his head.

For the first time in years, the boy who once refused to cry did.

Dusk

The chamber of the Secretariat was dim and austere that night, a hollow place of marble and shadow. The faint hum of Azur's power conduits pulsed through the walls, like a mechanical heartbeat marking the silence between men who had already said too much.

Lawrence stood at the center of it all—disheveled, sleepless, his uniform still stained from the aftermath on the Vesta. In his hands, he clutched Dawn's small, flower-decorated notebook, the petals smudged and wilted by the salt of his fingers. He ran a thumb over the embossed initials—**D.P.**—as if doing so could summon her back.

He looked up slowly, eyes burning beneath the weight of exhaustion and rage. Across the polished floor sat Lord Leveth and Sovereign Kit, their faces lit in the blue glow of the chamber's light.

"Her service is in two days," Lawrence said, voice

gravelled, half-broken but deadly calm. "Why is Ahmed being held?"

Lord Leveth didn't flinch. His composure was a blade—smooth, deliberate, sharp. "He was found with his biological mother," he said. "Both are considered accomplices to the raider's crimes."

Lawrence's jaw tightened. "Ahmed isn't a pirate. He sought help. He *found* his mother—he didn't conspire with her."

Leveth folded his hands. "Seems trouble found him instead."

From the corner of the chamber, a lazy trail of smoke rose. Balthazar sat half-slouched in a chair, the faintest smirk on his lips as he exhaled. The red glow of his cigarette tip pulsed like a heartbeat in the dark.

"She got what she deserved," he muttered.

The words hung in the air like acid. Lawrence turned his head slowly, eyes narrowing to a deadly slit. The air between them seemed to shift, heavy with heat and silence.

"You must find this amusing," Lawrence said, his tone low and venomous. "The only one brave enough to oppose you is gone, and you sit there—smoking—like a man relieved."

Balthazar's grin widened, crooked and cruel. "She brought it upon herself. No one forced her to die a hero."

"*Don't.*" Lawrence's voice cracked, but not with weakness—with fury barely restrained. He took a step forward, his shadow spilling across the floor like spilled ink. "You wouldn't know courage if it stood in front of you and bled out."

Balthazar rose, brushing the ash from his coat, his expression turning predatory. "Careful, Councilman" he said softly. "You're speaking to your superior. And if I recall correctly, *you're* the one who abandoned half your crew to die out there. Not me. Not Dawn. You."

That did it.

The world seemed to snap.

Lawrence moved like a storm uncoiled—his fist connecting with Balthazar's jaw in a single, violent motion. The crack echoed across the chamber as Balthazar flew backward, toppling over a chair and crashing to the marble floor. His cigarette skittered across the ground, sparks scattering like fireflies.

"Enough of this childish behavior!" Sovereign Kit's voice boomed through the room, but the troopers were already moving.

Two Azur guards seized Lawrence, dragging him backward as he struggled against their grip. His chest heaved, his eyes still locked on Balthazar, who wiped the blood from his mouth and smiled— a twisted, broken smile of someone who had wanted the fight.

Lawrence spat the words out like poison. "You're not a leader. You're a parasite wearing command stripes."

Balthazar leaned back against the pillar, voice low but cruel. "And yet the parasite survived."

Lawrence stopped fighting the guards. He straightened, shaking off their hands as best he could, his breathing ragged. He lifted Dawn's notebook one last time, clutching it to his chest as though it were a flag—or a grave marker.

"I've said my peace," he muttered. His voice had cooled to something even sharper than his anger. He turned for the door, every step echoing through the chamber like a countdown.

As the doors sealed behind him, the silence that followed was heavier than the violence that preceded it.

Lord Leveth sighed, eyes on the notebook Lawrence carried. "Grief makes men dangerous," he murmured.

Balthazar chuckled weakly, dabbing his split lip with a handkerchief. "No," he said. "Grief makes them honest."

And somewhere deep within the city of Azur, under the pulse of its perfect machinery, the world kept turning—cold, bright, and utterly indifferent.

* * *

The night was impossibly still. Azur glided like a ghost across the dark horizon, its lights shimmering over the water, a silent kingdom adrift among the stars. The air carried the soft scent of salt and metal. Lanterns floated along the dock, hundreds of them, their warm glow flickering like captive stars set free.

The people gathered in reverent silence. Men and women stood shoulder to shoulder, their faces pale in the celestial glow, their expressions hollowed by loss. At the center of the dock rested a single sea chest — polished, adorned with flowers, its surface carved with the crest of the Demeter.

It was not a coffin, not truly. But everyone knew what it meant.

Lawrence stood before it, shoulders drawn tight, Dawn's notebook trembling in his hands. The little book was frayed at the edges, its pages soft from years of handling, its cover still dusted with dried petals. Her handwriting filled every corner, looping and delicate, alive with her.

He swallowed hard before opening it.

"This was hers," he said softly. "Her words. Her final ones."

The crowd bowed their heads as he began to

read.

> *Find me on the edge of the world.*
> *I look and feel nothing.*
> *I've seen pain — the pain of others.*
> *Take it away so that I can smile.*
> *Push it away, so that I can pull in light...*

His voice faltered, catching against the wind, but he kept reading.

* * *

Ahmed lay curled on the velvet cot, his face buried in silken pillows that smelled faintly of lavender and brass polish. The brig of Azur was no dungeon — it was immaculate, softly lit by bands of azure light that pulsed gently along the curved walls. The air was perfumed and still, too beautiful for mourning.

The faint hum of the city's engines reverberated through the crystalline floor, a sound both soothing and cruel in its constancy. Beyond the latticed window, the vast expanse of clouds shimmered beneath the moonlight, the whole sky gliding by like a dream he could not touch.

He knew what was happening above. The funeral. Her funeral.

He'd begged to go. They told him he was nothing more than a prisoner.

He pressed his palms into his eyes until colors burst behind them — shards of light that felt like punishment. His breath came in ragged bursts, half sob, half prayer.

Somewhere above, faint but unmistakable, he could almost hear Lawrence's voice — distant, trembling — reading from her notebook. The words seeped through the silence like light through water.

Bring me peace in a world of war.
Bring me hope in a world of despair.
Bring me light in a world of darkness...

Ahmed bit hard on his knuckle, trying to choke back the sound clawing its way up his throat. But the sobs came anyway — deep, broken things that shook through him until the bedframe quivered. His tears darkened the sheets, and still he couldn't stop.

He wanted to scream. To tear apart the walls. To find her.

Bring me growth in a world filled to the

brink.
 Alone in a world, not safe.
 Not even for a flower.

The words lingered in the air like an afterimage — radiant and sorrowful — and the beauty of the place around him made them all the more unbearable.

He had never felt smaller within so much light.

* * *

Lawrence's voice trembled on the last line. The people stood motionless, bound together in the weight of it. Children wept openly, their small hands gripping each other for strength.

He closed the notebook slowly and laid it atop the sea chest, tucking a single white flower between its pages.

Then he whispered, "Goodbye, Captain."

The attendants released the chest into the dark water. Flames bloomed beneath it, orange and gold, devouring the wood as it drifted away from the dock. The fire's reflection shimmered across the faces of the mourners.

One by one, they released their flowers into

the air. The petals caught the lantern light and shimmered — rising, swirling, transforming into glimmering motes that looked like fireflies escaping the earth.

The wind carried them toward the stars.

* * *

Ahmed sat up slowly, his chest heaving, eyes red and raw. The air around him shimmered faintly — thin veils of light rippling across the curved crystal walls of the brig. Outside, through the wide, domed window, the night stretched open like a living sky.

Lanterns floated past the glass — hundreds of them — their golden glow drifting upward through the pale mist that cradled the city. Each one reflected across the surface of the window, scattering fragments of light over Ahmed's face like ghostly fingerprints.

He reached toward them, his fingertips brushing the cool glass. The city beyond glowed in solemn silence — its spires gleaming silver and blue, the bridges between them alive with slow-moving ribbons of light. From somewhere distant came the echo of bells, soft and mournful, carried on the wind.

He pressed his forehead against the window, watching as the last lantern rose higher, its glow thinning until it vanished among the stars that hung suspended over the horizon of clouds.

His voice broke when he spoke again, trembling with the weight of everything he could not say.

"Find me on the edge of the world."

And as Azur drifted onward — the radiant city gliding through an ocean of cloud and moonlight — Ahmed's tears continued to fall, silent and unending, like rain that would never reach the ground.

She WAS Dawn

The Terrarium stretched before them like a cathedral of light and life — a tunnel of glass and greenery that shimmered beneath Azur's night-dome. Water streamed gently down the crystalline walls, feeding the dense ferns and spiraling vines that climbed the pillars like living veins. The faint hum of energy beneath the floor resonated in Lawrence's chest as he walked beside Councilman Levy.

Levy held a slim clipboard in one hand, its surface glowing with faint blue light. He read as he walked, voice crisp and practiced.

"We've completed the evacuation," Levy said. "Everyone from that derelict vessel has been processed. Their belongings are being cataloged for redistribution."

Lawrence barely heard him. His gaze lingered on the suspended canopy above them — thousands of leaves swaying in the artificial breeze, illuminated by orbs of soft white light that drifted lazily through the air. For a city that floated on air and silence, Azur felt impossibly alive.

"You awake, Councilman?" Levy asked, his tone edged with impatience.

Lawrence's head snapped back toward him. "Don't badger me," he muttered, snatching the clipboard from his hands. The glow cast long shadows across his face as he scanned the manifest.

Levy folded his arms, watching. "Arjes is accounted for," he said. "He's been—"

"—confirmed dead," Lawrence interrupted. His voice was low, measured, but heavy with something darker. "I know. I was there."

For a moment, neither spoke. The distant sound of rushing water filled the silence between them — a quiet, eternal reminder that Azur's perfection never paused for grief.

"I watched him die," Lawrence said finally, his tone breaking just enough to betray what he'd tried to bury.

Levy's expression softened, but only slightly. "After all these years… he meets his end just before the Vesta finds its way home."

"They tried to use him," Lawrence said. "Turn him. They thought he could slip past our guard."

Levy shook his head. "He was past his prime. He must've known it. Men like him cling to glory until it crushes them."

Lawrence's jaw tightened. "He wasn't trying to reclaim anything. He was trying to protect what little was left."

Levy didn't answer. The path curved upward, and they walked in silence for several steps, their reflections gliding across the glass walls beside them.

Finally, Levy said, "I attended the ceremony tonight."

Lawrence's grip tightened on the clipboard. "You didn't have to."

"I didn't want to," Levy replied bluntly. "But protocol demands representation from the council. I stood there, watching them release lanterns into the air — hundreds of them — for a woman most of them barely knew." He gave a dry, humorless laugh. "You'd think she saved the world."

Lawrence stopped walking. The soft light caught in his eyes, turning them to molten amber. "She saved *mine*," he said quietly.

Levy turned, studying him for a moment. "You cared for her."

"She cared for everyone," Lawrence said. His voice was steady, but it carried a gravity that made the air between them feel heavier. "She believed people were still worth saving — even the ones who'd given up on themselves. That kind of faith..." He exhaled slowly. "It's rare."

Levy's tone remained clinical. "Faith doesn't keep the city running, Lawrence. Order does. Balance. She was a good woman, but sentiment like hers… it burns too bright. And when it burns out, it leaves nothing but ash."

Lawrence's gaze hardened. "You talk about her like she was a mistake."

Levy shrugged. "Perhaps she was. Or perhaps she simply belonged to a world that doesn't exist anymore."

The two men stood at the heart of the Terrarium, surrounded by the low hum of Azur's artificial paradise — a world untouched by the storms below. Beyond the dome, the city lights shimmered like constellations in motion.

Lawrence handed back the clipboard and turned away. "You're wrong," he said quietly. "She belonged to the world we're *supposed* to be building."

And with that, he walked on ahead, his footsteps echoing softly beneath the canopy — the sound of a man moving through paradise, still haunted by ghosts the city refused to remember.

Unraveling

Gates woke with a sharp gasp, the breath catching in his throat.

For a long, unanchored moment, he didn't know where he was — only that the light above him flickered in uneven pulses, and the world smelled faintly of antiseptic, ozone, and polished steel. Rows of beds surrounded him, filled with broken men and women — Renegades, their faces pale and still beneath thin medical sheets.

Every breath burned. Every sound felt distant.

He tried to move, but something held him. A thick plastic restraint looped around his wrist, binding him to the bedrail.

He tugged once. Then harder. No give.

Pain shot through his arm, sharp and merciless. He winced, the effort sending a cold sweat across his forehead. Somewhere nearby, a monitor beeped once, flatlined, and fell silent again.

Then he saw it — one bed near the far wall. Empty. The sheets hung half off, gathered on the

floor like shed skin. Someone had been there…
and left in a hurry.

The sight twisted something in his chest.

He looked back at his own wrist and exhaled
through his teeth. There was only one way out.

With a low growl, he turned his hand sharply
and popped his thumb out of its joint with a wet,
sickening crack. His vision flashed white. The
pain was instant, feral. But the restraint slackened.

He forced his injured hand through the plastic
loop, scraping skin and tearing the edge of his
palm open as he pulled free. When the tie snapped
back against the rail, he almost didn't notice — he
was already gripping his hand, panting through
his teeth.

"Come on," he muttered.

He braced his thumb against the edge of the
metal bedframe and pushed. The bone slid back
into place with another crack. His vision swam,
but the joint held.

He sat there for a few seconds, breathing
through the pain, sweat rolling down his temple.
Then he stood.

The floor was cold under his bare feet, the light
dim and humming overhead. He moved between
the rows of unconscious Renegades, their chests
rising and falling in shallow rhythm. None of
them stirred.

Only the empty bed seemed to watch him leave.

He slipped into the corridor. The air beyond was cool and perfumed faintly with lavender — Azur's strange blend of serenity and control. The hall stretched in gleaming glass and silver, his reflection warping in the curved surfaces as he moved.

He didn't know where he was going. Only that something was waiting for him out there — something that had been taken.

* * *

He ran.

The corridors of Azur twisted and gleamed like the veins of some living cathedral. Light pulsed faintly through the translucent walls, reacting to motion. He passed through sections of white marble, silver arches, and long panes of glass that revealed the city below — towers of gold and mist, the clouds painted by drifting lanterns.

People turned as he passed. Workers, engineers, couriers — all startled by the sight of a man in torn hospital scrubs sprinting through the royal corridors. None of them tried to stop him. They just moved aside, whispers trailing in his wake.

Gates didn't look back. His pulse thundered in his ears, echoing against the marble floors.

He turned a corner — and froze.

Kara stood at the far end of the hall, the soft blue light of the corridor glinting off her eyes. She was older now, sharper, her uniform pressed and spotless — a citizen of Azur, not the hardened Captain his people had terrorized.

When she saw him, she froze too. Her breath hitched.

"Help—" she started, but he moved faster.

He closed the distance in two strides and clamped a hand gently — but firmly — over her mouth.

"I'm not here to hurt you," he said, voice low, urgent. "I need your help."

Her eyes shimmered with tears. Fear radiated from her, but so did something else — memory. Recognition.

"Listen," Gates continued. "We can't let what happened before decide what happens now. Everything's changed. You know that."

Kara's breathing slowed, her trembling easing just enough for him to release her.

"Two boys," he said quietly. "They were left on your ship. One of them was hurt. Where is he?"

She didn't answer.

"Please." he said, more desperate now. "Is he

alive?"

Her eyes welled. The silence that followed told him everything he didn't want to hear.

The strength left his legs. He dropped to his knees, the sound of his breath breaking against the marble floor. His hands covered his face, but it did nothing to hide the grief that ripped through him.

Kara took one slow step back, her own face pale and trembling. Then another. She turned — and fled down the corridor, leaving him alone in the soft hum of the lights.

For a long time, Gates didn't move.

The silence pressed in on him like the weight of the sky above. Somewhere outside, the city hummed with life — but none of it reached him. None of it mattered.

* * *

When Gates finally stood, he did so without hesitation. The ache in his chest hadn't dulled, but something in him had solidified — a grim, cold purpose.

He found his way to the armory.

It was immaculate — every weapon, every tool,

arranged with surgical precision along the silver walls. Rifles gleamed under white light, plasma coils pulsed faintly behind glass cases. It wasn't just an arsenal; it was a museum of control.

But it was the far corner that caught his eye — a rack of parachutes, lined neatly beside the supply crates.

He ran his hand over the straps, his reflection staring back at him in the polished surface. Beyond the viewing window, the horizon stretched vast and dark, the lower clouds glimmering with the faint light of Azur's engines.

He took a long, steadying breath.

Below, the world waited — wild, unknown, unforgiving. But it was the only place that still held truth.

He turned from the window and looked down at the hatch built into the floor, its engraved letters glowing faintly in the low light.

DEPLOY HATCH.

The decision came without thought.

He crouched, resting a hand on the metal surface, feeling the faint hum of energy pulsing beneath it — the heartbeat of the city itself.

He wanted to leave more than ever.

Renegade Revolution

T alon ran.

Bare feet whispered against the polished floors of Azur's corridors, the rhythm of his steps swallowed by the city's soft mechanical hum. Pale light spilled through the high archways and glass-veined walls, casting rippling patterns across his small frame as he darted through the endless passages.

Behind him, the hospital wing was silent — rows of motionless bodies under sterile lights, the smell of medicine thick in the air. He'd slipped from his bed without a sound. The bed beside his had been empty, its blankets tangled and fallen to the floor. Something about that emptiness had felt wrong. So he'd followed the sound that called to him — faint, rhythmic, like the pulse of a heart buried deep within the city.

The further he went, the quieter Azur became. The polished walls turned colder, the air heavier. Blue light pulsed in the seams of the floor like veins of frozen lightning. Far below, turbines churned — a deep, living heartbeat that carried through the soles of his feet.

He turned a corner and stopped.

Ahead, the corridor narrowed to a single reinforced door under a flickering lantern. The golden letters etched into its surface caught the light: **BRIG.**

Talon hesitated. Then he reached into the folds of his hospital tunic and pulled something out — a small, silver access card, smooth and gleaming. He held it up in the dim glow, eyes tracing the insignia carved into its edge. It wasn't his. It had hung from a guard's belt, flashing in the corridor light when no one was looking.

He pressed it to the scanner beside the door. The lock clicked open with a soft hiss.

Inside, the brig was quiet — not the silence of emptiness, but of something contained, restrained. The air smelled faintly of water and oil. A faint ripple of condensation ran down the walls, catching the flicker of the lights above.

At the far end, a man stood at a narrow sink. He splashed water over his face, broad shoulders tense beneath his plain uniform. When he looked up, the reflection in the steel mirror caught a small figure standing by the open door.

Gunny War turned slowly. His eyes met Talon's

— a boy no taller than his chest, barefoot and breathing softly, the access card still dangling from his hand.

For a long, weighted moment, neither spoke.

Then Gunny smiled. It wasn't a cruel smile or even a warm one — just quiet, knowing, as if he understood far more than he should have.

"Well done," he said gently.

Talon said nothing. His fingers tightened around the card.

Gunny studied him for another breath, then nodded faintly, as though the boy had passed some unspoken test.

"Yeah," he murmured. "Real well done."

* * *

The locking mechanisms on the cells sighed as if remembering duty. Talon lingered by the doorway, fingers curled around the stolen access card, eyes wide as the far corner of the room filled with the hard angles of armored figures.

Azur troopers moved like a single animal down the corridor — disciplined, efficient, sabers clipped at their sides, helmets low against the dim light. Two of them paused at the far cell where a blanket lay abandoned on the floor. One peered in and barked, "Where is he?"

The question still hung when a hand like a shadow struck out from the darkness.

Gunny War stepped from the gloom as though he had always been part of it. He was all lean, coiled muscle and scarred intent. He moved with the quiet certainty of a man who had practiced violence until it became choreography. With an angular snap of his arm he knocked a trooper to the ground before the other could finish his alert. The saber came up in a flash; Gunny danced past it, palms open, catching the wrist and twisting. The trooper's weapon clattered away across the grated floor.

More troopers surged into the cell block, and the space filled with the metallic music of combat — the harsh bite of steel on steel, the thud of bodies, the grunt of exertion. Gunny War was everywhere at once: a shoulder into ribs, a sweep of his heel, a palm that pressed against a throat until the man beneath him lost hands and words.

"Renegades!" he barked after the first few fell quiet. The word rose and struck the men and boys inside the cells like a bell. It carried an accusation and an invitation all at once.

A dozen Emancipated figures answered. They had been dragged to Azur's wards as broken things — too young to be soldiers, too sharp to be children.

Gunny's voice cut above the chaos. "They'll try to crush you. They'll exploit your innocence, your hunger." He lifted a trooper's saber and held it aloft with the gravity of a standard. "Withstand their resistance — and stand. STEP!"

He moved down the line and worked the locks with a practiced hand, metal keys finding tumblers as if it had always been his job. The cells bled open and the Renegades poured into the corridor: small, lithe bodies springing as if from coiled springs, faces set and raw with the shock of sudden air.

"Embrace your new home!" Gunny shouted. His command was part promise, part provocation; he knew the sound would carry, the sound of a new order being born in the belly of Azur.

They spilled into the stone halls like a dark tide. Torches of emergency lighting strobed in their wake. Talon watched them pass — a child between worlds — clutching his access card as though it were talisman and proof.

Beyond the brig, the city's corridors were already filling with alarm. Gunny War led the Renegades down into the arterial corridors, boots thudding on polished stone. He issued orders with the confidence of a commander who trusted no one but the men at his back.

"C-Team, gather the residents," he told a wiry boy who had been given a name like a title. "Secure them in cells. Locate any communication devices. Destroy them."

Renegades fanned out, disciplined by necessity if not by training. Where they met troopers the collisions were sudden and brutal — disarming flicks, low sweeps, improvised tactics that turned weight and speed into leverage. Gunny rammed a trooper into a bulkhead, grabbed at his throat until the man coughed up his breath and his saber slid sliding from his hand.

"Where's your armory?" Gunny demanded as he wrenched a radio from a fallen guard, voice a rasp edged with triumph. Around him the Renegades tore into storerooms, overturning racks of reserve gear and stacking food packets into rough, uneven piles. They set small charges against comm panels, plastic fizzing and popping as wires snapped. The quiet, ordered world of Azur frayed at the edges and then split open.

The corridor filled with a new noise — not the steady hum of a city at work but the ragged chorus of uprising: shouts, the clatter of boots, the metallic ring of captured sabers. Gunny War moved through it like a surgeon through a wound, precise, merciless, and oddly protective. He didn't celebrate the damage; he made practical use of it.

As they pushed deeper, a Renegade found a locked supply vault and looked to Gunny with the almost childish light of a person told the truth behind a curtain. Gunny simply nodded. The door swung wide under a crowbar and the interior revealed racks of glinting rifles and sealed crates stamped with the royal insignia.

Gunny War's eyes swept the room. He saw the young faces, the hunger in their hands. He saw the empty beds in the hospital, the laundry on the floor where one small body had once lain.

He did not smile. He bared his teeth in something like a promise. "We take what we need," he said. "We go home on our terms."

Behind the rising din, for a breath, the floating city felt like a vessel tilting toward a storm — elegant and impossible, and suddenly very mortal.

Gunny War entered the armory like a man walking into memory. The door hissed shut behind him, sealing away the chaos of the uprising. The room was pristine—walls lined with racks of weaponry, every blade and rifle gleaming under the soft blue lights that hummed overhead. The air smelled faintly of oil and metal polish, the scent of discipline and readiness.

He moved through the aisles with slow, deliberate steps, his hand trailing across the edges of polished steel and chromed barrels. His boots clicked softly against the marble floor, echoing faintly in the silence that followed destruction.

At the far end of the chamber, a reinforced chest sat locked to the floor. Gunny crouched before it, running his fingers along the etched insignia of Azur's military crest — a reminder of the city that had taken so much and given so little.

"Still guarding your toys," he muttered.

The lock gave way beneath his code key and the chest opened with a muted hiss. Inside lay an arsenal that shimmered like treasure: rifles, sabers, compact explosives — and at the center, wrapped in dark cloth, his weapon.

The hook-sword.

Gunny lifted it reverently, the curved steel catching the light in a streak of silver-blue. The edge was flawless, its balance perfect even after years of neglect. It was a weapon that demanded respect — one that had ended rebellions, carved victories, and bled history into the soil of forgotten worlds.

He turned it in his hand, feeling its weight settle into his palm like something alive. His reflection shimmered along the blade's surface — older, harder, but unmistakably the same man who had once carried it into battle.

A proud, quiet smile tugged at the corner of his

mouth. "Welcome back, old friend."

He swung the blade once, a precise, controlled arc that sliced the air with a whisper. Then he sheathed it against his back, the motion practiced and instinctive.

Outside, the faint rumble of movement filtered through the floor — Renegades arming themselves, Azur's guards regrouping, the city trembling on the edge of open war.

Gunny War straightened, his expression turning cold and certain. He shut the chest, locked it again, and turned toward the door.

The uprising had begun. And for the first time in years, he felt whole.

Destiny

The brig shakes again. The walls quiver with the weight of distant explosions — rhythmic, deliberate, like the pulse of something breaking free. Smoke drifts faintly through the vents, carrying the scent of fire and chaos from the uprising beyond.

Ahmed sits on the edge of his cot, elbows on his knees, head in his hands. The alarms are meaningless now, just noise that blends with his heartbeat, relentless and hollow.

Alana moves quietly around the cell, her bare feet whispering across the cold metal floor. Her composure is calm, though her eyes betray the gravity of what she is about to say.

"He's going to tear this place apart," she murmurs, low and steady. "I can feel it."

Ahmed lifts his head, eyes dull. "It doesn't matter anymore. No one believed me from the start anyway."

Alana's gaze softens. "The *Legend of Sky City*

meant everything to you, didn't it? That dream… that hope. You fought for it."

Ahmed's lips twitch. "You mean everything to me," he says, voice breaking. "Dawn was—"

He stops, staring at the floor. "Dawn *meant* everything to me."

Alana steps closer, her voice urgent. "If he destroys this place, her sacrifice will have been for nothing."

He looks up. "He? Who are you talking about?"

She exhales, steadying herself. "Before I was imprisoned, Dawn saved us. She took me in, gave us refuge. We became a family. She pledged to protect us at any cost."

Her gaze hardens, the words heavy with memory. "Then he came — Gunny War. I was lost at sea when the Demeter Ark sank. I fell into the deep, dark water, alone and helpless. The currents tried to take me, and I almost didn't surface."

Ahmed's eyes widen.

"I remember gasping for air," she continues, voice trembling, "and then he was there. Gunny War pulled me from the ocean, dragged me aboard the Vulcan. He imprisoned me for hiding you from him — his own son."

Ahmed swallows hard. "My… father?"

Alana nods. "Gunnery Sergeant Warrinder Fasil. Gunny War. Your father."

Ahmed's world tilts. For a moment, he cannot breathe. "No. Why him?" he whispers. Then louder, almost shouting, "Why *him?*"

Alana steps closer, her expression soft but resolute. "I loved him once, but I couldn't bear to bring you into a world where you'd grow into the man he became. The war changed him. It made him cruel. Hungry for control. So I ran. I hid you. I thought I could keep you safe."

Ahmed presses his hands against his forehead. "He swore to find us, didn't he?"

Alana nods. "He vowed never to lose me again. And when he couldn't find me, he turned that vow into purpose. Into anger. Into violence."

Ahmed's lips part. "His destiny…"

"Destiny is what you make of it," Alana says firmly. "It doesn't choose you — you choose what to do with it. I believe I took you away from him for a reason."

Ahmed stares at the faint red glow flickering through the cell door. "I don't think I can fight my own father."

Alana places a hand on his shoulder. "Ahmed, you're not fighting your father. You're fighting the man he became. Destiny didn't lead you to find Sky City. It was preparing you — to *save* it."

Outside, the echoes of gunfire draw closer — each burst a heartbeat of the uprising unfolding

336

beyond the walls.

Ahmed lifts his head, the weight of blood and prophecy heavy in his eyes. The war outside rages on, but inside that cell, the true battle — the one that will decide the fate of both father and son — has just begun.

Oh Captain, No Captain?

The doors of the Secretariat groaned under the weight of unseen forces, their hinges straining as if they might give way at any moment. Outside, the sounds of chaos pulsed through the halls — the echo of running footsteps, shouts, the clash of metal on metal.

Inside, Sovereign Kit peered cautiously from behind a curtain, her expression tight. "Why haven't reinforcements arrived?" she asked, her voice barely more than a whisper.

Lawrence paced the room, the saber gripped so tightly in his hands that his knuckles whitened. His eyes darted to every shadow, every ornate detail of the lavish chamber, as if danger could spring from the gilded walls themselves.

"My guess," he muttered, voice low and tense, "they've probably cut off all communication with the other districts."

From the other side of the room, a sharp metallic scrape cut through the air. Lord Leveth strained against one of the heavy doors, only to freeze as a hook-sword slid dangerously close to his throat.

Gunny War stepped into the room, calm, precise, his presence a storm waiting to be unleashed. "Are you the Captain?" he asked, his voice low and controlled.

The Azur Troopers formed a protective circle, blades raised, ready to strike. Gunny War did not flinch. "Go ahead," he said. "Make a move and Captain loses his head."

Lord Leveth swallowed, eyes flicking nervously to the deadly edge near his neck. "There are no Captains here," he said, his voice tight.

"Looks like you could use one," Gunny War replied, his gaze never leaving Leveth.

The tension crackled like a live wire. Behind them, the doors shuddered as the rest of the Renegades flooded into the room, faces hard, eyes blazing with determination. They moved with a singular purpose, confronting the Azur Troopers who braced to defend their liege.

Gunny War's voice cut through the commotion. "Call your dogs back, or I'll pin your head to the wall."

Lord Leveth exhaled slowly, the weight of the decision pressing down. "Do it," he said, and reluctantly, the Azur Troopers lowered their weapons, forming uneasy, tense lines along the walls.

Lawrence watched the scene unfold, disbelief flickering across his face. "A fake Captain leading a kingdom," he muttered under his breath.

Gunny War turned, eyes locking on Lawrence. "You talk way too much," he said, his tone a lethal promise. He pushed Leveth toward another Renegade and pivoted, readying for the next move.

Lawrence's pride flared, and he lunged, striking at Gunny War. But the attack was deflected with fluid precision, and before he could recover, Gunny War shoved him into the wall with such force that the impact reverberated through the chamber.

Balthazar used the distraction to slip away into the shadows, leaving Lawrence alone in the storm of violence. Gunny War did not pause. Each movement was measured, devastating — a calculated dance of power and wrath. Lawrence retaliated, fists and saber swinging, but each attack met an immovable force, each counter a lesson in futility.

With a final, brutal maneuver, Gunny War seized Lawrence and hurled him across a massive table. The wood splintered under the impact. Lawrence struggled to rise, blood streaking his face, vision blurred, every breath a labor.

Gunny War loomed over him, towering, unyielding. The hook-sword dropped from his hand as he gripped Lawrence, squeezing with bone-crushing strength. Pain exploded in Lawrence's chest and lungs, every inhale ragged, every heartbeat a hammering drum.

Lawrence clawed at Gunny War's arms, trying to twist free, but the grip only tightened. His muscles burned, his vision narrowed, and the world seemed to tilt around him. The echoes of the Renegade uprising — shouts, steel clashing, alarms ringing — faded into a distant, muffled roar.

Every nerve in Lawrence's body screamed. His limbs trembled uncontrollably. The ornate walls of the Secretariat blurred as darkness clawed at the edges of his vision.

And then, with a final, suffocating squeeze, the pain became absolute. Lawrence's teeth ground against the pressure, his chest heaving impossibly, every second stretching into agony. He couldn't think. He couldn't move. Only suffering remained, sharp and unrelenting, as if the very air around him conspired to crush him.

Reinforcements

Ahmed moved through the dimly lit corridor of Azur, shadows clinging to his frame like a second skin. The soft hum of the city's energy pulsed beneath the floors and walls, a constant reminder that they were trapped within a living, breathing fortress. His eyes tracked the Renegades as they maneuvered through the halls, their movements cautious but desperate, each one armed with weapons scavenged or taken from the Azur Troopers. Jaxon led the small group, swinging a saber with reckless confidence, his youthful energy a stark contrast to the lethal precision in his hands.

Ahmed pressed a hand against the smooth wall, motioning for Alana to stay hidden in the shadows. He inhaled, the scent of ozone and polished metal filling his nostrils, and stepped forward. The corridor opened before him, and the Renegades' heads snapped up, alert.

"Where's Gunny War?" Ahmed demanded, his

voice sharp, unwavering, cutting through the low hum and distant clatter.

Jaxon's lips curled into a cocky smirk. "Well, if it isn't Mr. Peter Pan himself."

"This isn't a game," Ahmed said, fists tightening until his knuckles ached. "We need to stop him."

"You? You're not one of us anymore," Jaxon shot back, the edge of scorn in his voice.

Ahmed's jaw clenched, and the tension coiled in his chest like a spring. "Gunny War left Dover. You don't think he'll leave you too?"

Jaxon lunged with a feral shout, the saber swinging in a wide arc. Ahmed pivoted on his heel, sidestepping with practiced precision, and grabbed the boy's arm, twisting and flipping him onto the cold metal floor. The corridor echoed with the sharp clangs of metal as they struggled, their movements a chaotic dance of strikes and blocks.

Jaxon kicked, aiming low, but Ahmed caught the leg, twisting, and with a sharp grunt, sent the boy sprawling into the wall. The other Renegades hesitated, their eyes flicking between Ahmed and Jaxon, uncertainty in their posture.

Ahmed pressed forward, his voice low but dangerous. "Where is he?"

One of the younger Renegades, barely more than a child, spoke up, voice trembling. "Last we heard… he's got the leaders hostage."

Ahmed's gaze hardened, the weight of responsibility pressing against his shoulders. "If he destroys this place, we're all finished," he said, his tone carrying the gravity of inevitability.

The Renegades exchanged worried looks. "He ordered us to disable the tower in the ship dock," another added. "If you can get it back online, reinforcements can stop him."

Ahmed's chest rose and fell with rapid breaths. He nodded once, sharply. "Destiny is a choice," he said, voice resolute. "We need to make things right."

He pivoted, scanning the corridor for any movement, for any sign that Gunny War's shadow lurked nearby. A stray panel slid open, a faint glow from the dock below spilling upward. Ahmed's pulse quickened. The Renegades shifted behind him, a tense line of silent, waiting figures.

He moved again, faster this time, weaving through the corridors, flipping tables and knocking aside obstacles with precise strikes when a Renegade panicked and tried to block him. The corridor had become a maze of shadow and metal, each turn threatening a new ambush, but Ahmed's focus never wavered. Every heartbeat, every decision, sharpened the urgency in the air.

Finally, he paused at a junction, the faint hum of

the tower below growing louder with each passing second. He turned to the Renegades behind him, meeting their hesitant gazes. "We move together. One chance, one shot."

And then, as the metallic echo of distant footsteps vibrated through the floors above, Ahmed led the way toward the dock, every step a battle between fear and determination, every breath carrying the weight of the city—and the lives at stake.

By the time Ahmed reached the dock, the Renegades had fanned out with careful precision, their movements deliberate as they inspected the satellite panels. Every footstep echoed faintly across the polished metal floor, punctuated by the soft hum of the city's power coursing through the infrastructure. Ahmed's eyes swept over the group, noting who guarded the controls and who was poised to react at a moment's notice.

A sharp voice broke the tense silence. "Peter Pan!" one of the older teens shouted, charging forward with a saber raised high.

Ahmed reacted instantly, sidestepping and parrying with fluid, controlled motions. The clang of metal rang through the hangar as sparks danced along the edges of their weapons. Two more Renegades lunged at him simultaneously. He tripped one with a swift kick and sent the other sprawling with a sharp, calculated strike. Another leapt toward him in a chokehold; Ahmed twisted under the boy, flipped him over, and disarmed him, the motion precise and unhesitating. Each movement was a rhythm, a pulse of calculated force.

Finally, he reached the console beneath the towering satellite. The mechanisms hummed beneath his fingers as he yanked a lever, the machine roaring to life with a sudden, mechanical force. The satellite began to spin, its lights flaring across the dock in urgent, blinding arcs. He snatched the intercom, voice cracking with tension and command.

"Um, hello? Can someone send help?"

"This is district three. Repeat your last transmission," came the calm, clipped response.

"There are um, pirates and—stuff. Like, right now!" Ahmed shouted, the desperation clear in his voice.

"I repeat—"

"Ugh!" He barely had time to curse before a Renegade lunged from behind, seizing him and throwing him hard to the ground. The impact jarred his shoulder, and he gritted his teeth against the pain, rolling to his feet in a single, fluid motion.

The Renegades converged, forming a tense

circle around him, poised to strike. But a new sound cut through the tension—the deep, rhythmic thrum of jumpers touching down on the dock. The Renegades froze, uncertainty flashing across their faces, and then bolted in every direction, scattering like startled birds.

From above, the hangar doors swung open with a metallic roar, and a wave of Azur Troopers poured in, their movements precise and disciplined, forming lines that cut through the chaos with methodical efficiency. The dock, once dominated by scattered panic, now hummed with the organized force of the city's defenders.

Ahmed pressed himself against the shadows, chest heaving, as the glowing satellite tower continued its relentless spin above him. Its lights cast sharp beams across the floor, illuminating the Renegades who now surged forward, emboldened by the shift in momentum.

A triumphant smile tugged at Ahmed's lips, fleeting but fierce. For a brief, suspended moment amid the noise, the clanging sabers, and the echoing footsteps, he allowed himself to believe that victory was within reach, that the uprising— the culmination of every risk and every desperate plan—might finally succeed.

Yet even as the Renegades moved like a single, unstoppable force, a lingering tension remained

in the air, a reminder that the fight for Azur was
far from over.

Mutiny

Lawrence crashed through the table with a violent thud, splintered wood splintering beneath him, shards embedding in the floor. His face was swollen and streaked with blood, copper tang coating his lips, a dull ache radiating through his skull.

Gunny War loomed over him, eyes cold, the hook-sword clattering to the floor as he seized Lawrence with unyielding strength. With a sharp, brutal motion, he hoisted him into a blood choke, squeezing until Lawrence's lungs screamed for air. Lawrence's fists hammered against Gunny War's forearms, but it was like punching iron. His knees buckled under the pressure, his body trembling violently.

Before he could recover, Gunny War slammed him against the wall, the impact rattling his teeth and leaving a stinging line of pain across his back. Lawrence slumped, dazed, but Gunny War's grip never relented. He twisted Lawrence sideways, slamming him into the corner of a table, sending a splintered leg skittering across the floor.

Lawrence clawed at the walls, at anything to free himself, coughing and choking as bruises blossomed across his torso. A grim, almost predatory smile tugged at Gunny War's lips as he tightened his hold, biceps bulging under the strain, relishing every second of dominance.

A sudden glimmer through the tall viewing window snapped Gunny War's focus. The shadows of jumpers streaked across the night sky, moving in precise formation, impossible to ignore. Gunny War's grip faltered for a heartbeat, calculating. Reinforcements. They were coming.

Seizing the opportunity, Lawrence gasped and twisted, driving his elbow into Gunny War's ribs. Gunny War staggered, releasing just enough to let Lawrence crumple to the floor, coughing, wheezing, struggling to draw in precious air. But the reprieve was temporary. Gunny War lunged, knees driving into Lawrence's side, fists hammering his back, each blow a reminder of his unrelenting power. Lawrence gritted his teeth, blood mixing with sweat, rising shakily to his feet again and again, refusing to yield entirely.

Finally, Gunny War drew back, his gaze locking on the approaching armada, awe and calculation flickering in his eyes. Lawrence's body sagged, bruised and battered, every breath a ragged effort. He clutched his ribs, staggering, knowing he had survived—but only barely. Outside, the jumpers streaked through the sky, a looming, unstoppable force, and Gunny War's attention was drawn fully to the threat.

Lawrence's eyes met Gunny War's one last time. He was alive—but the cost had been immense, and the standoff was far from over.

A surge of Renegades burst into the Secretariat, their footsteps echoing against the polished floors as the room erupted into chaos. Gunny War's expression darkened the instant they appeared, his eyes narrowing.

"Why aren't you at the dock?" he barked. "We've got incoming!"

One of the older children, barely more than a teen but carrying the weight of urgency in his stance, stepped forward. "We need your strength out there. We can't hold them off alone."

Gunny's jaw clenched. "My place is here."

The Renegade glanced at his companions, uncertainty flickering across his face. "We'll be forced to surrender if you're not with us."

Gunny's voice dropped low, hard as stone. "Renegades don't surrender."

A brief silence followed. Then the young boy,

gathering courage from somewhere deep within, spoke again. "They also don't abandon their own."

Gunny's teeth gritted in anger. "Do as I say and get out there!"

The boy hesitated, the saber trembling in his grip, before finally dropping it to the floor. One by one, the other Renegades followed suit, laying down their weapons. Gunny War's chest heaved as he watched them, a mix of disbelief and anguish flashing across his face.

Somewhere down the corridors, the disciplined march of Azur Troopers filled the air, their movements precise and unyielding as they subdued the disarmed Renegades in coordinated sweeps.

Gunny War took a step back, his gaze sweeping over the fallen children, his face shadowed with frustration. "Gutless," he muttered, the word barely audible above the din. Then, with controlled resolve, he retreated from the room, disappearing into the deeper corridors of Azur.

Lawrence struggled to his feet, bloodied and bruised, just as Lord Leveth barked across the room. "Shut the dock down! Don't let him get in there!"

The heavy doors of the dock began to slide closed with a grinding thud. But Gunny War moved with a predator's grace, slipping through the narrowing gap with barely a whisper of movement. With a final resounding latch, the doors sealed behind him, leaving him alone inside the dock with the hum of machinery and the tension of impending confrontation.

Gunny War's eyes swept across the hangar, taking in the jumble of jumpers, Renegades, and spinning satellite panels. Every sense was sharpened, every nerve on edge. And then he saw him—Ahmed, crouched in the shadows, watching, waiting, calculating.

Time slowed. The distant chaos of the uprising faded into a tense, heartbeat-filled silence. Two forces, father and son, poised on opposite sides of the dock, each aware that the next moment could decide everything.

Gunny War raised his hook-sword, a single word slicing through the air, thick with warning and command.

Ahmed's fists clenched, his breath shallow. His eyes never left Gunny War's. The dock seemed impossibly wide, yet impossibly small, each of them the center of the storm.

And in that suspended moment, the world held its breath—waiting to see which of them would move first.

The Edge of the World

Ahmed stood across from Gunny War, the dock lit by flickering blue sirens and the pulse of spinning satellite light. The clang of distant alarms echoed through the chamber, the tension between them almost unbearable. Gunny War's hook-sword gleamed at his side, its curved edge catching the light like a predator's smile.

"Did you forget who taught you how to fight?" Gunny War taunted, voice low, dangerous.

Ahmed's breath came hard through gritted teeth. "You killed her."

Gunny War tilted his head, unflinching. "Casualties of War."

The words hit Ahmed like a blade to the chest. His grip tightened around his saber until his knuckles whitened. "You abandoned me!"

Gunny's expression hardened—then, unexpectedly, he lowered his weapon slightly, studying Ahmed with quiet scorn. "Well, look at that," he murmured. "You look just like your mother."

A scream ripped from Ahmed's throat as he lunged, sabers colliding with a flash of sparks. The clash of steel rang through the dock—furious, relentless. Ahmed's strikes came fast, desperate, his anger giving him speed but no precision. Gunny War met each blow with ease, parrying, twisting, then driving his boot hard into Ahmed's chest.

"Destiny chose you as my heir," Gunny snarled, forcing Ahmed back toward the edge of the dock, "but you were never ready!"

Ahmed roared, charging again. His blade connected, slicing across Gunny's shoulder—a rare hit that drew blood. Gunny answered with a brutal counter, grabbing Ahmed by the arm and hurling him across the deck. Ahmed slid dangerously close to the drop-off, his saber skittering out of reach.

Gunny War stalked forward, his breath heavy, pain flickering behind his fury. He hooked Ahmed's fallen blade with his own, flinging it over the edge, then drove a powerful kick that sent Ahmed sprawling near the brink. The abyss below yawned wide and dark.

Before Gunny could strike again, a figure stepped between them—Alana. Her hand pressed firmly against Gunny's chest.

"Stop this, please," she pleaded, voice trembling.

"Get out of my way, wretch!" Gunny roared, his face twisted with rage.

"You betrayed me!" he spat. "Took him, and turned him against my destiny!"

"I made a choice," Alana said softly. "Not for us… but for him."

Her words struck something deep within him. For a moment, Gunny War's expression faltered—his fury cracking, revealing something almost human beneath.

Alana stepped closer, eyes glistening. "But now, for as long as I'm here, I won't stop until we figure this out. Together."

Gunny War's gaze softened. His hand lowered slightly. "You're right," he murmured.

Alana managed a faint, hopeful smile—

—and then Gunny War's hand shot out, seizing her by the throat.

Her gasp choked in the air as he lifted her effortlessly, hoisting her over the edge of the dock. Her boots scraped against metal, one shoe slipping free and tumbling into the vast blue abyss below.

"Mom!" Ahmed shouted, horror twisting through him. He lunged, saber flashing, slashing Gunny War across the face.

Gunny staggered back with a roar, clutching his face as blood poured between his fingers, one eye now a mangled ruin. Alana dangled helplessly over the edge, her fingers slipping.

Ahmed threw himself forward, reaching out. "Hang on!"

Gunny War staggered behind him, half-blind, snarling in pain, dropping his trusty hooksword to the floor. Ahmed ignored him, stretching further, his voice cracking. "Take my hand!"

Alana's eyes filled with tears. "No, you'll fall too!"

"Mom, please!" Ahmed cried.

For a heartbeat, the world seemed to stop. The alarms, the wind, the flickering lights—all fell away. Just a mother and son at the edge of the world.

"You can't," she whispered. "Run!"

"Yes, I can!" Ahmed yelled, gripping her hand.

Alana hesitated—then grabbed him. The strain sent Ahmed sliding forward across the deck, boots scraping, muscles burning as he fought to hold her weight.

Then—a sudden pull at his leg.

A hook wrapped around his ankle. Gates stood at the ledge, the hook-sword anchored to a jumper's landing strut, veins bulging with effort.

"Let's go! Pull!" Gates shouted.

Ahmed gritted his teeth, hauling Alana up inch by inch. Gates pulled Ahmed, the hook creaking under the strain, their muscles locked in desperate synchrony. Finally, with one last surge, Alana was back on solid ground, collapsing against Ahmed, gasping for breath.

Ahmed turned to Gates, their eyes meeting with shared relief and disbelief.

Then Gunny War moved.

Without warning, he drove his boot into Gates's chest—hard.

"GATES!" Ahmed screamed.

Gates's body sailed off the platform, swallowed by the open sky.

For the Love a Chase

The dock shuddered as the heavy door exploded inward, torn from its hinges by the sheer force of Azur Troopers storming through. Smoke and debris billowed into the air, the sharp scent of metal and fuel thick in the chaos.

Through the haze, a jumper ignited—its engines roaring to life. The sleek craft blasted from the hangar with a deafening boom, streaking toward the open sky before the troopers could even take aim.

"Shoot it down!" one of the troopers shouted, raising his weapon.

"No!" Alana cried out, her voice raw, desperate. She stumbled forward, shoving through the line of armored soldiers. "Ahmed's inside!"

The troopers hesitated, weapons trembling in their grips as the jumper vanished into the light beyond the hangar bay doors. The air hummed with the fading echo of its engines—a sound that carried both relief and dread.

Alana's knees nearly gave beneath her as she clutched the railing, eyes locked on the distant sky where the jumper had disappeared.

* * *

Inside the jumper, the cabin rattled with the roar of engines and the low hum of turbulence cutting through the clouds. Gunny War sat hunched near the cockpit wall, hastily tearing a sleeve from his tattered blouse. Each movement was sharp, deliberate—more survival than care. Blood seeped through the makeshift bandage as he pressed the torn fabric against the ruined socket of his eye.

Across the narrow cabin, Ahmed watched him in silence. His knuckles whitened around the hilt of his saber, breath steady but burning with fury. The dim emergency lights flickered across his face, carving deep shadows beneath his eyes.

Gunny War adjusted the cloth and grunted, not looking up. "You're just like her," he muttered. "Always too stubborn to stay down."

Ahmed's rage boiled over. He lunged forward, springing off the bulkhead and vaulting clean over Gunny's head. The saber caught a glint of crimson light as he swung midair, aiming for the exposed flank.

Gunny moved with soldier's reflex—fast, brutal. He spun on his heel and slammed the flat of his hook-sword into Ahmed's side, sending him crashing into the metal wall. The blow reverberated through the cramped space, rattling loose panels.

Ahmed hit the floor hard but didn't stay down. With a fierce cry, he pushed off the deck and drove the tip of his saber into Gunny's boot. The steel pierced through leather and flesh.

Gunny snarled—a guttural sound torn between pain and fury—as he stumbled back, clutching at the wall for balance. The jumper rocked violently, the controls whining as turbulence rattled the cabin around them.

Neither man moved for a heartbeat, their heavy breaths filling the space. Then Gunny War raised his head slowly, the crimson-stained cloth pressed against his eye, and bared his teeth in something between a snarl and a smile.

"You've got fight in you, boy," he rasped. "Let's see how far it gets you."

The jumper tore through the night sky, shuddering with each gust of wind that rattled its hull. Inside, the air was thick with sweat, smoke, and the violent chaos of a father and son locked in desperate struggle.

Ahmed lunged again, his small hands gripping the saber with every ounce of fury his body could summon. Gunny War met the strike with his hook-sword, the clash of steel ringing through the cabin like a bell of judgment. Sparks flared and died against the blood-streaked walls.

Gunny shoved the boy back, his boot grinding against the deck, blood still seeping through the torn cloth that covered his ruined eye. "You think this ends with me, boy?" he growled, voice rough with exhaustion. "You've got no idea what's coming."

Ahmed's response came through clenched teeth, breath trembling with rage and grief. "You destroyed everything that mattered!"

Gunny swung low. Ahmed ducked, the blade cutting a shallow line across his shoulder before embedding in the wall. The jumper lurched violently—alarms shrieked from the cockpit, and the comms unit crackled to life overhead.

"—Alpha Hemi, get ready to engage!" a voice barked through the static.

Gunny froze for half a breath, head turning toward the sound. Outside the narrow viewport, streaks of light carved through the dark horizon— shadows of incoming jumpers.

Then another voice came, clipped and cold:

"Fire when ready."

The world erupted.

A blinding flash tore across the sky, followed by the thunderous roar of impact. The jumper jolted sideways as an energy blast ripped through its left wing. The cabin exploded into chaos—metal screamed, panels burst loose, and weight vanished.

Ahmed and Gunny were thrown from their footing, crashing into one another midair. Fire and smoke filled the confined space. They struck the ceiling, then the floor, grappling wildly as the ship spun out of control.

Gunny pinned Ahmed against the bulkhead, his weapon hooked against the boy's throat. "This is what survival costs," he hissed, his one good eye burning.

Ahmed gasped for breath, tears cutting through the soot on his face. "Then maybe it's time you paid it," he spat, driving his knee hard into Gunny's stomach.

Gunny reeled back just as the jumper pitched forward nose-first. Both were hurled into the cockpit, crashing through shattered glass and twisted metal. The comms crackled again between bursts of static:

"Target hit! Confirming impact—he's going down!"

The windshield filled with light. The Vulcan Ark loomed ahead—massive, cold, and merciless.

Gunny War clawed for the controls, his wounded hand slick with blood. Ahmed gripped the railing beside him, his knuckles white as fire and wind roared through the ruptured hull.

For a single suspended heartbeat, everything stilled—the Ark's colossal frame filled the view, and Gunny's eye locked with Ahmed's. There was no hate left, only the weight of everything they had lost.

Then came the crash.

The jumper struck the side of the Vulcan Ark with catastrophic force, bursting into a bloom of fire that lit the clouds like dawn. Metal shrieked. Glass shattered. And the world was swallowed in white flame.

"Gates" of Heaven

Earlier

Gates plummeted through the night, the world spinning in a blur of steel-gray clouds and the endless sweep of dark ocean below. The air howled past his ears, sharp and merciless, tugging at his limbs as gravity pulled him toward the deep. For an instant, panic surged — raw and primal — but it burned out as quickly as it came.

Then came the calm.

He spread his arms, surrendering to the fall. The wind tore at his jacket and roared through his hair, the sheer velocity numbing his senses. The world around him became nothing but cold air and motion — freedom in its purest, most violent form.

With a swift, practiced motion, Gates yanked the chute cord. The parachute burst open above him with a thunderous snap, jerking his body upward and slowing his descent to a steady glide. His breath came hard, ragged — a mixture of relief and awe.

Far below, the sea shimmered like liquid obsidian under the fractured light of the moons. But it wasn't the water that caught his eye — it was the massive shadow breaking through the mist ahead.

The Vulcan Ark.

Its surface stretched across the clouds like a continent of steel, its lights burning faintly through the smoke and debris. Gates drifted toward it, the faint hum of its engines vibrating through the air.

A grin crept across his face — not of safety, but of recognition.

He was close.

The chute swayed, the wind shifting as the Ark's pull grew stronger. He adjusted the straps, steadying himself as the titanic structure loomed beneath him.

For a heartbeat, everything went quiet — the kind of silence that sits right before impact, right before fate decides what comes next.

Then the wind surged again, carrying him forward into the dark.

War Ship

The wreckage of the Vulcan Ark burned from within like a dying star. Flames licked the steel corridors, their reflections dancing across the rising water that flooded through ruptured hulls. Smoke curled through the broken beams and twisted bulkheads, heavy and choking.

Ahmed emerged from the shadows, staggering into the flickering light. His face was smeared with blood and soot; every movement carried the weight of pain. He clutched his hand to his chest — one finger broken and swelling fast — but he pressed on through the haze.

A crack of light caught his eye. Amidst the rubble, the saber lay half-buried beneath debris. He reached for it, grimacing as the metal burned hot against his palm. The ship groaned around him, a deep, dying sound that echoed through the corridors like a wounded beast.

He pushed forward. The smoke thickened, and every step sent ripples through the shallow, rising flood that hissed and steamed across the floor.

At last, he found an opening — a jagged hole torn through the side of the hull. Ahmed crawled through it, dragging himself onto what remained of the upper deck.

Outside, the night was chaos.

The sea churned below, black and furious. The ship listed hard to one side, half-swallowed by the waves. Lightning flickered across the low clouds, casting the world in stuttering flashes of white.

Ahmed collapsed to his knees, breath trembling. He lifted his head toward the storm-swept sky — searching, praying for a sign of life.

That's when he heard it.

Bootsteps. Heavy, deliberate.

He turned.

Gunny War stood behind him, rising from the haze like a phantom — burned, bloodied, and unbroken. His coat hung in tatters, and his one good eye gleamed like molten iron.

Ahmed steadied himself, saber in hand.

"It's over," he said, his voice hoarse.

Gunny's lips curled into something between a smile and a snarl.

"I never wanted you," he said quietly. "Never. You were a disappointment to my legacy."

Ahmed's throat tightened. "Dawn wanted me," he shot back. "She loved me."

Gunny's eye darkened. "She owes you a thank you," he hissed. "I'll gladly send you to her myself."

Ahmed charged first — a blur of movement and fury. Gunny met him with raw power, striking him hard across the face. The blow sent Ahmed sprawling, blood bursting from his lip. But the boy rose again, eyes burning through the pain.

He lunged. Their blades collided with a sound like thunder — saber against hook-sword — each strike echoing through the dying ship. Sparks flashed. Steel clashed. The deck tilted beneath their feet as the ship's final breaths shook the air.

Gunny swung high. Ahmed ducked low, spinning with a burst of strength. The saber flashed once — clean, sharp, decisive.

Gunny froze.

For a long moment, he didn't move. Then he looked down, disbelief in his one good eye, as blood poured from where his hand had been.

A strangled cry escaped him as he fell to his knees. "You… took my ship," he gasped, clutching the mangled stump. "You took my men… you stole my destiny!"

Ahmed's chest heaved. His fingers loosened around the saber's hilt. He tossed it aside.

"As nature intended," he said softly.

Before either could move, the ship convulsed. A deafening explosion tore through the hull, fire bursting through the deck. Both were thrown backward, tumbling across the tilting metal.

The Vulcan Ark was dying. Fast.

Water surged across the deck, sweeping debris into the churning black sea. Ahmed struggled to his feet, climbing toward the taffrail as the entire vessel began to sink nose-first into the depths.

"Gunny!" he shouted over the roar of collapsing steel. "We have to go!"

Gunny didn't move. He knelt amid the chaos, one arm pressed to his side, the other gone. The water rose to his waist, but his eyes never left the burning horizon.

"I rise with it," he said, voice barely audible over the storm. "I fall with it."

Ahmed's throat tightened. He wanted to reach for him — to pull him away — but the next explosion ripped through the deck, forcing him to leap aside.

And then, through the veil of smoke, a light appeared in the distance.

A raft.

"Peter Pan!"

The voice cut through the wind. Gates stood at the helm of a small rescue craft, guiding it through the burning debris. His face was streaked with soot, eyes blazing with determination.

"Let's go!" he shouted, steering closer.

Ahmed hesitated, one last glance toward Gunny War — a man who had been father, teacher, and monster all at once. Gunny didn't look back. His gaze was fixed on the flames, on the ship that had carried his empire and his ruin.

Ahmed took a breath that trembled in his chest. "Goodbye," he whispered.

Then he jumped.

The water hit like ice, dragging the air from his lungs. He kicked hard, breaking the surface as debris rained down around him. Gates reached out from the raft, hauling him aboard with a grunt of effort.

The moment he landed, an eruption split the night. The Vulcan Ark exploded from within, a column of fire rising into the storm. The shockwave sent the raft lurching backward, waves slamming against its sides.

Ahmed sat motionless, drenched and trembling, staring at the inferno consuming the ship.

For the first time in what felt like forever, he let out a breath — not of fear, but release.

In the distance, the faint hum of engines grew louder. Several jumpers cut through the clouds, their lights shimmering like constellations reborn.

The sky burned. The sea roared.

And amid it all, the boy who had been forgotten drifted toward a future that finally belonged to him.

Epilogue

Trial

The morning light filtered through the grand windows of the Secretariat, casting long gold beams across the marbled floor. The air was still, solemn, carrying the faint hum of distant machinery and the murmurs of assembled guards.

At the dais, Sovereign Kit sat upon the high seat, his posture rigid yet weary. Beside him stood Lord Leveth, adorned in the regalia of judgment — a mantle of deep indigo embroidered with the sigil of Azur. Before them knelt the Renegades, bound in iron restraints, their heads bowed low. The scent of salt and oil clung to them — remnants of their rebellion and of the sea that nearly swallowed them whole.

Lord Leveth regarded them with a mixture of disdain and duty. His voice, when it came, filled the hall with cold precision.

"Proper punishment is imperative for rehabilitation," he declared. "For the preservation of order, the law must speak clearly and without hesitation."

Gates stood at the periphery, silent and uneasy. His gaze flicked between the young captives and the Sovereign, guilt and conflict etched into his features.

Leveth lifted a parchment from the podium and read aloud with finality:

"You are all hereby sentenced to twenty years in the Azur Correctional Sector, where your penance shall reflect the cost of your disobedience."

A murmur rippled through the hall — not of protest, but resignation. The Renegades bowed their heads as one, the weight of the decree settling over them like a shroud.

For a long moment, the only sound was the steady rhythm of the sea beyond the glass walls. Then, quietly, Lawrence rose from his seat among the council. His movements were measured, deliberate.

"My lord," he began, his tone firm yet respectful, "may I propose an alternative path — one that seeks not vengeance, but restoration?"

Lord Leveth turned sharply, his gaze piercing. "You contest this verdict?"

"I contest the notion of confinement," Lawrence replied. His voice carried across the chamber, calm but unwavering. "These are not strangers to Azur's soil. They are its sons and daughters. They have erred — gravely — but so too have they been shaped by the failures of those who led them."

Whispers rose from the gathered attendants, soft as shifting tides.

Leveth's brow furrowed. "These individuals bear responsibility for their deeds. What alternative do you propose?"

Lawrence clasped his hands behind his back. "The opportunity to make amends," he said. "Let them rebuild what they destroyed. Let them learn service, not through walls and chains, but through work — through purpose. Give them the chance to shape their own destinies, as we all must."

The hall fell silent.

Sovereign Kit studied Lawrence for a long moment, the light catching faintly on the circlet upon his brow. His expression softened — ever so slightly. Then his gaze turned to Leveth.

The old lord exhaled, the sound heavy and weary, yet not without thought. "You speak of mercy," Leveth said slowly. "A noble sentiment — though not one easily granted."

Lawrence bowed his head. "Mercy," he said, "is the truest measure of strength."

The Sovereign leaned forward, his voice cutting through the quiet.

"Then let it be so," he declared. "The Renegades shall labor under the Crown's watch — not as prisoners, but as servants to the restoration of Azur. Their sentence will not be chains, but duty."

The guards hesitated, exchanging glances. The Renegades lifted their heads, disbelief mingling with relief.

Lawrence turned to face them. His expression was solemn, but in his eyes burned something brighter — conviction, perhaps even hope.

Outside, the bells of the upper wards began to toll, signaling the new dawn. Through the wide glass of the Secretariat, the light grew stronger — golden and steady, cutting through the remnants of smoke still hanging over the city.

Azur lived on.

And though the scars of war remained, so too did the faint, stubborn promise of peace.

* * *

A New Destiny

Lawrence walked down the narrow corridor of the Azur brig, the metallic floors polished and meticulously maintained, the hum of ventilation systems filling the controlled silence. Rows of cells lined the hall, each identical, doors glinting with freshly oiled mechanisms. The prisoners were orderly, seated or standing within their confines, the weight of their chains stark but disciplined.

He stopped before one cell. Inside, Balthazar sat rigidly on the bench, his posture taut with suppressed fury. Even here, the organization of the brig seemed to mock him: each prisoner treated according to protocol, every motion monitored, every detail precise.

"Perspective," Lawrence said lightly, a measured smile on his lips.

Balthazar's gaze snapped to him, sharp and bitter. "Yeah. I bet this is funny to you."

"Funny? Yes," Lawrence replied, moving a chair and placing it just outside the cell. "But *appropriate* is more like it. How does it feel, to be the very thing you despised? To sit here in order and routine, treated better than those you tormented, while you are forced to confront your own failures?"

Balthazar's jaw tightened. "They're no saints," he spat. "They're no different from me, from my vision. Order. Discipline. Purpose. I gave you that once, remember?"

Lawrence leaned forward, eyes sharp. "You gave me chains. You gave me blood on my hands. And now, even in confinement, you are a lesson in what blind authority costs."

Balthazar laughed, bitter and hollow. "I had a job to do."

"And so do I," Lawrence said, rising. "Mine is to rebuild. There are people out there who need us. That's my purpose, my destiny — to save them, not control them."

He slid the chair aside and walked away, the precise click of his boots echoing in the ordered hall. Behind him, Balthazar remained seated, staring at the neat rows of cells and the unwavering rules of the brig, a silent witness to the irony of his own downfall.

The polished corridors of the Azur brig faded behind Lawrence as he stepped into the open air of the Sectors. Here, the city felt different—less suffocating, more alive, yet still precise, structured, and impossibly vast. Sunlight spilled across the terraces, reflecting off the sleek lines of buildings and the polished hulls of parked jumpers. Even the air carried purpose, thick with the hum of activity and disciplined motion.

He paused a moment, watching a squad of troopers glide past with measured precision, their movements fluid, coordinated, and exact. The contrast to the brig was stark. Here, freedom had boundaries, but those boundaries were guided, not imposed.

Gates stood nearby, fingers brushing the stitched name tape on his fleece cap. "Dover," he murmured, tracing it absentmindedly, eyes distant yet grounded. A faint, bittersweet smile tugged at his lips as he stole a glance toward the horizon, where sunlight danced across billowing clouds.

A firm knock on the side of the training pavilion broke his reverie.

"You ready?" Lawrence asked, voice calm but resolute.

Gates nodded, determination and vulnerability mingling in his expression. "Yeah. I've never felt more ready in my life."

By nightfall, Lawrence led the Renegades to the dock, their new trooper uniforms crisp and spotless against the dark gleam of the hangar. The jumpers were lined and ready, gleaming like polished beasts poised for flight.

"Alright, everyone," Lawrence said, voice carrying authority. "First day of training."

The Renegades gathered, standing at attention, a mix of anticipation and awe in their eyes.

"Our approach may be different," Lawrence continued, pacing in front of them, "but the goal remains the same. We're here to save lives."

Gates offered a quiet nod, absorbing every word.

"Remember," Lawrence said, voice rising with conviction, "this isn't just a duty—it's a service to humanity. Every action, every choice, shapes the lives of those who cannot defend themselves. Our purpose is to protect, to act, to endure."

He gestured toward the waiting jumpers. "Move out."

The Renegades boarded with practiced precision, their earlier uncertainty replaced by focus, determination, and a growing sense of unity.

* * *

Green

Ahmed stepped into the vast terrarium, the soft hum of life filling the air. Sunlight filtered through the glass canopy, scattering across vibrant leaves and delicate blossoms. A symphony of unseen birds and insects wove through the warm, fragrant air. Everywhere, life flourished—lush, untamed, yet carefully tended.

Ahmed's gaze swept over the greenery in awe. "What's in here?" he whispered, his voice small against the living cathedral around him.

His eyes fell upon a small potted plant set on a raised pedestal, a neat label reading *Dawn*. His breath caught. He froze, every memory crashing over him—the Vesta, her smile, her courage, the quiet way she had always nurtured life even in the darkness.

He stepped closer, his fingers hovering over the glass as if afraid to touch yet desperate to connect.

The plant's leaves were vibrant, the flowers delicate and full of life. It was as though she were there, tending it herself. Every small blossom seemed to pulse with memory and hope, a living echo of her presence.

Ahmed gently brushed a finger along a leaf, feeling its smooth texture beneath his touch. His eyes misted as he whispered, "It's like she's still here."

For a long, quiet moment, he simply stood there, letting the serenity of the terrarium wash over him. The soft rustle of leaves, the subtle hum of life, the delicate glow of sunlight through the canopy—it all felt like her, guiding him, reminding him of what he had fought for, and what he still had to protect.

He traced the contours of the glass, each curve and vein of the leaves reflecting in his eyes, a mirror of both grief and hope. A wistful, small smile tugged at his lips. In that living tribute, surrounded by the quiet pulse of life, Ahmed felt her presence—not as a memory alone, but as a force that endured, a reminder that love, courage, and care could survive even the harshest storms.

He exhaled slowly, a gentle, almost reverent sound, letting the plant and the living world around him anchor his heart. Dawn was here. In him. In everything that grew and thrived. And for the first time in a long while, Ahmed felt a profound, peaceful hope.

About the Author

W.W. Mitchell is a storyteller with a boundless imagination and a love for exploring the human spirit through every world he creates. His stories range from raw, emotional journeys to thrilling adventures across distant galaxies—each one pulling readers into vivid, cinematic experiences that linger long after the last page.

Born in Newark, New Jersey, and raised in Orlando, Florida, Mitchell's passion for storytelling began early and only grew stronger during his years in the United States Marine Corps. Traveling across the world, he gathered the kinds of stories, faces, and moments that now fuel his writing—giving his work a rare mix of grit, heart, and perspective.

After his service, Mitchell turned his creative drive toward screenwriting, blending the rhythm of film with the depth of fiction to craft stories that feel alive on the page.

Today, he continues to write with the same energy and curiosity that's defined his journey from Marine to author, creating powerful, imaginative tales that invite readers to see the world—and themselves—a little differently.

Also by W.W. Mitchell

Cataclysm Kin
Two sisters born of stars. One destined to burn the world.

Edith and Bethany once fled their dying celestial realm to find peace on Earth. But centuries later, betrayal and the sins of their father have turned sister against sister.

Edith hides her divinity behind compassion. Bethany, cursed and vengeful, carries the fury of a forgotten people.

When ancient creatures rise to reclaim their bloodline, the sisters are forced into a final reckoning—where love and ruin collide, and even in darkness, some flames refuse to die.

9 781958 148235